A WEAKNESS FOR SWEETS

"Vanilla?" Melody rolled her eyes skyward. "How exciting."

She turned to the teenager behind the counter. "I'll have two scoops of chocolate chip cookie dough. No, make it two scoops of peanut butter cup. What the heck, give me one scoop of each on a sugar cone."

Grant's eyes narrowed. "Thought you were only into healthy stuff?"

She smiled sheepishly as the teen held out her cone. "For the most part, I am. However, I'm still trying to lick sweets, no pun intended." She sampled the ice cream cone and her face split into a grin. "They're my weakness."

He recalled the sweet taste of her lips. This woman was fast becoming *his* weakness. "I'll keep that in mind."

A Moment on the Lips

Phyllis Bourne Williams

LEISURE BOOKS NEW YORK CITY

For Byron,
who held my hand
from page one to the end.

A LEISURE BOOK®

February 2006

Published by

Dorchester Publishing Co., Inc.
200 Madison Avenue
New York, NY 10016

ISBN 0-8439-5659-3

The name "Leisure Books" and the stylized "L" with design are trademarks of Dorchester Publishing Co., Inc.

Printed in the United States of America.

Visit us on the web at www.dorchesterpub.com.

A Moment on the Lips

CHAPTER ONE

"It's an offer you can't refuse," he said into the speakerphone.

Grant Price leaned back in the leather office chair and locked his hands behind his head. His persistence was about to pay off.

It had taken him weeks to track down elusive Wall Street legend Melody Mason to a nowhere town in Tennessee. Then he'd pulled together the ultimate compensation package to lure her to his family's Boston-based investment firm, including a signing bonus, penthouse condo, and company jet privileges.

Grant grinned as he propped his Bally-clad feet upon his polished oak desk. She'd go for it, all right. He and Melody were two of a kind. Although he hadn't seen her since college, he knew when it came to business she was like him— competitive and downright ruthless.

"So what do you say?"

"No."

Grant jerked ramrod straight in his chair and planted his feet firmly on the plush carpeting. He took the phone off speaker and snatched up the receiver.

"Pardon me?"

"I said no."

Blindsided by her casual dismissal, Grant scrambled to recover. "If there's something about the package that's lacking, I'm sure we can negotiate and come to terms."

"That won't be necessary."

"Is this about what happened between us in college? Because if it is . . ."

She interrupted before he could finish. "I assure you it isn't."

Grant didn't think so. Melody was too shrewd to allow personal feelings to interfere with good business. Still, he had to be certain she wasn't nursing an old grudge.

"Offers like this don't come along every day. Perhaps you should take a few days to mull it over."

"There's nothing to think about. My answer is no."

A click sounded in Grant's ear and he glared at the phone in disbelief. "What the—?" She'd actually turned him down. In fact, she'd barely heard him out.

He was still staring dumbfounded at the telephone when his father knocked on his slightly opened office door. The older man smiled broadly.

"Is it time to uncork the champagne?"

Grant looked up at the patriarch, who led their

family as well as the country's largest African-American-owned mutual fund firm. Like his son, John Price stood over six feet tall. At sixty-nine years old, deep lines etched his brown skin, and gray battled to overtake the black in his hair.

Still, his father's business acumen was as keen as it had been thirty years ago when Price Investments had begun operations. Through hard work and sheer determination his father had turned the firm into an industry leader. Now millions of small investors entrusted everything from their children's college funds to their retirement to Price Investments.

John Price had dedicated his life to the company. Grant knew his father expected nothing less than the same devotion from him.

"Well?" the elder Price asked in the booming voice known to make grown men cower.

"She rejected our offer." The knots in Grant's stomach constricted as he watched displeasure replace his father's victorious grin. He hated disappointing the old man.

John Price seated himself in a chair on the other side of Grant's desk and sighed heavily. "What happened?"

"I wish I knew." Grant reached into his top desk drawer and pulled out a bottle of aspirin. Shaking the last two out of it, he gulped them down dry.

"Maybe her hands are tied by a noncompete clause in her old contract?"

Grant shook his head. "It expired six months ago."

"She knows she's a hot property. Maybe she's holding out for a better deal?"

"No doubt she's had plenty to sift through," Grant said, tapping the eraser end of his pencil against his desk. The tempo kept time with the pounding in his skull. "There was something about the way she sounded on the phone. I can't put my finger on it."

He reviewed the situation aloud, to see if his father could detect anything he might have overlooked. "Okay, so we know she abruptly resigned from her job last year and dropped out of sight. But why?"

John Price propped his elbows on Grant's desk, tenting his fingertips. "Nobody knows, but according to the grapevine, she took a leave of absence and a few weeks later turned in her resignation. I heard her former company tried everything in their power to keep her."

"It doesn't make sense. She's at the top of her game, and she turns her back on a tremendously successful career. For what?"

"You were friends in college. What do you think?"

"Well, we weren't exactly friends—"

His father eyed him sternly. "Don't tell me this deal got screwed up over some juvenile love affair?"

"Nothing like that." Grant couldn't help chuckling. He could call what went on between Melody and him a lot of things, but a romance wasn't one of them. The idea of him linked to the serious

4

bookworm he remembered was ridiculous. "The only thing between us was a rivalry."

The expectant look on his father's face indicated he required more of an explanation.

Grant pushed away from his desk and began pacing around his office as he continued. "From freshman year until the day we graduated, Melody and I were locked in a fierce battle of one-upmanship. We competed against each other for awards, honors, everything."

"Wait a minute. Is she the same girl who beat you out for student government president and a space on your school's brain bowl team?"

Grant stopped mid-pace and frowned at his father's selective recollection of events. "I did happen to best her once in a while, you know. I snagged the internship with the Federal Reserve Bank and graduated with a higher GPA too."

"No need to get defensive, son. All I'm asking is are you sure she isn't holding the past against you?"

"She says she isn't."

Grant glanced down at the half dozen financial magazines scattered across his desk. Melody stared back at him from the covers. The photos were nearly identical. In each one she wore a stiff designer suit and a crisp white shirt. Her bone-straight black hair was smoothed back from her heart-shaped face into a knot at the nape of her neck. Everything from her humorless amber eyes to the slash of red on her unsmiling lips was all business.

Though she'd apparently given up the thick spectacles, she looked as uptight now as she had back when they were students at Howard University.

For a fleeting moment, he wondered if she ever threw her head back and really laughed, allowing her raven mane to tumble down onto her honey-brown shoulders. He imagined those serious golden eyes of hers sparkling with passion, then quickly banished the thought. It didn't matter. He needed her in his boardroom, not his bedroom.

Grant picked up an old issue of *Black Enterprise* and examined her image closely. "What's your deal, Melody?"

His father cleared his throat. "More importantly, what are you going to do to rectify the situation? I don't have to remind you that your Miss Mason would have brought countless new investors and millions of dollars to the firm on her name alone."

Grant's first instinct was to tell his father that Melody was not *his* Miss Mason, but he knew his father well enough to know that once he had an idea stuck in his mind, there was no changing it. "I'm well aware of it."

Melody's track record wasn't something of which he needed to be reminded. In their business, it was legend. Despite the ups and downs of the stock market, the mutual fund Melody had managed for her former firm continuously beat the S&P 500. A savvy investor who had stashed ten thousand dollars in it a decade ago would now be a millionaire.

"Well, then you're also aware that I was counting on you to come through. I don't want to turn on the Bloomberg Report and hear about her going to Vanguard or Fidelity."

The elder Price rose from his chair. "In a few months, I'll be seventy."

Grant nodded. According the company bylaws, his father's retirement was mandatory the day he turned seventy years old.

"I have to know the son I choose to succeed me can handle the job." John Price leveled a stare at Grant. "Your failure in this matter will definitely factor into my decision."

Subtlety certainly wasn't his old man's forte, Grant thought. The presidency of Price Investments was a carrot his father had dangled in front of his boys since they were youngsters. And like a horse with blinders on, he'd always chased it.

Grant had given up his own dreams for the promise of running Price Investments. It was too late to turn back now. Like it or not, the company was both his duty and his destiny.

He held up his hand. "Wait, Dad," he said. "I'm not ready to give up just yet."

"What's your next move?"

"Put the champagne on ice, and order the nameplate for her office door. She doesn't know it yet, but Melody Mason is coming to Boston and Price Investments."

Melody Mason rolled her eyes heavenward and sighed.

"Another job offer?"

Hanging up the phone, she nodded at her best friend, Joyce. Ever since she'd retreated to the childhood home left to her by the grandmother who had raised her, there had been a steady stream of employment opportunities. When was corporate America going to get the message? She wasn't interested in returning to her old life. Not now. Not ever.

Melody plopped down in the kitchen chair across the table from Joyce, and then remembered what she'd stood to do before the phone rang. "Oh, I was going to make tea."

Her friend stopped her before she could get up. "I'll do it. You've got puppets to knit."

Melody sat while Joyce pulled a box of tea bags from the pantry and turned on the burner under the kettle. The usually soothing click of her bamboo knitting needles did little to quell Melody's excitement over the blast from the past she'd just received. Grant Price. She hadn't seen him since her undergrad graduation.

"What are you grinning about?"

"I'm not grinning." Melody glanced up from the yellow yarn to the scrutiny of Joyce's curious glare.

"Are you sure there wasn't more to that call than a job offer?"

"Of course I'm sure," Melody replied a bit too quickly, hoping Joyce didn't detect the defensiveness in her voice or notice she'd nearly dropped a stitch.

Besides, the call *was* only about a job. That was

all. A job she had no intention of taking, no matter who was offering it. Neither money nor a silly crush on a guy who used to be hot in college would sway her decision. She'd been blessed with a second chance, and she wouldn't squander it. This time she'd focus on the truly important things in life.

"What kind of perks did they try to entice you with this time?" Joyce opened a cabinet door, but shut it when she saw it held skeins of red wool yarn instead of mugs. She opened another, which was stuffed with balls of cotton fleece yarn.

"I'm not sure. I wasn't paying attention."

Melody dropped the strand of yellow yarn and joined in orange to form the bill of the duck puppet she was making. "Try the bottom cabinet on your right."

"I don't get it. Every time I turn around somebody offers you a dream job with a fat salary." Joyce retrieved two mugs, dropped in the tea bags and filled them with hot water. "How can you be so blasé?"

Melody broke from her knitting long enough to add a generous squirt of honey to her tea. "Easy. I'm not interested."

She blew on the hot tea and took a tentative sip. She doubted she could make even her best friend understand why no amount of money enticed her. Some things were more important than money.

Her gaze settled on Joyce. Her extraordinarily pretty features played out on flawless dark skin. She hadn't changed much since she'd been crowned homecoming queen more than twenty years ago. She was still beautiful, and continued to turn heads everywhere she went.

The two of them had been inseparable from the time they were little girls. Physical opposites, Melody was as tall and thick as Joyce was petite and pixieish.

Joyce was the beauty, and Melody was the brain.

While being referred to as pretty or smart may have appealed to some, both had similar reactions to the labels others had thrust upon them: "It ain't what it's cracked up to be," they often laughed.

Joyce had married immediately after high school and remained in town, while Melody had gone off to Howard University on a scholarship, then on to Harvard for her MBA. Through the births of Joyce's four children and Melody's climb up the career ladder, they had maintained their connection with frequent phone calls and e-mails.

"Aren't you the least bit tempted?" Joyce asked.

Melody recalled Grant's deep baritone on the phone and suppressed a shiver. If his authoritative tone was any indication, he hadn't changed since college. He was still a man accustomed to getting whatever he wanted. Not this time.

Even if he was every bit as handsome as she remembered, not Grant, nor anyone else for that matter, could persuade her to return to the rat race. Her career had already cost her too much.

She'd spent her twenties and most of her thirties crunching numbers behind a desk. Now, at thirty-nine, inching closer to forty, her chances of having a husband and family dwindled with each passing year. Her grandmother used to warn her about the consequences of making a hard bed. Now Melody had little choice but to sleep in hers. Alone.

"The only thing tempting me is this homemade coffee cake you brought over here," she said, putting her knitting aside. "I wish you'd quit fooling around and cut me a piece."

"Girl, I thought you'd outgrown your sweet tooth." Joyce chuckled and passed her a plate bearing a hunk of cake, then helped herself to a significantly smaller slice.

Melody's stomach growled in anticipation. In the year since her health scare, she'd managed to clean up her diet, stop smoking and start exercising.

However, she knew there was no way she could ever resist the temptation of sweets. They were her weakness. There wasn't a cookie, cake or pie invented she could walk past without sampling, and she carried ten extra pounds on her size-twelve frame to prove it.

Cutting into the thick, pecan-laden cake with her fork, she caught a whiff of cinnamon as she put it into her mouth. She closed her eyes, taking a moment to savor the rush of sugary sensations assaulting her tongue.

"Delicious," she declared.

"I was downtown earlier, and I drove past the old toy-store building," Joyce said.

"Don't keep me in suspense. What did you think?"

"I barely recognized it. I swear, it looks like an entirely different place."

"That's because it is a different place. My place."

Her place. Pride filled Melody when she thought about her new venture. Upon her return she'd purchased the building that had housed the long-abandoned toy store. With the help of a contractor, she'd revived the dilapidated eyesore. Now in just a few weeks, her yarn shop, The Knitty Gritty, would open for business.

"It used to be the ugliest building on the town square. Now it makes the renovated town hall look shabby."

"I can hardly wait to open."

"Is everything still on schedule for the grand opening?" Joyce sipped her tea and grimaced.

"I went over my checklist earlier, and so far it looks good." Melody chewed on her bottom lip. "And you can make all the faces you want; I don't have any coffee. Green tea is better for you anyway."

Joyce took another sip of tea. Apparently giving up on acquiring a taste for the brew, she slid the offending cup to the center of the table. "You're going to be a smashing success."

Melody signed. "I want The Knitty Gritty to be more than just a yarn store. I'm hoping to create an environment for knitters to steal some time for themselves to unwind or maybe just work on their latest project."

"Well, the word is already out. You've got half the women in town digging out their mother's and grandmother's old knitting needles."

Already down to her last bite of coffee cake, she motioned for Joyce to serve her another slice. "So what's going on with you? Any word on your college application?"

Melody watched her friend's eyes cast downward and feared the worst. Devoting the past two decades to raising four children and boosting her husband's career, Joyce had delayed pursuing her own educational goals.

"Not yet," she replied unenthusiastically.

"Then why so glum?"

Joyce blew out a tired breath. "I don't know. It's been years since high school. I can't even remember the last time I studied. Maybe I should forget the whole thing."

Reaching across the old but sturdy table, Melody clasped her friend's hand. "That's just nerves talking."

"I hope so. Plus, to say Kevin isn't wild about the idea is an understatement."

Melody nodded, but kept her lips buttoned. She and Joyce were tight, but it wasn't her place to offer marital advice. "Everything will work out," she finally said, giving Joyce's hand a squeeze.

"I know this sounds selfish, but I'm glad you aren't taking those jobs. I like having you around."

"Don't worry. I'm not going anywhere."

The Red Sox had dug themselves a hole that not even a grand slam home run could help. Grant shut off the satellite radio in his rented Camry and hoped he'd have better luck.

13

Not that he'd had a choice. He couldn't strike out with Melody again.

A year ago the woman had had the financial world at her feet. What on earth had made her come to this place? The town, located about a half hour from Nashville, was barely a blip on the radar.

Though she had sounded firm on the phone, he was sure he could change her mind. Everyone had their price. And there wasn't anything he wasn't willing to pay to bring her into the firm and make his old man happy.

Grant rubbed his lower back and squirmed in the driver's seat. The nagging ache had started up again this morning on the company jet flight to Nashville and hadn't let up. His doctor had warned him repeatedly to change his lifestyle in order to reduce his stress level. No chance of that happening anytime soon.

He'd read about executives who sat around swank country clubs in tennis whites making deals over three-martini lunches, but he wasn't one of them. He reported to the office every morning at seven and rarely left before midnight. A jam-packed schedule and fast-food meals wolfed down at his desk were all part of his business. He hadn't taken as much as a day off in years.

Like his father and brother, Grant worked his butt off.

Besides, his stress level would drop dramatically after he convinced Melody to come to work for the firm. The sooner he returned to Boston with her, the better.

* * *

Melody felt the knitting needle slip from her hand and caught it before it hit the floor. She pushed aside the pig finger puppet she was knitting.

She gently massaged her weakened left hand with her right. Sometimes her left side seemed to have a mind of its own. She wasn't surprised when it went out on her; however, she would never get used to feeling not quite in control.

"At least your reaction time is getting better," she muttered to herself.

A knock sounded at the front door, startling her. Although she'd been home for months now, she was still surprised when someone dropped by out of the blue to say hello. The friendly, small-town practice was only one of the things that had drawn her back to her hometown. She'd lived in her New York apartment for years and had never even met her neighbors.

Knowing how she loved sweets, folks often brought a homemade treat along. Her mouth watered at the possibility that it was her grandmother's best friend, Ruth, and one of her blue-ribbon-winning peach cobblers.

"Coming," she yelled in the direction of the front door, which she'd left open to allow the summer breeze to drift through the screen.

Melody took one look at the man darkening her front entrance and froze.

"What are you doing here?"

15

CHAPTER TWO

Grant Price.

Melody had underestimated him. For someone supposedly so smart, she'd been dumb. She could kick herself for allowing him to catch her off guard, then give him a swift kick for showing up on her doorstep uninvited.

Pigheaded as ever, the man still hadn't learned to take no for an answer.

It was the story of her life. Melody sighed. Men only pursued her when they wanted something. When she was a kid, the boys were only nice long enough to get a peek at the smart girl's homework. Later on, men tried to get close for a chance she'd use what Wall Street watchers called her "Midas Touch," to make them rich.

Part of her wanted to tell him to get lost and slam the door right in his smug face. However, she knew the only thing she'd get out of it was momentary satisfaction. Whenever she opened her door again, he'd be standing there waiting.

Exhaling sharply, she pushed open the screen door and stepped out onto the porch. "I don't like surprises."

"Melody?" Grant's whiskey-brown eyes swept over her before meeting her gaze.

His penetrating stare sent a tingle of awareness down her spine. It had been years since they'd last seen each other. Not since the only two summa cum laude graduates in their class stood side by side at college commencement.

Melody automatically reached up to smooth her unruly mass of kinky curls away from her face. When she realized what she was doing, she abruptly stopped and jammed her hands into her skirt pockets. The last thing she wanted was for the man to think she was primping for him.

Melody grudgingly noted how kind the years had been to her former classmate. The subtle changes in his appearance were all flattering. Life wasn't fair. If people got what they truly deserved, Grant surely would have ended up with male pattern baldness and a gut hanging over his belt buckle.

Instead age had matured the features of a skinny, good-looking kid, who could barely walk across campus without a pretty cheerleader, AKA or Delta clamoring for his attention, into those of a strikingly attractive man.

Tall and lean, he wore the double-breasted, navy Armani suit like he had been born in it. His pristine white shirt emphasized skin the color of black coffee. But it went beyond designer attire. Grant

Price had presence. Melody was sure he could wear rags and not dilute the commanding aura of power and confidence surrounding him.

One thing remained the same: Grant Price hated to lose. He especially detested losing to her, and the feeling was mutual. She had no doubt he would try every trick in the book to persuade her to do his bidding.

Thank God he'd never discovered the huge crush she'd had on him back in college. If he had, he'd probably find a way to use it now.

"I told you on the phone, I'm not interested in your job." She figured she'd save them both wasted time if she stopped him before he even got started. She could return to her knitting, and he could go back home.

His bewildered expression relaxed into an easy, this-is-a-done-deal grin. "How can you be so sure?"

"Good-bye, Grant." Melody turned toward the door, but he moved deftly in front of it, blocking her path. The masculine scent of his cologne stirred her senses.

Shooting him a withering glance, she tried not to notice how his height forced her to tilt her chin up to face him. At five-eleven, she looked down on most people. Standing near him made her feel almost diminutive.

"Is this any way to greet an old friend?" he finally asked.

Melody frowned and propped her hand on her hip. "Your charm doesn't work on me, so you might as well move out of my way."

"This job will make you a wealthy woman."

"I'm already a wealthy woman," Melody countered, her patience waning.

"Just listen, that's all I'm asking."

Melody sighed. "Give me one good reason why I should."

She looked different. Softer somehow, Grant thought as he stared at the woman on the verge of shutting the door in his face.

Looking at her now didn't bring to mind the relentless competitor he remembered from college or the stone-faced, unapproachable businesswoman he'd seen on CNBC and countless financial magazine covers.

Maybe it was the sun-kissed glow radiating from her honey complexion, or the way her hair surrounded her face in a seductive halo of curls. He couldn't be sure. All he knew was he found the effect extremely attractive.

He looked into her golden eyes, which flashed back at him in annoyance. His gaze slid down the statuesque length of her. She'd traded in her conservative suits and sensible pumps for an orange gauzy skirt that skimmed her ankles. Hot orange toenails peeked at him from her strappy sandals and a sexy gold bracelet encircled her ankle.

"Well?" she asked, her hand still perched on her hip. "I'm waiting. You were about to explain why I should listen to you?"

"Because I'm here to offer you the opportunity of a lifetime." He swallowed hard, trying not to stare at her full lips, which were painted a lush tropical color.

"I've already told you there's nothing . . ."

Grant's cell phone rang. "Excuse me." He reached into his inside suit jacket pocket to retrieve it.

"Yes," he barked into the phone. He'd been away from the office only a few hours and already his assistant, Barbara, was calling with problems needing his immediate attention. The knot in his gut pulled tighter.

"Let Dad or Thomas handle it," he told her.

"But Mr. Price, you insisted on attending to these matters personally," Barbara protested.

Grant ran his free hand over his coarse, close-cut hair and released an exasperated breath. He'd chewed Barbara out when she'd gently suggested he not be so hands-on, obsessive, as she'd put it, and delegate more of his duties. "Nothing is more important than what I'm doing right now," he said brusquely.

"Yes, sir," he heard her say in an I-told-you-so tone, before he pressed a button and ended the call.

He sighed and turned back to Melody, who still looked less than pleased to see him. At least she hadn't gone back into the house or called the cops on him for trespassing. "As I was saying, I presented you with an extremely generous opportunity."

"Which I promptly rejected."

"I'm prepared to up the ante."

Melody shook her head. "Let me break this down. I don't want to work for you or anyone else," she said in the slow, precise tone adults used to reason with naughty children.

"I've come a long way. Please, at least listen to what I have to say."

"You're wasting your breath."

"Why don't you let me be the judge of that?"

She heaved a sigh. "Go ahead," she grumbled. "The sooner you get started, the sooner you can leave."

Grant ran his finger along the inside of his shirt collar and loosened his tie. He suddenly felt the heat of the day. The shade of the covered porch blocked some of the sun's blaze, but provided little relief from the stifling heat. To top it off, his head was pounding. He was aware of Melody watching him warily as he pulled a new bottle of aspirin from his shirt breast pocket and popped the seal.

"Do you always keep aspirin so handy?"

"Headaches and ulcers are all part of the game," he replied jokingly.

"So when is the last time you took any time off or had a vacation?" For a split second he thought he saw something akin to sympathy touch her face. Just as quickly her expression turned back to stone.

Grant snorted. "Vacation? Who has time for a vacation?"

"That long, huh?"

"I don't have to tell you about this business."

"No, I remember all too well," she said softly. "My head hurt for a week straight after shares of

Adkins Computers plummeted and they were delisted from the stock exchange."

"What kind of stake did you have in it?"

"Enough." Her brow furrowed, and she shivered visibly, as if she were trying to shake off a bad memory. "I'll get you something to drink."

She went into the house, letting the screen door slam behind her. He shrugged off his suit jacket and took a seat on the wooden porch swing. The swing, like the rest of the modest wood-frame house, was painted white with black trim and shutters. He gently pushed off, allowing the swing to rock with the slight breeze.

Melody returned with a frosty glass of lemonade, which he gratefully accepted. Eyeing her over the rim of the glass, Grant took a long, slow swig to wash down the aspirin. This wasn't turning out to be as simple as he had originally thought. She hadn't even blinked when he offered to sweeten the pot.

"Make your pitch," Melody said, sitting down next to him on the swing. "However, I won't change my mind."

Money and perks hadn't even persuaded her to hear him out, so there was little chance they'd sway her. Grant decided he'd try another approach, one that might convince her to seriously consider what could be a very lucrative situation for both of them.

"First, I want you to know that my company does more than make money for investors," he said. "We're very proud of both our scholarship and in-

22

ternship programs for business and finance students at historically black colleges and universities."

Although she tried to hide it, her eyes brightened. He had her attention. Now if he could only hold on to it. "We've not only contributed money, books and computers loaded with the latest software to these schools, but our time. Our managers are given paid leave to give hands-on seminars at HBCUs."

Melody nodded and graced him with an approving smile. It was the first one she'd given him since he'd stepped on her porch. It made him feel good.

"I can't tell you how rewarding it's been to watch those young people step into top jobs across the nation and even go on to start their own businesses," he said. "It's even more gratifying to watch them reach back and pull others up the ladder."

Grant took another gulp of lemonade. "These are wonderful programs, but it takes money to run them. If you were to come to work for me, you could help us expand them to reach even more students."

Melody was silent.

"What do you think?"

Grant felt like an elephant was performing a tap dance on his gut as he waited for her answer. Melody's eyes were closed and her lips firmly pressed together. The fact that she hadn't said no yet made him feel guardedly optimistic. She was thinking about it all right. Finally, she opened her eyes and fixed her gaze on him.

23

"Grant, your offer is extremely generous and your firm's commitment to our HBCUs is admirable," she said. "Still, my answer remains no."

Grant sat dumbfounded, staring at his old classmate. The Melody he remembered would have jumped at a plum position like this one. Shaking his head, he threw up his hands in frustration. "You worked hard to get to the top, and your aptitude for stock picking is nothing short of a gift. I don't get you at all."

"You wanted me to listen to your offer and I did." She rose from the porch swing. "Why I said no is none of your concern."

Instinctively he stood and laid his hand on her arm. "It is when you're hiding out in the sticks letting those degrees you busted your butt to earn go to waste."

She shrugged his hand away and strode over to the porch railing. "Go home, Grant."

Grant wished he could do just that. Life would be a lot simpler if he turned around and walked away. A small part of him envied Melody for stepping back from it all. But he knew he never could. His duty was to his father and Price Investments.

"At least help me understand why. What's holding you here?" He followed her, taking in his surroundings. All he saw was an average house with a postage-stamp yard on a block with two dozen homes just like it. For the life of him he didn't see anything that would compel her to reject a million-dollar job.

He turned to Melody for an explanation. Her

lips were pressed into a firm, stubborn line, and he could feel the scorch from the fire flashing in her golden eyes. Still, if he had to go back to his father empty-handed, then he wanted to know why.

"I'm here because I want to be. This town is my home. I have every right to live and work right here."

Dread seeped through his veins. She was working? No wonder she'd barely listened to his spiel. "You already have a job?" he managed to croak out.

"Of course."

"What kind of job?"

"I'm opening a yarn shop," she said with so much enthusiasm he thought the market had just soared three hundred points. "In addition to selling yarn, I'll be teaching both knitting and crochet classes."

Grant released the breath stuck in his chest. Unfortunately, he couldn't stop the chuckle that followed it. "A yarn store?" he muttered more to himself than to her.

She propped a hand on her hip. "What's so funny?"

"I never pictured you as the knitting type. At least not for another thirty or forty years."

"What rock have you been hiding under?" she nearly shouted. "The popularity of knitting has surged. Everyone from supermodels to business executives is knitting nowadays. It's calming and relaxing. It's the new yoga."

"Well, why didn't you say so?" Grant asked. The Melody he'd known wouldn't just sit out in the sticks and let her brilliant mind turn to mush. She was capitalizing on a new trend and was about to become to knitting what Starbucks was to coffee. "How many stores? Are you thinking about franchising or keeping them company-owned?"

Melody held up both hands. "Slow down. I said I was opening a *single yarn store*, not a knitting empire."

"Only one store?"

"That's right."

"In this town?"

"Right again."

The moment of clarity he thought he'd experienced shriveled up before his eyes, leaving him just as confused as before.

"I find that hard to believe," he said, mentally searching his brain for her angle.

He watched her pluck a withered rose from the vine crawling up the white wooden trellis. "It's not complicated. I like to knit."

"There has to be more to it. This yarn thing couldn't possibly satisfy you. A woman like you needs more."

"We haven't seen each other in years. How would you know what I need?"

"You need *real* work, Melody," he said. "The competition. The challenge. You thrive on them."

"Thrive?" she asked incredulously, crushing the rose in her palm. "My work was literally a pain in the neck. In my head. In my back. Not to mention the eighteen-hour workdays and sleepless nights that accompany the burden of being responsible for people's life savings."

"Oh come on. *Business Week* named you best fund manager five years in a row. Your fund never suffered a losing year. Even when the market dived, you had double-digit returns."

"None of it matters anymore. I've kissed the financial world good-bye." She advanced on him, poking her finger at his chest. "You're looking at a new me. No briefcase. No cell phone. No Blackberry. No agenda."

His gaze locked with hers. "Who are you trying to convince, me or yourself? Lady, you're a shark. And like all sharks, sooner or later you'll get hungry."

"Wrong."

Grant laughed and shook his head. "Stop fooling yourself. I know you," he said. "We're two of a kind."

She lifted a brow. "So you're telling me you're enjoying yourself?"

"Thoroughly."

"And I suppose you also enjoy the headaches and feeling like your stomach's turning into one big ulcer?"

Grant felt himself flinch.

"Ahhhh, hit a nerve, didn't I?" Melody asked. "Don't bother denying it. I've been there."

"Any stress-related problems I'm experiencing could be easily alleviated if you'd agree to join the Price Investments team."

Melody eyed him meaningfully before she spoke. "Okay, fine," she said smoothly.

A bit too smoothly as far as he was concerned. "What's the catch?"

"I'll only do it for a week."

"What? You're kidding, right?"

"It's no joke. Here's the deal: I'll come to Boston and conduct a weeklong workshop for your fund managers. I'll also review their portfolios and make suggestions. But first, you'll spend a week here with no pager, no cell phone, no laptop and absolutely no contact with your office."

"What kind of business deal is that?" Grant sputtered.

"Believe it or not, I'm doing you a favor, one I wish someone had done for me. Unfortunately, I had to learn my lesson the hard way."

Grant shook his head and rubbed the back of his neck. She was smiling as if she were actually pleased with herself. "I'm going to rescue you," she said.

"Rescue me?" Grant couldn't help chuckling, although he was anything but amused. "From what?"

"Yourself."

Grant closed his eyes and squeezed the bridge of his nose with his fingertips. In a matter of seconds, their conversation had taken a turn from business to sheer lunacy. Opening his eyes, he fixed them on her.

"Melody, I haven't a clue as to what you're talking about."

"It's simple. You are going to learn how to relax."

"That's ridiculous," Grant growled. "I want you in Boston, permanently running a Price mutual fund. And as far as my staying here, it's out of the question."

Shrugging her shoulders, Melody turned to her front door. "Suit yourself."

"No, wait. Let's discuss this," he said. He hoped as long as they kept talking, he had a chance of convincing her to see things his way.

"My terms are nonnegotiable."

"Your terms are also impractical, as well as impossible. Even if I wanted to, there's no way I could leave work," Grant stammered.

"No one is indispensable, Grant, and nothing is impossible."

"But . . ."

"Take it or leave it."

Grant tried to slow his thoughts. Something was better than nothing, he realized. Now, at least, he had two weeks to change her mind. And with her onboard, his father was sure to turn over the reigns of Price Investments to him.

"You've given me no choice. I'll take it."

CHAPTER THREE

Was she out of her mind? What had she just done?

Melody hoped the carefully schooled expression pasted on her face didn't reveal the commotion going on inside her head, a battle royal between her common sense and her conscience. And her common sense, which was shouting at her to send this man packing, had fallen victim to a silly crush.

She thought she'd gotten over her infatuation with Grant. Yet one look at him and decades-old feelings came rushing back with a vengeance.

He offered his hand and she briefly shook it, sealing their agreement to a deal she should have never made. Her store would open in less than a month. That was what she should be concentrating on, not Grant Price.

Besides, if Grant wanted to dig himself a stress-induced grave, she had no right to interfere. He was a grown man.

She opened her mouth to tell him to forget it,

but couldn't force the words through her lips. Melody understood that time changed people, but there was something missing from the picture Grant tried to paint of the contented workaholic. Sure, he still had the drive, but he seemed to be merely going through the motions. The passion for what he did was noticeably absent.

The saddest part was, she doubted whether he even realized it.

He reminded her so much of herself just before her world had come crashing down. The memory made her shudder. She had also run the treadmill of long hours, pain relievers, junk food and little or no sleep. She had done anything to stay a step ahead of the competition, only to wind up lying helpless in a hospital emergency room, rethinking the life she'd taken for granted.

Now the piece of her heart that cared for Grant wouldn't allow her to look away while he walked the same treacherous path.

"So what now?" he asked.

What now, indeed. Melody examined the man whose unannounced visit had thrown her day and now the next week into chaos. She swallowed hard as the reality of having him around for the next few days hit her. She didn't like the way her pulse skittered when she looked at him or how the skin on her forearm tingled where he had touched it.

She cleared her throat and spoke with an authoritative self-assurance she didn't feel. "I'll give you a few moments to notify your office you'll be out of touch for the week. Then you can hand over your briefcase and electronic gadgets."

Melody bit her lip to keep from laughing at Grant's fierce scowl when, after two heated but short phone conversations, he reluctantly relieved himself of the items.

"Is this all of it? Or do I need to search you?"

His scowl deepened. "Don't push it."

"You'll have all your toys back at the end of the week," she said. "And who knows, by then you might not want them."

"I wouldn't bet on it."

Joyce Holden looked from her youngest son's hopeful face to the sealed envelope lying on the kitchen table. The postman had dropped it off hours ago, yet every time she picked it up her hands started shaking.

"Come on, Mom. Open it!" David prodded.

"I will; just give me a moment." She chewed anxiously on her bottom lip as she rearranged the bowl of fruit on the counter. It wasn't like she hadn't been through this before. She'd walked three of her four children through the college application process. Well, with the twins it had been more like shoving them through, she chuckled to herself. Still, this time it was different. This particular envelope, with a return address from the office of admissions, was addressed to her.

Joyce grabbed a dish towel and swept it across her already spotless granite countertop. Getting into college hadn't been at the top of her priority list when she'd graduated high school. Back then she had been too busy preparing to wed her high-school sweetheart, Kevin. At the time, her parents had been dead set against the union. They hadn't approved of Kevin or his family. Kevin's parents had stayed either drunk or in jail, leaving him for the most part to raise himself.

"The apple doesn't fall far from the tree," her father had warned.

But she and Kevin had been young, in love, and believed they had life all figured out. First, she'd go to work to support them while Kevin attended college on a scholarship. He'd graduate, get a good job and work while she earned her nursing degree.

Unfortunately, their perfect plan left no contingency for babies or Kevin going on to law school. So Joyce put her education on hold to raise their sons and boost her husband's career.

Not once had she regretted her decision. Both marriage and motherhood had been wonderfully fulfilling. However, her babies didn't need her so much anymore. Their oldest son and the twins had already left the nest, leaving only David at home. Kevin had launched his own firm, and it was doing well.

Finally, there was enough time and money for her to pursue her deferred dreams.

"Whatcha waiting on?" David snatched a Granny Smith apple from the bowl she kept on the counter, and bit into it.

What was she waiting on? Joyce peered up at her

son, who in the short time he'd returned home from football practice, had devoured two sandwiches, a dozen cookies and half a bag of potato chips. At fifteen, he already towered a foot over her and outweighed her by a good hundred pounds. And like her other sons when they were his age, he was always hungry.

"Do you want me to make you another sandwich?"

"Quit stalling, Mom." David picked up the envelope and held it out to her.

"Fat is good, right?" Her hands trembled as she dropped the dish towel and took the heavy envelope from him.

David shrugged in typical teenage fashion. "I guess."

Joyce slid her index finger underneath the envelope flap and pulled out the enclosed sheaf of papers. She peeked at the opening line of the cover page.

"Our Admissions and Academic Standards Committee has reviewed your application for admission," she read aloud, her voice quivering along with her hands. "With pleasure, I can inform you that you have been approved . . ."

She stopped, giving herself a second to absorb the words, and then let out a yell. "I'm in! I'm in!" She threw her arms around David, enveloping him in a bear hug. "Your mother's going to college!"

Releasing him, she read the letter again, and flipped through the attached papers outlining registration, campus and class information. "I can't believe it," she whispered.

"Way to go, Mom." David patted her on the head, playfully ruffling her close-cropped curls.

"We're going to celebrate big tonight!" she announced breathlessly. "How about we meet your dad in Nashville for dinner? We can go to that fancy seafood place at Opryland?"

"Cool," David said. "I'm starving."

"You go change your clothes, and I'll give your father a call."

"Change?"

Joyce surveyed her son's grass-stained and dirt-covered T-shirt and scrunched up her nose. "And shower too," she called out to him as he headed to his room. "No baggy jeans or sneakers, please."

The phone rang before Joyce reached it. To her delight, Kevin was on the other end. "Just the man I wanted to talk to," she said, still reeling from the news. She felt like a just-opened bottle of bubbly champagne at midnight on New Year's Eve. "I was about to call you."

"You're in a good mood," Kevin said. The timbre of his smooth voice sent a delicious shiver through her body. After more than twenty years together, her husband still excited her like crazy.

"Well, you happen to be talking to an incoming college freshman," she said proudly.

"Huh?"

"I got accepted to nursing school!" Joyce gushed. "The letter came today. I keep pinching myself to make sure I'm not dreaming. Oh, honey. I'm so happy!"

In her jubilation, Joyce didn't notice the dead silence on the other end. "Hon?" she asked after a few moments, thinking they must have gotten disconnected. Then she heard a heavy sigh. While Kevin hadn't exactly encouraged her decision to apply to college, she'd expected a more enthusiastic response.

"Look, Joyce, I'm already late for a meeting. I was calling to let you know Paul Wilson's in town," he said. "I need you to pull together a dinner party for tonight."

Her husband acted as if he hasn't heard a word she'd said. Disappointed, she felt her exuberance begin to ebb away.

"Tonight?"

"Yes, tonight," he said shortly.

"But I was hoping we could celebrate tonight," she said softly.

"Wilson Electronics is a major client for the firm," Kevin said. "Besides, all Paul's done is rave about the fabulous dinner you made last time he was here. He even brought along some of his partners. I can't very well take them to a restaurant, now can I?"

Joyce glanced up at the clock. It was already nearly four. "Kevin, I don't know if there's enough time to prepare anything elaborate."

"You'll pull it off. I can always depend on you to come through."

"Kevin, about school—" Joyce began. Her heart sank when her husband cut her off midstream.

"I have to get to that meeting. See you tonight."

Joyce crammed her college paperwork back

into its envelope and stashed it away. Yanking open the freezer door, she looked to see what she could pull together for dinner, not bothering to brush away her tears.

"Damn," Kevin Holden muttered disgustedly, setting the phone back on the hook. The joy and expectation crackling through the phone lines when Joyce picked up had disappeared by the time he ended the call. He could feel the chill in her voice, and the temperature was bound to drop below freezing by the time he got home.

Propping his elbows on his desktop, Kevin rested his head in his hands. Sometimes he didn't understand his wife at all. Why was she so anxious to go college, of all things? And at her age! Sure, they'd agreed he would go first, and then she would go to nursing school. But that was ages ago, when they were just kids.

He dropped his hands and looked up at the framed law school diploma hanging on the wall. The slip of paper represented years of hard work and sacrifice on both their parts. Together they had proven wrong everyone who had said she was tying herself to a man destined to end up a drunk like his parents.

Now they had it all: plenty of money; a spacious home in the right neighborhood; two luxury cars in the garage; a solid marriage and four great sons.

Kevin pushed away from his desk and slipped on the suit jacket draped across the back of his chair. He glanced at his wife's photo before heading to the conference room. Her dimpled cheeks and beautiful face tugged at his heart.

"I'm doing all I can to make you happy," he told the photo. "Why isn't that enough for you?"

Despite fuzzy directions consisting of hints like "turn left at the old Leary place" and "make a right at the war memorial statue," Grant managed to maneuver his rental car fairly easily through the one-stoplight town. In a matter of minutes he parked in front of the quaint bed-and-breakfast where Melody had arranged for him to stay. He shut off the engine, but remained in the car.

Nestled in a carefully tended yard of vibrant summer blooms, the pale yellow wood-frame cottage looked as if it had been ripped from the pages of a children's storybook. Grant hoped the cheerful, old-fashioned house would be equipped with a fax machine, computer and Internet access.

Automatically he reached for his cell phone, then remembered Melody had confiscated it. He drummed his fingers against the steering wheel. No sweat. He'd use the phone in his room to check in with the office.

"There's more than one way to skin a cat," he chuckled to himself. And fortunately, Melody couldn't watch him 24/7.

Grant opened the trunk and grabbed the Coach overnight bag he'd brought along in case he had to spend the night. He hadn't anticipated being stuck for an entire week.

The curtain in one of the house's windows moved and he knew he'd been spotted. Within moments, an elderly woman appeared on the porch. She wore jeans and a pink shirt on her spry frame. Her silver hair was drawn into a French braid that hung down her back. She had to be the Miss Sharp about whom Melody had told him.

She squinted, then shaded her eyes with her hand. "Well, come on in, young man. I've been expecting you."

Grant strode up the walkway. He dropped his bag on the porch and extended his hand. "Hello, Miss Sharp. I'm Grant Price. It looks like I'll be your guest this week."

The woman put her small hand in his. "I've got a room all fixed up for you," she said. "You're just in time. I have a peach cobbler cooling."

Grant picked up his bag and followed her into the house. The aroma of the deep-dish fruit pie hit him the moment he crossed the threshold, and his stomach growled. He hadn't had homemade cobbler in years—not since his mother died.

Grant brushed aside the memories beginning to assault him. He didn't have time for them or cobbler, no matter how wonderful it smelled. He needed to get to his room and check in with Barbara. The office must be crazy without him.

"No thanks, Miss Sharp. I'm anxious to get to my room."

The older woman nodded, and if Grant wasn't mistaken, her lips curled into a smirk. "Sure, follow me," she said, climbing the staircase with the energy of a woman half her age. "And you can drop the Miss Sharp. Call me Ruth."

He thanked Ruth and quickly shuttled her out of the small, tastefully decorated room. He tossed his bag on the quilt-covered, king-sized bed and collapsed beside it.

He blew out a heavy breath. "What a morning."

Staring up at the ceiling fan leisurely spinning above him, he rested his forearm against his head. His father had not been pleased when he'd called to let him know he'd be out of the office for the rest of the week. The pressure was on for him to change Melody's mind about working for the firm, and he was determined to do just that.

But how? he wondered. She was so keyed up over this yarn-store deal. He recalled seeing the same sparks in her amber eyes when they had gone toe-to-toe back in college. He also wondered why he never noticed until today how pretty they were.

"Where did that come from?" he muttered, startled at the direction his wayward thoughts were taking.

He pulled himself up to a sitting position on the bed. The best way to get his mind back on business was to check in with his office. He reached for the phone on the nightstand. Dead.

"What the . . . ?"

He descended the stairs two at a time. "Ruth," he called out.

He found her in the dining room, where she'd already set out two slices of cobbler.

40

"Oh Grant, I thought you might change your mind about tasting a bit of my cobbler."

"Ma'am, the phone in my room is dead."

"Of course it is. Melody told me you wouldn't be needing one." The smile on her crinkled bronze face might have been innocent, but her eyes sparkled with pure devilment.

Grant frowned and headed toward the door. "I'll just have to find a pay phone," he grumbled.

Ruth shook her head. "The only pay phone in town is at the diner, and it's been out of order for years. Everyone has cell phones nowadays."

Her grin broadened as she continued. "I may have mentioned your situation to Edith Riley when she stopped by to pick up the pies I baked for the church. Don't get me wrong, Edith is a dear, but she spreads news like butter. By now there's not a soul countywide who would allow you to touch their phone, or, for that matter, computer or fax machine. Heck, I doubt the little Johnson twins would let you play on their toy walkie-talkies."

Grant sighed and released his grip on the doorknob. He turned to his hostess, who had just set a decanter of fresh-brewed coffee on the table and poured herself a cup.

Resigned to his fate, he trudged over to the dining table and sat down. The cobbler did smell good. He reached for the coffee decanter and was rewarded with a lightning-fast smack on his hand.

"Ouch! What was that for?"

"No coffee for you. There's milk in the kitchen."

Grant pushed away from the table, rubbing his stinging hand as he headed to the kitchen.

"You might think you're one up on me now, Melody," he growled. "But you've got another thing coming."

Conflicting feelings of dread and spine-tingling anticipation assaulted Melody as she stopped her bicycle in front of Ruth's house. She'd expected her counter-proposal to send Grant running. Instead he'd called her on it, in effect, cashing a check she should never have written in the first place.

She hopped off the bike, reached into her fanny pack for a stick of cinnamon-flavored gum and came up empty.

She blew out an exasperated breath and smoothed a kinky curl that had escaped the confines of her white scrunchie behind her ear.

It was days like this that made her regret kicking cigarettes. One puff was all she needed, just one tiny puff to fortify her. Melody shook her head, banishing the thought. Giving up cigarettes had been one of the hardest things she'd ever done. Besides, if she hadn't put an end to her two-packs-a-day nicotine habit, she'd eventually have a bigger problem on her hands than Grant Price.

Leaning the bike against Ruth's porch, Melody didn't bother chaining it to the railing. Just like she knew her name, she knew it would be there when she returned.

"Hello?" she called out as pushed open the unlatched screen door and walked inside.

"We're out here," Melody heard her friend call back from the direction of the backyard patio. Thank goodness Ruth was home. Melody pushed the errant curl away from her face again. What was the matter with her? Her career had demanded she work closely with plenty of men. Why did this one make her so uneasy?

Rubbing her palms against the denim capri pants she'd changed into for her bike ride, Melody walked through the house to the patio.

Ruth was relaxing in a cushioned yard chaise, thumbing through a cooking magazine. She looked up, acknowledging Melody with a slight nod before returning her attention to the glossy pages of the magazine. The older woman's cool was a stark contrast to the man pacing the confines of the stone patio like a caged panther. He spotted her and came to an abrupt stop.

Melody met Grant's unwavering stare, telling herself she only imagined the shiver of unbridled excitement it sent coursing through her. Commanding her traitorous knees to stop knocking, she struggled to keep her face impassive. The last thing she needed was to appear nervous. If he detected any fear or uncertainty on her part, he'd surely use it to his advantage.

"I don't suppose you're here to tell me you've come to your senses and decided to accept my offer?" Grant's brow lifted inquiringly.

He'd shed his tie and rolled up the sleeves of his white shirt, revealing impressively firm forearms covered with a light dusting of baby-fine hair. Melody swallowed hard. She'd heard of men labeling themselves as breast, leg or even butt men when it came to their favorite parts of the female anatomy. She bit the inside of her lip. If the same could be said for ladies, she was definitely an arm woman. Her mind drifted as she fantasized how it would feel to be wrapped inside those strong, sexy arms.

"Well?" Grant asked.

Swallowing again, she shook her head no. It was a good thing he couldn't read her thoughts. She cleared her throat. "I wanted to check to see if you were settling in okay."

"I would have called with an update, but I don't seem to have phone privileges."

"If you can't hang, I'll gladly return your gadgets, and you can hightail it back to Boston," she answered sternly.

"I can hang just fine, and when I leave"—his deep baritone lowered an octave as he pinned her with his gaze—"you'll be right beside me."

"Only for a week," she amended.

"We'll see."

Melody let it go, refusing to be drawn into a debate. It would be enough to make it through the week with this man, exasperating as he was gorgeous, underfoot.

"I rode my bike over. I figured we could ride while I show you around town." She motioned toward a storage shed in the yard. "Ruth keeps bicycles on hand for guests."

He looked down at his still-crisp shirt and dress slacks. "I didn't bring anything casual."

"Do you even own casual clothes?"

He shrugged his broad shoulders. "I have no need for them."

Melody frowned. She'd figured as much. His matter-of-fact statement bolstered her resolve to save this man from himself.

"You can pick up a few things while we're in the square," she said.

"Fine. Let's go."

"That was easy."

"Don't read too much into it. I'm just going nuts here thinking about all the work I left on my desk."

"Oh, I'll have to ride home and get my SUV," Melody said, turning to leave.

Grant pulled a set of keys from his pants pocket and jangled them in front of her. "I'll drive."

Surely this was the land time had forgotten, Grant thought as he took in the town square.

Four main streets flanked a landscaped park filled with shade trees and dotted with wooden benches. The town hall, a movie theatre and a variety of storefronts lined the blocks. Red-and-white striped awnings hung over the windows of each structure, and a large gazebo sat in the middle of it all.

"I thought Mayberry only existed on TV," he said.

Melody motioned for him to park in a vacant space in front of the town hall. "We're more contemporary than that," she said.

Contemporary wasn't a word Grant would use to describe the late 1800s architecture dominating the buildings on the square. Yet it was what he didn't see that gave the place a cozy, old-fashioned air.

"No Golden Arches?"

"So far, the town's managed to steer clear of fast-food joints and national chain stores," Melody said. "I didn't like that decision as a kid, but now I can appreciate it."

He followed her inside the town hall and into the mayor's office.

"Hi, Cara," Melody greeted the receptionist.

"Hey there." The receptionist continued to type, her eyes never leaving her computer monitor. "We ran out of M&Ms, so the mayor authorized me to try those."

Melody helped herself to two pieces of candy from the dish on the counter in front of the receptionist's desk. She held one out to Grant. "I'll feel less guilty if I share."

"Thanks," he said, accepting the treat. "Do you have business with the mayor?"

Melody shook her head. "I stop by for candy whenever I'm in the square. I've been doing it since I was a kid. Free candy in the mayor's office is a town institution."

She told the busy receptionist good-bye, and Grant followed her out the door.

"I've been trying to get this sweets monkey off my back." She unwrapped her candy and popped it into her mouth.

Grant watched an expression of pure bliss slowly take over her face. He couldn't help but marvel at how the woman infused the simplest things with passion. Even back in college, her enthusiasm would peek from beneath her schoolgirl shyness when she did something important to her.

He wondered if she realized how appealing it made her.

"Something wrong?" she asked.

"No," Grant said abruptly. Embarrassed at being caught staring, he shoved his hands into his pants pockets. He retrieved the piece of candy out of one of them and gave it back to her. "You take it."

Her eyes lit up. "Are you sure?"

"I'm not hungry," he said, when in reality he simply longed to put that look of pleasure back on her face.

She didn't disappoint him. She ate the second Tootsie Roll with the same relish as she had the first.

"Mmmmm," she crooned. "You don't know what you're missing."

Silently he questioned if he had indeed missed out decades ago when he didn't take a closer look at her.

Later Grant found himself standing at the counter of a general store that carried everything from battery jumper cables to baby clothes.

"Thanks for shopping with us." The salesclerk

gave him a receipt to sign and returned his credit card. She passed the plastic bag over the counter. "Once you get out of that suit and into these, you'll have no problem relaxing."

"Who said I needed to relax?" he asked, already knowing the answer.

"Edith Riley mentioned it when she stopped in earlier today," the clerk replied.

Grant shot Melody an inquiring look.

Melody shrugged. "It's a small town. Everybody knowing everybody else's business comes with the territory."

That was an understatement, he thought as he signed the receipt and took the bag. While there was a charge for merchandise, the shopkeepers in every store they'd entered had given plenty of free advice. At the shoe store, his new athletic shoes had come with the suggestion that he take up fishing. The man who'd sold him a three-pack of T-shirts insisted Moon Pies and Coca-Cola were the ultimate stress-busters.

The fact that he was a complete stranger didn't deter them or passersby on the street from tossing out their opinions.

"You got some real bargains," Melody said as they walked along the sidewalk with several bags in tow.

Grant spied her ponytail out of the corner of his eye. Its bounce kept time with the gentle sway of her hips. He couldn't help but notice the way the soft wisps of hair that had broken free from the confines of the ponytail framed her heart-shaped face.

They skirted out of the path of an oncoming pack of giggling teenage girls with eyes only for a nearby group of sulky-looking boys around the same age. Clad in dark denim pants that stopped inches above her ankles, a white T-shirt and sneakers, Melody didn't look much older than them.

"I never would have guessed you were so into shopping," Grant said after the adolescents had passed. Melody was bubbling over with enthusiasm. The spark in her eye over the relatively small price reductions she'd haggled over wasn't lost on him.

They walked to the gazebo situated in the center of the square's park. They seated themselves on one of its benches, and he gratefully dropped the shopping bags at their feet.

"I'm not, really," she said thoughtfully. "I guess I just love getting a good deal."

"Are you sure it isn't the *art* of the deal you're missing?"

Melody fixed him with a frown. "Positive."

"I don't know. You seem worked up to me."

She blinked away what appeared to be regret. "You're wrong," she said, averting her eyes.

Hope surged through Grant. She could deny it, but her protest belied the flash of longing he'd detected. He might be making some progress.

With a light touch of his finger, he lifted her chin and tilted it toward him. Attraction hit Grant

49

full force and caught him totally off guard. His gaze swept over her, lingering on her full, lush lips.

"I don't think I am." He took his hand from her face, hoping it would break the spell she'd cast over him. It didn't.

A curl fell across her forehead. Automatically, he reached out and pushed it aside. The moment he touched her again, he knew it was a mistake. Caught within the depths of her golden eyes, he voiced the question running through his mind.

"When was the last time a man told you how beautiful you are?"

Abruptly, Melody jerked away. In a split second, he watched her warm and inviting expression cool to downright glacial. "When he wanted the same thing as you: for me to make him a lot of money."

CHAPTER FOUR

Melody wasn't about to be the same fool again.

She'd been deceived twice by smooth-talking men who'd pledged their love. But underneath the sweet conversation, all they'd really cared about was what they thought a relationship with her could do for their social status or bank balance.

Melody knew she was being unfair to Grant, who remained silent as he drove. He was no doubt wondering why she'd gotten so upset. The confines of the sedan made it impossible for her to keep a physical distance from him; still, she scooted as far away as she could as if it would ensure her emotional space.

She bit down on her bottom lip, but the pain didn't keep the past at bay. Two broken engagements still haunted her.

First there had been Eric, a saxophonist she'd met when a girlfriend had invited her out to a jazz brunch. The mellow notes from his magical sax had caught her attention, and his easy, bad-boy smile had captured her heart.

Their whirlwind romance spun out after she refused to cosign a six-figure loan to buy the club where he worked. He said he couldn't marry a woman who wouldn't support his dream and promptly dumped her.

Her second close call with marriage had come with Rob, a man she'd met on a blind date. A family practice physician, Rob had a deep baritone that put Barry White to shame. It turned out he spent more time day-trading online than he did with patients. He'd tried picking her brain for tips, but she begged off. When his portfolio collapsed along with the tech bubble, he gave her an ultimatum.

"If you love me, you'll help me," he'd said.

Again, it had all come down to money. Melody risked a glance at Grant, then turned her attention back to the passenger-side window. Now the first man she'd ever really fallen for was finally pursuing her—solely for financial reasons.

She had intended to show him the building where her yarn shop would soon open, but instead she'd allowed herself to be distracted. For a few moments, she'd been gullible enough to think the adoring look she'd seen in his velvety brown eyes was genuine.

The man was tall, dark and to-die-for handsome. He'd had his pick of the prettiest girls back in college, and she doubted he lacked female attention nowadays. What would he want with her?

Of course. He'd already told her. He wanted her to accept his job offer and proceed to make his investors a lot of money.

Somehow with her and men it always came down to money.

"I apologize for upsetting you," Grant said, breaking the awkward silence that had hung between them since they'd left the square.

"Accepted."

"But make no mistake, I'm only apologizing for upsetting you. I'm not sorry I said you were beautiful."

Melody looked over at him. His expression seemed sincere, and the woman in her wanted nothing more than to believe him. But she didn't trust him. Moreover, she couldn't trust herself. Ironically, the dead-on intuition that had served her so well in deciding which stocks to buy for the fund she'd managed was worthless when it came to matters of the heart.

"I already told you to save the butter-wouldn't-melt-in-my-mouth charm for someone else."

"What's so awful about calling you beautiful?" he asked incredulously. "You're an attractive woman. I'm sure it's nothing you haven't heard before."

Melody snorted and rolled her eyes. "Yeah, I've heard it all before."

"What's that supposed to mean?"

"It means flattery will get you nowhere with me." A bitter edge crept into her voice. "I'm no Halle Berry look-alike, and I know it."

He spared her a glance. "Look, Melody, the last thing I want to do is offend you."

"Forget it." She leaned against the headrest and closed her eyes. It wasn't his fault. If she wanted to be angry with or blame someone, she should start with the woman in the mirror.

Grant probably thought she was nuts. One minute she was gawking at him dreamily and the next she was practically biting his head off. Melody felt her face grow warm as she recalled her reaction to him. Embarrassed that a simple touch had her practically melting into a puddle at his feet, she was determined not to let it happen again.

Men would always try to get next to her for financial reasons, she decided. She couldn't control them, but she could control herself. Her well-being was her responsibility, and it was up to her to protect it.

Opening her eyes, she exhaled. "We have a long week ahead, so we're bound to step on each other's toes."

As they neared the fork in the road, she gestured for him to make a left. "It's getting late. You can just drop me off at home. I'll get my bike tomorrow."

Melody didn't know if it was hormones or some phase of the moon that had her acting like those teenage girls they'd seen earlier. She didn't know what was drawing her to this man like a magnet, but she intended to put a stop to it.

She bit down on her lip. It had been a long day, and she was just tired. A hot shower and good night's sleep and she'd forget she had ever entertained the silly idea of being attracted to Grant Price.

Grant pulled the car in front of her house and cut the engine.

"You don't have to see me in," she said. "I'll see you in the morning, bright and early."

He got out of the car, walked around and held open her door, as if he hadn't heard a word she'd said. "I told you this wasn't necessary," she said.

"Despite your obviously low opinion of me, I'm a gentleman. I've never dumped a lady off at the curb, and I don't intend to start now."

Grant extended his hand and Melody reluctantly took it as she rose from the car. She refused to look up at him. It would be too easy to get lost in the sensuous depths of those brown eyes. Melody dropped his hand the moment she got to her feet, telling herself it wasn't his touch that sent a surge of warmth from her fingertips down to her toes.

She attempted to walk ahead of him, to put physical distance between them, but her steps were no match for his long stride. The short walk to her doorstep seemed as long as a mile. She felt a whoosh of relief when they reached the front door.

"Well, thanks for the ride," she said hurriedly, carefully avoiding his gaze.

Grant nodded, but made no move to leave. She pulled her key from her fanny pack and unlocked the door. When she crossed the threshold, she heard him softly call out to her. Goose bumps popped up on her arms at the sound of her name on his lips.

"Yes?" With the barrier of the screen door between them protecting her from the strange yearnings he brought out in her, she allowed herself to look him in the eye.

"Good night," he said simply, then walked away.

A part of her had expected him to kiss her. What she hadn't anticipated was the intense pang of disappointment she felt when he didn't.

Three A.M.

The clock's red numbers pierced the darkness, glaring at Grant. He'd spent the night rolling from one side of the bed to the other and tossing from his left side to his right. He flipped from his back onto his stomach and shifted the pillow beneath his head.

"Damned lumpy bed," he muttered aloud. He turned on the lamp on the bedside table.

Throwing back the quilt, he swung his legs over the side of the bed. He knew the bed wasn't really the problem. It was comfortable enough, but it might as well have been a slab of cement.

Grant rose and padded barefoot across the hardwood floor to the bathroom adjoining his room. He turned the sink faucet on full blast and splashed his face with cold water. No stranger to sleepless nights, he'd spent plenty of them with his mind on work. No woman had haunted his dreams like this, not even Celeste.

As the cold water hit his face, he flashed back to the way Melody's golden eyes had blazed angrily at him after he blurted out she was beautiful. It was as if he'd slapped her.

She didn't believe you.

Yet at the moment he'd said it, he'd wanted nothing more than to feel those kissable lips of hers against his.

He peered at his reflection in the mirror and shook his head in disgust. "You're letting her get in your head, man," he grumbled.

Why now, he wondered. Why Melody?

He'd dated Celeste for five years, and she'd never had this effect on him. Celeste had always been so sweet and understanding. He couldn't imagine the former Miss Massachusetts doing something so ridiculous as to confiscate his electronic gadgets or ban him from getting in touch with anyone at the office.

From the day she'd walked into Prices' offices with her beauty-pageant smile and model-like beauty, his father had encouraged his pursuit of her.

"Now that's the kind of woman you need on your arm," John Price had said after he'd hired Celeste to revamp their outdated decor.

His father had been right. In their years together, Celeste had never balked over his long hours or when business forced him to break a date. She didn't argue with him, challenge him or leave him perplexed like Melody had managed to do in just one day.

He sighed at his bleary-eyed reflection. The predictable routine of his and Celeste's relationship hadn't required much effort at all on his part. If it hadn't been for her sister's wedding, they would more than likely still be together in the same comfortable routine.

Had he made a mistake in letting her go? he wondered.

Turning off the faucet, he dried his face with a fluffy towel from the nearby rack. It wasn't like him to have second thoughts. What was wrong with him lately? He was on the brink of getting the job he'd been groomed for his whole life. Yet doubts niggled at him. Was it what he really wanted?

He wasn't so sure anymore. Not since he'd watched Frank Scott pitch a no-hitter and win the World Series last October. Over forty years old and the guy was still throwing smoke. Nobody could get a hit off of him.

"Except you," Grant mumbled.

He'd played Little League and high school baseball against Frank. Even back then old Frank's arm was like a rocket launcher. Grant had been the only kid in the conference to get a hit off him. He even got a few home runs.

Both he and Frank had been offered baseball scholarships to college. Frank took his and eventually made it to the majors. Grant turned his down after his father pointed out that he needed to forget baseball and concentrate on business-school studies.

"Get out of the way-back machine." Grant shook his head as if it would help him get back into the right frame of mind. His father had done the right thing. Grant needed to prepare for a future of running Price Investments, not chasing some baseball pipe dream.

And this thing with Melody. He'd only been here a day, and now his mind was on this blasted, stubborn woman instead of his duty.

That was completely unacceptable.

He lowered himself back onto the bed and turned off the light. He wanted her only for Price Investments. All he cared about was what was best for Price Investments.

CHAPTER FIVE

When Melody pulled her Ford Explorer into Ruth's drive early the next morning, the rising sun had begun to burn off the blanket of fog coating the rural landscape. Despite the dense haze, she quickly spotted Grant pacing the well-tended yard.

Melody sighed. On the way over, she'd told herself this attraction she'd felt toward Grant yesterday was just her imagination, and his guest appearance in her dreams last night was merely a coincidence. She'd convinced herself it was true.

Until she saw him again.

He'd traded his suit and tie for sneakers, khaki shorts and a black T-shirt. The change into casual clothing gave him an entirely different persona. She nearly bit her tongue to keep from saying it aloud. *He looked good.*

Melody popped the lock and Grant slid into the SUV's passenger seat. The tiny hairs on the back of her neck tingled at his close proximity as he adjusted the leather bucket seat to accommodate his masculine frame. His presence made her Explorer's spacious cockpit feel downright claustrophobic.

"Good morning," she said brightly, hoping to put the awkwardness from last night behind them.

Grant grunted something that sounded like a greeting, then pulled the seatbelt across his broad chest and clicked it into place.

"So I'm guessing you're not a morning person," she offered.

"What tipped you off?"

"It was a toss-up between that scowl you're wearing and the way you're practically growling at me."

"You take your chances when you take away a man's morning coffee," he grumbled. "Mind explaining why you summoned me at the crack of dawn?"

"Oh, come on. I'll bet you're usually up at this hour." Melody countered. If he thought grouchiness was going to dissuade her, he was mistaken. They'd made a deal, and she intended to uphold her end of it.

"Well, yeah, but . . ."

"I know, you're reading the *Wall Street Journal* or checking CNBC," Melody said, answering her own question.

"That's important. It's part of my job."

"For now, consider this your top priority. Today, you're doing something for you."

"So you've told me. You can save the rest of the sermon. I've been drafted into your relaxation boot camp, and you're going to show me the error of my ways."

"Something like that," Melody replied matter-of-factly. "It might not feel like it now, but I really am doing you a favor. Trust me."

"You haven't given me a choice."

Ruth stepped outside. "You taking him to yoga class with you?" she asked, inclining her head toward Grant.

Melody shook her head. "No, I think yoga is probably too tough for him," she said. "So we'll power walk around the square instead."

"Stop in when you're done. I'll have breakfast ready," the older woman said.

Melody's stomach growled at the prospect of Ruth's cooking. The older woman had been her grandmother's best friend and a fixture in her life ever since she could remember. Although they weren't connected through blood, Ruth Sharp was family. With her grandmother gone now, she was all the family Melody had left. "That'll be great. We'll see you in a bit."

She waved goodbye to Ruth and backed the car out of the driveway.

"What was that you said about yoga being too hard for me?" Grant asked.

Melody sighed and clicked on her turn signal. "All I meant was, it can be tough for a beginner."

"For all you know, I could be some kind of yoga guru."

"Are you?"

"No, but there's no need for you to alter your routine because of me. If you can do yoga, so can I," he challenged.

"Have you ever tried yoga? It's not easy," Melody said. It was too early in the morning for fragile-male-ego drama.

"No, but my assistant, Barbara, sometimes takes a class over her lunch hour. If you two can survive it, I can too."

"Fine, but don't say I didn't warn you," Melody said, then lowered her voice to a mumble. "Maybe it'll improve your grouchy disposition."

"That's what coffee is for, but thanks to you and Warden Ruth, it's forbidden."

Melody bit her bottom lip to keep from laughing aloud. "Warden Ruth? Grant Price, you should be ashamed of yourself. She's just a sweet old lady."

"Humph. My hand's stinging from her brand of sweetness."

This time Melody did laugh. "She *is* a hand-smacker."

He cracked a smile. "Thanks for the warning—too late."

"Sorry," Melody said contritely. "But I can empathize with you there. She popped my hands a time or two when I was a child."

"Really?" Grant chuckled. "How come?"

"It's a long story."

"You have a captive audience."

"Well, Ruth was always baking for the church or county fair, and she'd set her cakes and pies out to cool on her windowsill. And boy, they always smelled so good. All the kids in town would gather around for a whiff. My best friend, Joyce, and the other kids were too scared, but I could never resist sneaking a sample."

Melody continued as she maneuvered the SUV along the road's twists and turns. "For a while, she never knew I swiped a taste here and there. But one day, just as I was about to stick a finger into one of her apple pies, she caught me with a smack so quick if I'd blinked I would have missed it." Melody looked down at her hand, which stung at the memory. "But I felt it all right."

Grant's chuckle exploded into a full-fledged laugh, his deep, rich baritone filling the interior of the SUV. He had a nice laugh, Melody noted. Too bad he didn't use it more often.

"Sweets have always been my weakness," Melody confessed. "Still are."

"So was it worth it?"

"Have you tasted her peach cobbler yet?"

A hint of a smile crossed his face. "I guess she's not all bad," he conceded. "But she should be running a jail instead of a bed-and-breakfast."

"She'll grow on you."

Melody stole a glimpse of the man sitting on the passenger's side, only to find him watching her pensively. She could feel her cheeks heating up and hoped he didn't notice. "What's the matter?"

"Nothing's wrong. I'm curious, that's all."

"About Ruth?"

"No. You," he said. She could almost feel his gaze on her skin. "What brought about the complete turnaround? You're one of the most renowned mutual fund managers in the country.

Why are you so determined to toss away everything you sweated for and worked so hard to achieve?"

She flipped down the visor to keep the rising sun out of her eyes. His question was legitimate and deserved an answer. She'd eventually give him one, just not yet. Right now she wanted to keep the focus on him.

"It doesn't matter. This week isn't about me. It's about you," she said.

A few seconds later, Melody brought the Explorer to a stop in front of the town hall building. "I was thinking a nice walk would be better for both of us this morning," she said, offering Grant an out.

Grant leaned in, bringing his face mere inches from hers. "Don't patronize me, Melody. If yoga is what you usually do, that's what we'll do."

The masculine scent of his cologne sent a charge from her fingertips down to her toes. Her gaze unwittingly slid from his eyes down to his mouth. The soft warmth of his breath gently caressed her jaw, and she couldn't help but wonder what it would feel like to kiss him.

He abruptly pulled away. And Melody busied herself unbuckling her seatbelt. What was it about this man that made her feel like a schoolgirl with a bad case of puppy love?

It's the job, stupid!

Grant silently scolded himself as he stepped into the community recreation room. He had only got in Melody's face to tell her he had no intention of wimping out on the yoga class. Instead, he'd almost kissed her—again.

He had to get his mind back on business and convincing Melody to take the job. Letting his father down was not an option.

He scanned the large room, taking in the two dozen or so people gathered for the class. Folding tables and chairs had been pushed out of the way and stacked along the concrete block walls to clear space. Thin rubber mats in a variety of colors littered the tiled floor.

The right side of his mouth quirked upwards. He'd twist, bend or walk on his hands if he had to. In the end, it would all be worth it. Two weeks from now, he and his father would enjoy a good laugh about this over celebratory flutes of champagne.

"Hello, Melody." A man with a beard and sandals approached them, suspending the mantra running through Grant's mind.

"Hi, Mr. Gise."

Mr. Gise motioned toward Grant and looked back at Melody curiously. "Who's your friend?"

Grant was surprised. The man had to be the only person in town who didn't know who he was and why he was there.

Melody glanced from the man to Grant. "Well, he's . . ."

Picking up on Melody's trouble explaining his presence, Grant interjected. "Grant Price." He extended his hand and the other man shook it. "Melody and I are old classmates."

"The name's Austin. I was Melody's high-school chemistry teacher. I've been trying to get her to call me by my first name for years now. Her class was my first right out of college, so I'm only a few years older."

Melody smiled. "I'm working on it, Mr. Gi . . . I mean, Austin."

Austin gave Grant a quick once-over. "You're new to yoga, right?"

"How did you know?"

Austin laughed. "You have an 'I've been dragged here' look on your face."

"Is it that noticeable?"

Melody and Austin looked at each other and back at Grant. "Yes," they said simultaneously.

Austin assured him he was going to love yoga, then moved on to the other side of the room. Grant doubted it, but didn't have any alternative. If he was going to convince her to take this job, he'd have to appease her. For now.

Melody elbowed him lightly in the ribs. "It's going to be fun."

"You don't hear me complaining. Bring it on."

"Good. Yoga seems to be improving your karma already. You're only half as crabby as you were when I picked you up."

Scanning the room, Grant noted a diverse group of students. The room contained people old enough to be grandparents, a few college-aged kids and everything in between. It should be easy enough. His eyes stopped on a familiar-looking man with a stocky build. "Hey, that guy looks like

Dirt Ramey," Grant mumbled aloud, not believing his eyes.

"Who?"

"My God, it *is* him."

"Oh, you mean Dirk, not Dirt," Melody corrected.

"That's *Dirt* Ramey," he said, looking in awe at his childhood hero. "In his day, he broke all kinds of stolen base records."

"I'd heard he used to be a ball player or something like that."

"A baseball player!" Grant said. "There wasn't a boy alive who didn't want to be Dirt Ramey."

"Even you?"

"You'd better believe it. My brother, Thomas, and I would take turns pretending to slide into home plate."

"I didn't know you were such a baseball fan."

Pangs of longing mixed with regret stabbed at Grant. He rubbed the back of his hand against his chin. "It was a long time ago. I was just a kid."

"Do you get out to many games now?"

"Work keeps me pretty busy. I don't have a lot of time for leisure pursuits." The explanation sounded flimsy to his own ears. He could only imagine what was going through her head.

Melody pinned him under the scrutiny of her golden gaze. "So you work hard so you can't enjoy the things you love?"

Her question hung in the air. While he didn't answer, it echoed in Grant's mind. Why didn't he make time?

He watched Melody unfurl a rubber mat from

the case she'd carried in and roll it out onto hard wood floor. "This is a sticky mat. It keeps your feet from slipping in standing postures and cushions you from the floor in sitting ones," she explained. "I'm sure Nona has an extra."

"Nona?"

"Our instructor."

Melody called out to a thin, barefoot woman wearing a black leotard and shoulder-length dreadlocks tied back with a multicolored scarf.

"Ahhhh, I'd heard Melody had a visitor. You must be Grant," Nona said, not waiting for him to confirm it. Grant raised a brow. CNN could take lessons from these people. "Well, you've come to the right place. Yoga is a great way to clear your mind and release tension. It'll help you deal calmly with issues in your life."

From what he'd experienced so far, small-town life definitely wasn't his speed. He'd never get used to strangers sticking their noses in his business. There was something to be said for big-city anonymity.

"As a matter of fact, why don't you see me after class. I've been reading up on acupuncture, and I know just the thing for those headaches of yours," Nona said. "Just a needle here and maybe a few here, then no more pain."

He looked over Nona's shoulder to see Melody shaking her head vigorously. She needn't have bothered. While yoga, acupuncture and a whole host of new-age therapies were the current trend, he didn't plan to jump on their bandwagons anytime soon.

"Thanks, but I'll stick, no pun intended, with aspirin."

Nona shrugged. "Suit yourself, but if you change your mind my offer stands."

It took the two women only moments to produce an extra mat. Grant unfurled the black mat in the vacant spot next to Melody.

"I'll demonstrate modifications on some of the postures as we go," Nona said. "Push as far as you can, but remember that yoga isn't competitive. Respect your limits. Your body will tell you how far to go. All you have to do is listen."

Grant nodded. It wasn't if they were about to run a marathon. Despite his tight schedule, he did manage to make it to the gym every once in a while. Not as often as he should, but enough to make it through this easily enough.

"Oh, you'll have to take off your shoes," Melody said, kicking off her sneakers.

Grant complied. At this point, he just wanted get it over with. Nona turned on a CD player, filling the room with the soulful voice of Al Green, then positioned herself at the front of the room.

"Okay, let's get started," she said. "We're going to begin in mountain pose. That's feet shoulder-length apart with arms at your sides and toes pointing forward. Hold it for six breaths. Breathe in, allowing your stomach to expand, then exhale."

Standing and breathing. Grant smiled to himself. He hoped he didn't fall asleep during class.

"Let's begin Sun Salutation by moving into prayer pose. Feet together and hands at your sides.

Take a deep breath, exhale, and put your hands together." Nona demonstrated the motions as she spoke. "We're going to do a half dozen sun salutes before moving on to the other asanas."

Nona looked to her new student and continued, "Grant, I want you to just observe the first couple of times and join in when you feel comfortable. I'll be working my way around the room to help."

He watched as Nona stretched like a cat and bent her body into a series of movements. The moves seemed simple enough when Nona demonstrated them.

Forty-five minutes later, sweat streamed from every pore in Grant's body. Yoga? Boot camp was more like it, and there was nothing laid-back or remotely relaxing about it. No area of his body escaped the continuous series of challenging and fast-moving poses.

He should have opted for the walk, Grant thought, though he would never admit it aloud.

Classic R&B tunes played in the background. Any other time, Grant would have enjoyed the variety of artists ranging from early Luther Vandross to the Ohio Players. However, he was too busy trying to keep up to appreciate his old favorites.

While Nona displayed some less challenging modifications for his benefit and even came over a few times to show him proper alignment, she never let up on the intensity. Following her cue, Grant twisted his body from something she called triangle pose into exalted warrior pose. His legs wobbled in the wide stance as he lifted his arms overhead.

"Everything okay?" Melody asked.

Bending over into what Nona had called the downward facing dog, he figured it would have been easier to run a marathon. "Yeah, just great," he said, as they were directed into a standing pose. Then he spied Melody out the corner of his eye.

Grant froze. Last night, he'd called her beautiful. In the light of day, he realized it was an understatement.

Mesmerized, he couldn't tear his gaze away. Melody wasn't a thin woman, yet she executed the yoga moves with ballerina grace and fluidity. The shapeless gray T-shirt and cotton drawstring pants she wore worked hard to camouflage the voluptuous figure underneath. However, her sinfully sexy curves wouldn't be hidden. His Adam's apple bobbed in his throat.

He ordered himself to stop gawking and turn away, but like his traitorous mind, his body rebelled. She turned to him and flashed an innocent smile. Thank God she couldn't read his thoughts.

Price Investments was the last thing on his mind.

"So how'd he take to yoga?"

Melody savored a melt-in-your-mouth bite of banana-pecan pancakes. To her delight, Ruth had had breakfast prepared when they got back to her place. The pancakes and freshly squeezed orange juice were dished up in the sun-drenched dining room on cheerful yellow fiesta dishes. A vase filled with a splashy mix of Gerber daisies served as the centerpiece. The table reflected the pride the older woman took in her exceptional culinary skills.

The meal was a scrumptious break from Melody's usual breakfast of orange juice and a piece of fruit.

"He did just fine," Melody replied.

"I'm impressed," Ruth said.

"He'll never admit it, but I actually think he liked it."

"Are you two going to continue to talk about me as if I weren't sitting here?"

"Sorry," Melody offered, attempting to look contrite.

"Humph," Ruth grunted. "Doesn't seem like it improved his disposition any. He's as cranky now as he was when you picked him up this morning."

Melody took a sip of orange juice, catching Grant ogling the generous stacks of pancakes on her and Ruth's plates. He looked so pitiful, she felt a smidgen of guilt as she doused hers with a coating of berry maple syrup.

"Maybe I'd feel more jovial if I was wolfing down pancakes too," Grant said.

Ruth helped herself to a piece of sausage. "Mind your own plate."

"What plate?" Grant asked, looking down at the solitary bowl of oatmeal sitting before him.

Melody peered at the bowl of oatmeal. Despite the touch of diced peaches and cinnamon, next to the pancakes it looked pretty bland. And she ought to know. Ruth had spooned enough of the stuff into her when she'd first returned home.

"With all that trashy junk food you eat, I can almost hear your arteries crying out for a healthy bowl of oatmeal," Ruth said matter-of-factly. "It's good for you."

"It doesn't taste like it," he grumbled. "And how come she gets pancakes?" He motioned toward Melody, momentarily distracting her from her plate.

"Leave me out of it."

"Leave you out of it? You're the reason I'm eating baby food."

Ruth cleared her throat. "Melody is only trying to save you from the very thing that almost killed her. You know what hell she went through."

"No, but why don't you tell me?" Grant said slowly, his interest piqued.

"She almost worked herself into an early grave. She . . ."

Melody cut the older woman off with a silencing wave of her hand. She planned to tell Grant everything eventually, but for now she just wanted to take him out of his workaholic grind for a few days. She hoped he'd discover there was more to life than work and money.

"Never mind. It's her business to tell and I suppose she'll do it when she's good and ready," Ruth said. "No pancakes for you and that's that. You might as well finish up your oatmeal before it gets cold."

"No big deal, Ruth," Grant replied casually. "I've been tempted by better-looking pancakes than those anyway." Grant winked at Melody and she saw a sinful smile cross his handsome face.

"Have you really?" The older woman visibly stiffened, her lips thinning into a line. Melody decided to take Ruth's admonishment to Grant to heart and mind her own plate. She didn't want any part of this conversation.

"Yes, indeed. Light, fluffy ones," he mused. Stirring his oatmeal, he swallowed a spoonful. "Really tasty, too."

"A few moments ago, you were practically begging for them."

"I was raised to be a gentleman. I was merely being polite, that's all."

"Humph," Ruth sniffed. "One bite of my pancakes will have you so smitten, you'll be on bended knee, begging me to marry you."

"While I might be tempted to ask for your hand"—Grant winked—"I can assure you it won't be over those."

Ruth cut into a layer of pancakes, stabbed a chunk with a fork and held it out to him. "Eat!"

"If you insist." Grant dropped his spoon into his half-full bowl of oatmeal. He cut a sly look at Melody before accepting the morsel. Melody waited for his face to break into the wide smile that only the older woman's delectable cooking could summon. However, his face remained unreadable as he slowly chewed.

"Well?" Ruth inquired.

"I'm not sure," Grant said innocently. "Maybe another taste will help me decide."

Melody broke her self-imposed silence. "Ruth, can't you see what he's doing? I don't believe it!

It's the oldest trick in the book, and you're playing right into his hands."

"I'm doing no such thing," Ruth replied. "Now hush up so he can tell me what he thinks."

Ruth held out another piece of pancake on a fork, this time practically jamming it into Grant's mouth. Melody rolled her eyes skyward.

"But he's got you feeding him," she objected in vain.

Ignoring Melody's protests, Ruth fixed Grant with a pointed stare. "Well?"

Grant sighed thoughtfully. "Not bad," he finally said.

"Not bad?" Ruth mimicked. For a moment, Melody thought she spotted smoke coming from her friend's ears. "Those are the best pancakes you ever tasted and you darn well know it."

Ruth continued to rant. "I don't have time for this today. I have five cakes and three pies to bake for the festival," she said as she stood to clear her plate and the platter of leftover pancakes from the table.

"Oh, the festival!" Between preparing for her shop's opening and Grant's unexpected arrival, the festival had totally slipped Melody's mind.

"Don't tell me you forgot about it," Ruth said. "Weren't you knitting a batch of puppets and dish-cloths as giveaways to promote your store?"

"I'm just about done."

"Good," Ruth said, as she headed toward the kitchen.

"Festival?" Grant asked.

"The town holds an end-of-summer festival every year. A big chunk of the proceeds goes to buy supplies for the schools," she said. "It's a pretty big deal around here."

"This isn't going to conflict with our agreement, is it? You gave me your word you're coming to Boston next week."

His question hit Melody with an unexpected twinge of disappointment. The festival wasn't the only thing she'd forgotten. Grant wasn't here for social reasons. This was business for him. She mustn't forget his bottom line.

"It won't interfere. The festival is Saturday. I'll return to Boston with you on Sunday as planned," she said. "I have no intention of reneging on our deal."

"Neither do I." His chocolate-brown eyes met hers. The intensity of his gaze made the hair on the back of her neck tingle.

She turned away from him, hoping to hide the flush she felt warming her cheeks, and rose from the table. "I'm going home to shower, then I thought I'd show you around town."

"Actually, Dirt invited me to go check out the local minor league team's practice."

"I have an errand to run myself, so I'll meet you back here in a couple of hours."

He reached out and touched her arm, sending the delicious tingles on the back of her neck sliding down her spine. "Are you okay, Melody? Did I say something wrong?"

"Everything's okay," she heard her own voice say

aloud, while the tiny voice deep down whispered that her simple and uncomplicated life would never be okay again.

Grant hadn't been to a ballpark in years.

He took a deep breath, savoring the scent of the freshly mown field. Excitement coursed through his veins. Even in this tiny venue, he felt like the prodigal son who had finally returned home.

Initially, he'd turned down Dirt's invitation. Now he was glad he'd changed his mind. Not only was it an opportunity to talk with one of his childhood heroes, he could use the time to rethink his approach to persuading Melody to take the job.

Her newfound, small-town life couldn't be as idyllic as she pretended, Grant thought. There had to be something wrong with it. Something he could use to help him change her mind. He raised his hand to his forehead to shield his eyes from the sun. All he had to do was figure out what it was.

"Glad you could make it," Dirt called out from the bleachers. As he approached, Grant noticed for the first time the former athlete walked with a slight limp.

Grant's gaze dropped to the cell phone clipped to Dirt's belt. He rubbed the back of his neck with his hand. What he wouldn't give for five minutes, just enough time to check in with the office.

"I hate to ask, but . . ."

Dirt shook his head no before he could finish the question. Damn, they'd obviously gotten to him too. "No can do, man. I can't cross Ruth and wind up on her bad side," he said sheepishly.

It didn't take a rocket scientist to figure out how a man once crowned major league baseball's rookie of the year, who had a hall of fame plaque with his name on it in Cooperstown, had been muscled into doing Ruth's bidding. "So what did she get you with, peach cobbler?" Grant asked.

"No, I'm hooked on her sweet potato pound cake."

"Pound cake?" Grant's curiosity was aroused along with his taste buds. He had no idea there was a cake version of one of his favorite pies.

"Yeah, she bakes them every year around Thanksgiving," Dirt said. "And while I sympathize with your plight, there's no way I'm going to chance missing out on cake."

"I understand." Grant thought back to the light, buttery crust on Ruth's melt-in-your-mouth peach cobbler and heaved a defeated sigh. "If I were you, I wouldn't risk helping me either."

Dirt tossed him a new baseball cap he'd been holding in his hand. "Figured you might need this. The sun is merciless this time of day."

Grant slipped the red cap, emblazoned with the minor league team's logo, on his head and adjusted it. "Thanks, man. It gets hot back in New England, but nothing like this."

The two walked along the edge of the ball field. "You still a baseball fan or were you just eager to catch a break from the ladies?" Dirt asked.

"Both." Grant chuckled.

"You used to play, right?"

An unexpected pang of envy hit Grant as he watched the players emerge from the clubhouse and take the field. He shrugged. "Just a little high-school ball."

"Were you any good?"

Grant rolled off a couple of his old high school stats. Dirt's brow lifted. "Damn, you were better than good."

"A couple of scouts were interested, and I was offered a scholarship to play in college."

"How come you didn't pursue it?"

"I went into the family business." He stared out at the players warming up on the field. A part of him wished he could turn back the clock.

"So how was it?" Grant finally asked.

Somehow Grant knew Dirt would understand exactly what he meant. Although they hadn't known each other long, they both loved the game.

"What part do you want to hear? The good, the bad or the ugly?" Dirt joked.

"All of it." It would be the closest he ever got to finding out what he had missed, Grant thought.

Dirt paused and tossed back to him a ball that had rolled between an outfielder's legs. "Well, the good is almost indescribable. The camaraderie. The competition. Bringing a packed stadium to its feet when you hit a ball out of the park or catch the game-winning out," he said. The wistful look on his face echoed in his voice. "Even after nine innings under the blazing sun, you feel like a kid whose mother just called him in to dinner. You hate to stop playing."

Grant found himself hanging on to Dirt's every word. In the back of his mind, he imagined what his life would have been like now if he had chased his own dream instead of following the path his father had mapped out for him. Would he now be playing Monday morning quarterback with the decisions he'd made for his life?

"From what you've just told me, I find it hard to believe there could be any bad." To Grant it sounded perfect, everything he'd ever imagined.

"For one, the salaries thirty years ago weren't anything like they are now. Back then, you didn't retire from the game set for life."

"But I'm sure your autograph is still in demand."

"Yeah, there are a few fans out there who still remember an old-timer like me."

Dirt sighed. "The other bad thing was the travel during the season. It was hell on my family. While little boys everywhere watched me play, my own barely saw me. My poor wife finally got fed up with being both mother and father to them," Dirt said, kicking at a stone embedded in the grass. "I'll never forget coming home from back-to-back games against the Pirates to find changed locks and divorce papers."

As a kid, Grant had envied Dirt Ramey's sons. His childhood hero's revelation gave him a new respect for his own father, who made time for both him and Thomas no matter how busy he was.

"My kids and I have grown closer over the

years," Dirt said, "but I can never get back the time we lost. I wasn't there for most of their firsts—first steps, first words, first day of school. . . ."

Dirt turned to Grant. "What about you? Do you have kids?"

Grant shook his head. "Never been married. No kids."

"That's too bad."

Grant didn't bother asking what Dirt meant by that statement. He'd been plagued with enough doubts lately. He didn't need to unleash another Pandora's box of possible regrets.

"So you're probably wondering what the ugly is all about?"

"I'll admit, I am curious," Grant said.

"Injuries."

"Oh yeah, that's right. You retired after having knee surgery."

"Two right knee surgeries, elbow surgery and a host of dislocated joints, popped ligaments and pulled muscles," he added. "There are a few guys who are still playing in their forties, but basically it's a young man's game. The body can only take so much."

"With those past injuries, I'm surprised you're doing yoga. That class is pretty vigorous," Grant said. This morning he'd watched Dirt twist and hold his body into positions that had left him trembling.

"Five years ago, I was walking with a cane and had the range of motion of an eighty-year-old. Then Nona convinced me to give her class a try," he said. "Mind you, it didn't happen overnight and I couldn't tell you how it works, but that yoga changed my life."

A stray ball rolled past Grant's foot. He stopped, picked it up, and threw toward the infield.

"Looks like you still have a good arm," Dirt said. "Are you sure you don't want to work out a bit with the guys?"

Grant shrugged off the suggestion. "Man, I haven't picked up a bat in years. Those guys have a game to get ready for. They don't need me getting in their way."

"This will probably be the Cosmos' last season here."

"Really? I thought you said the team sells out their home games."

"They do." Dirt nodded sadly. "But the current owner is getting on in years. He says he's ready to let it go."

"That's too bad." Grant reminded himself it wasn't his problem. If he had his way, the minor league team wouldn't be the only thing kicking the dust from this town off its shoes. At week's end they'd be saying goodbye to another resident—Melody.

Joyce held up the backpack stuffed with note-books, pens, a ruler, calculator and every other school supply imaginable.

"It's absolutely perfect, Mel."

"It's been a while since I was a coed, but I think there's enough in there to at least get you started."

Joyce hugged the bulging backpack to her chest. "I love it! Thanks so much."

Melody bit back a giggle as she watched her best friend sling the pack over her shoulder and model the gift. She had bought the backpack and supplies the day Joyce had sent off her college application. While Joyce may have sat on edge for weeks wondering if she'd make the cut, Melody had had no doubt she would be accepted.

"Congratulations, girl." Melody gave her friend a quick hug. "It takes a lot of courage to start school at our age. I'm proud of you."

"Well, you and my youngest are about the only ones."

"Kevin?" Melody had detected the disappointment in Joyce's tone when she'd called yesterday to tell her the good news. She figured her husband hadn't been pleased.

Joyce nodded. "Let's not stand out on the porch. Come on in. I've got leftover cinnamon rolls in the kitchen."

"No, thanks."

"You're turning down cinnamon rolls?" Joyce asked incredulously. "Are you feeling okay?"

"I'm fine. Ruth stuffed me with banana pecan pancakes earlier."

"Well, let me set this inside and we can walk down to the square. I need to stop by the deli, and you can burn off those pancakes." Joyce shrugged off the backpack and set it inside her house. Then the duo headed down Joyce's block toward the square.

Kevin and Joyce's two-story brick home was located in the newer, upscale part of town close to the square. Joyce had tried talking her into moving into the exclusive gated community where each house was like a mini mansion, but Melody had decided against it. For the time being, she still needed the warmth surrounding her grandmother's old place.

"So what did Kevin have to say after the dinner party?" Melody asked.

"Not much more than when I first called to read him my acceptance letter. Needless to say, things were pretty tense between us last night," Joyce said as the two walked past the tennis courts and through the community's gates.

"And dinner?"

"Despite him giving me practically no notice, it went off without a hitch. As usual, I was the perfect hostess. His clients never noticed the tension between us." Joyce sighed.

"Kevin didn't even thank me. He simply took for granted I'd take care of everything. No matter how last minute or inconvenient it was to pull off."

Melody wasn't sure what to say. She hadn't seen this side of Joyce. She'd always assumed her friend had reveled in the role of super wife. "I'm sure Kevin's grateful . . ." she began.

Joyce waved her hand in a dismissive gesture. "But I don't want to talk about Kevin anymore. Tell me more about this hunk who came all the way down here just for you."

Melody shrugged. "There's nothing to tell, really. He's not here for me. He's here about a job. It's about money. It's always about money."

"Maybe not. He's still here. Since you've been home, others have knocked on your door with offers and you practically kicked them out of your yard."

Melody brushed her hair back from her face. The deluge of employment opportunities didn't mean anything to her, because she wasn't that person anymore. She wasn't the *Money* magazine cover girl who spent hours upon hours researching a company. She no longer had the urge to discover a stock market hidden jewel and catch it on the rise.

"I don't know." Melody kicked a pebble on the sidewalk with the toe of her shoe. "I see so much of the old me in Grant. You of all people should remember, you could barely hold a conversation with me. All I thought about was which trends or stocks would boost my fund's returns."

Joyce touched her hand. "Are you sure there isn't more to it?"

"Like what?"

"Don't play coy with me. I remember you being bonkers over a guy named Grant when you were away at school," Joyce said. "Is this the same Grant or a big coincidence?"

Melody half groaned, half sighed. How could Joyce remember back so far? she wondered. Had she really talked about Grant that much back then?

"Same guy," she finally admitted.

"I heard he's fine. It didn't sound to me like he

was about to pass out or be carted away in an ambulance."

Melody bit down on lower lip. Okay, so one look at the man on her doorstep sent her heartbeat into overdrive. Still, it wasn't the reason she'd made a deal with him. Her intention was only to help him avert disaster. At least, that's what she kept telling herself. "I didn't look like that either, but it happened."

"If you say so." Her friend sounded doubtful.

"Really, this has nothing to do with how I felt about Grant in college. That was a long time ago," Melody contended, as they walked past the construction site of the new elementary school. "Wouldn't you take the car keys from a drunk driver or snatch a loaded gun away from a child?"

"Of course."

"That's exactly what I'm doing. Only in Grant's case unchecked drive, stress and ambition are the car keys and loaded gun." Melody knew her argument was weak, and the more she said the more obvious it became that the torch she'd carried for Grant still burned.

"Okay, maybe right now it's about this job for him and you're only trying to help, but who knows? It could turn into more," Joyce said with a wink.

"Joyce, please."

"Maybe you should tell him how you feel."

"I already told you . . ."

"Yeah, I know. You told me it's simply a rescue mission," Joyce said. "But that dreamy look on your face when you talk about him says something different."

The duo walked to the town hall and into the mayor's office. Cara wasn't at the desk so they each grabbed a piece of candy before heading out to the deli.

"You know my track record when it comes to romance," Melody said, unwrapping her Tootsie Roll.

"Just because things didn't work out with Rob or Eric doesn't mean you should give up on love."

"I faced the facts a long time ago. I know I'm no beauty. Men only want one thing from me, financial help. It's like the worn-out line that won Cuba Gooding, Jr. an Oscar: They only want me to show them the money."

"Oh, Mel, any man would be damned lucky to have you."

Melody wished she could believe Joyce. However, her history with men had tainted any fantasies of settling down. Cheated out of a real family by her parents' deaths, she wondered if she would ever have one of her own.

"Well, Grant Price isn't the man. He only wants me to make money for his investors."

Everyone said when it came to money, she had the Midas touch. It may have been a blessing financially, but as far as her love life went, it was nothing but a curse.

CHAPTER SIX

Hours after they'd parted, Joyce's thoughts were still on her friend. Opening the refrigerator, she pulled out the deli cold cuts and set them on the counter with a thump. She just didn't get it. How could a woman as intelligent and sharp as Melody actually believe no man would love her for herself?

"Pure baloney," Joyce muttered, looking down at the lunch meat on the counter. Melody had everything going for her, and Joyce knew there was a good man just waiting for a special woman like her.

She eyeballed the clock and figured she'd better get a move on. Her son, David, would be home from football practice soon and food would be the first thing on his mind. He'd mentioned bringing home a few of his teammates to play video games, so she knew from the experience that comes along with raising teenaged boys, she'd better prepare to feed a small army.

Joyce shook her head as she began to assemble

an assortment of sandwiches. Melody didn't realize how lucky she was to be known as smart and really great at something important. Melody had gone out into the world and made something of herself. Now the world was beating a path to her doorstep, begging her to share her skills and talent.

Sighing, Joyce sliced into a tomato. No one sought her opinions on anything of any relevance. She was the pretty little girl who had simply grown up to be the pretty little wife and mother. Her husband of all people should know that she needed something more.

"The only thing anyone asks me is 'where are my socks?' and 'what's for dinner?'" She finished cutting the tomatoes and divided the slices over her makeshift sandwich assembly line.

Joyce thought about the backpack Melody had brought her and how thoughtful it was. Why couldn't her husband have done something like that? It wasn't so much the gift, but the meaning behind it. Her friend had been a source of support and encouragement, while the man she'd spent over half her life loving gave her the cold shoulder.

She didn't expect or deserve his frosty attitude. She had been nothing but supportive when he wanted to sacrifice a well-paying job to start his own firm. She had smiled, cooked and entertained her tail off over the years, whether or not she was in the mood.

What was so wrong about her doing something for herself? Joyce covered the platter of sandwiches with plastic wrap and placed it in the refrigerator. Yesterday, her husband had successfully avoided talking about it, but this evening would be different. She was going to get to the bottom of his resistance to the idea of her finally pursuing her education.

"We're going to deal with this tonight."

Kevin tossed the legal brief across his desk in frustration. He'd tried reading it several times in the last half hour, but it was no use. While he was physically in his office, his brain was someplace else. As hard as he tried, he couldn't push his wife or the issue of her planning to start college out of his thoughts.

"Mr. Holden?"

Startled, he looked up to see his secretary standing before him with a sheaf of papers. He wasn't certain how long she'd been standing there or how many times she'd called him before he'd heard her. "What do you need?"

"I have those deposition transcripts you asked for," she said.

"Fine," he said absently. He took the stack of papers and dropped them on his desk.

"Uh . . . I don't mean to pry, but are you okay?"

He'd known his secretary long enough to know she wasn't the nosy type. She was merely concerned. After all, he was usually all business, but today he couldn't seem to concentrate on work.

"Everything's fine," he said in what he hoped was a reassuring tone.

He watched her leave, then swiveled his chair around to face the windows overlooking downtown Nashville. He stared out at the BellSouth building, his mind still firmly focused on Joyce. The previous evening's dinner for the head of Wilson Electronics had been a success. As usual, his beautiful wife had been the consummate hostess, making sure everyone who entered their home was entertained, well-fed and left with a smile on his or her face. In more than two decades of marriage, she had never ceased to make him proud. And in those years, they rarely went to bed angry.

Last night was the rare exception.

Pulling off his reading glasses, Kevin massaged the bridge of his nose with his fingertips. There was no argument or heated discussion, but they'd retreated to opposite ends of their king-sized bed not speaking or touching.

"All because of this school business," he grumbled aloud.

He knew what Joyce wanted from him. She expected him to be filled with the same excitement about it she felt. While he hated disappointing her, he couldn't pretend something he didn't feel. Not only was he not pleased, he wished he could find a way to persuade her to drop the whole thing.

Pivoting his chair back around, he faced the photograph of her on his desk.

"Three of the boys are out on their own. David's growing up." He spoke to the radiant, smiling woman in the photograph as if she could hear him. "We've barely spent any time alone since we've been married. Hell, we didn't even go on a honeymoon. This was supposed to be our time."

How could they make up for lost time if she was busy with classes, studying, labs and all the other grueling requirements needed to become a nurse? And it wasn't for a few months or a year, she was talking about four long years.

Kevin leaned back in his chair. Maybe there was a way to get her to postpone and rethink this school thing. He smiled as an idea developed. Maybe he could make both himself and Joyce happy at the same time.

He summoned his secretary back to his office and instructed her to clear his schedule for the day. He stood, shrugging on his suit jacket and reaching for his briefcase at the same time. His mind had already fast-forwarded to blue skies, sandy beaches and his gorgeous wife wearing a sexy bikini or—even better—nothing at all.

First, he would stop by the travel agency and then make a quick trip to the florist for the biggest bouquet of tropical flowers he could find.

A long-overdue honeymoon to Hawaii was sure to put a grin back on his wife's pretty face.

"How's this for transportation?" Melody asked.

Grant squirmed on the narrow and annoyingly hard seat. He hadn't ridden a bike since he'd turned sixteen and got his driver's license.

"Hey, Birdy." Melody waved to a housecoat-clad woman out watering the roses in her front yard.

Then she turned to Grant. "I'll bet it beats cramming yourself into a sardine can and fighting rush-hour traffic, huh?"

He followed her as she veered right. Sure, why wouldn't he prefer riding a bicycle to the supple leather seats and climate-controlled comfort of his special-edition, S-Class Mercedes? "Oh, yeah. Just great."

Seeming oblivious to his sarcasm, she continued to greet passersby with a wave or a nod. You'd think they were riding a float down a parade route.

"I figured we could ride down to my shop. The sign goes up this afternoon. I'm dying to see it."

Grant felt the muscle in his jaw twitch. This yarn store enterprise definitely presented a problem. It would be fine for anyone else, but not for Melody. The lady had a sixth sense when it came to the stock market. She knew it like a mother knows her child. Melody belonged at Price Investments.

He thought back to when shares of Sears had dropped below twenty dollars, and everyone was dumping their shares. Melody had increased her fund's stake in it. As the share price soared to over a hundred dollars, her fund produced twenty-nine percent returns for the year, and Melody had made the cover of *Business Week* as the year's best fund manager.

She seemed to know exactly when to buy, when to sit tight and when to sell.

He cast a glance at the curvaceous woman riding alongside him. How could she turn her back on her gift for a knitting store? There had to be more to it. What was she running away from?

"I designed it myself."

"What?" Grant hadn't heard a word.

"The sign for the store," she said. "THE KNITTY GRITTY is spelled out in a red script that looks like it's unwound from a ball of yarn. The yarn is the same red as the trim on the building and the awning over the windows."

He opened his mouth to give her a dozen reasons why a yarn store wasn't right for her. Then he glanced over at her. Those golden eyes held a spark that lit up her entire face. Her smile was positively entrancing. She had him almost as excited as she was about yarn.

His discouraging words caught in back of his throat.

Again, he wondered how he hadn't noticed back in college that there was more to this woman than brains. How could he have missed the way she carried her nearly six-foot form with such grace, or the incredibly long lashes framing her almond-shaped eyes?

He turned sharply after his bike nearly veered into a parked car. Focus, he reminded himself. Somehow he had to make her see how wrong it was for her to hide herself and her skills in this tiny town, but for now he simply wanted to bask in the glow of her spectacular smile.

"I'm sure it's a very nice sign," he said.

"Let's hurry. I want to watch them hang it."

Grant pedaled faster to match Melody's pace.

The ride had seemed a lot shorter when they drove it yesterday.

Another neighbor had her hand in the air, only this woman wasn't waving in greeting like the others they'd passed. She flailed her arms about frantically. The woman ran from the edge of a driveway into the street, nearly colliding with them.

"Oh, Melody. Thank goodness you rode by," she said breathlessly.

Melody laid a hand on the frazzled woman's shoulder. "What's going on, Liz?"

"My sister just called. She's in labor. I have to get over there right away and take her to the hospital. I need someone to keep an eye on the boys." She tilted her head toward the yard she'd come from, where two overall-clad little boys crawled through the grass, pushing toy dump trucks.

Grant watched Melody's face blanch.

"I can't," she hedged. "I have to be down at the store. They're hanging the . . ."

"Please," the woman begged before Melody could finish. "I know the twins can be a handful, but it's only until the baby-sitter gets here."

"How long do you think she'll be?"

"Not long at all," Liz said. "Melody, I wouldn't ask you to do this, but I'm desperate. The boys will be on their best behavior. Promise."

"Okay," Melody said, getting off her bike.

Grant followed Melody and the harried woman.

"I was just about to make their lunch when she called. There are some kid frozen dinners in the freezer, if you'd just pop them in the microwave."

"Sure," Melody said. "And the sitter is on her way."

"She'll be here any minute."

The woman called the boys over. "Mommy has to go. I want you two to be good until I get back." She turned to Melody. "My cell phone and Doc Gallagher's numbers are on a corkboard in the kitchen."

Melody remembered how Joyce had had Dr. Gallagher on her speed dial when her twins were boys and emergency room regulars. "They'll be fine. Go see about your sister."

"Thanks. You're a good neighbor, Melody. You too, Grant," Liz said. This time Grant didn't think twice about someone he didn't know calling him by name. Ruth was right. He hadn't run into Edith yet, but she could indeed spread news like butter.

"I almost forgot—if they offer you a drink of water, don't take it." The woman jumped into her car and backed out of her driveway.

"I wonder what that cryptic warning was all about," Grant said.

"With these two, it's probably better if you don't know."

"Relax, Melody," he said. "Their mother said the baby-sitter is on the way. It'll be a piece of cake."

So far, so good.

Melody released a sigh of relief as she sat the nuked meals in front of the twins. She peered at her watch, hoping the baby-sitter would show up soon. Her knowledge of kids was limited to the gifts a personal shopper at the toy store had selected and mailed off to Joyce's boys when they were young.

She looked up at Grant, who was sitting on the opposite end of Liz's kitchen table. "Tell me you have a host of nieces and nephews who have turned you into an expert on children."

"I'm afraid my experience with kids extends only to how to set up their college funds."

She poured milk into the boys' matching *Sesame Street* cups. So what if they didn't know much about kids, she thought. How hard could it be? They were mature adults, with advanced university degrees, who'd been responsible for handling millions of dollars. Surely, they could take care of a pair of three-year-olds for an hour.

"Melly, I want spagettees." Joe frowned at the plate of macaroni and cheese in front of him.

"Joe, you said you wanted macaroni and cheese, remember?"

"How can you tell them apart?" Grant interrupted.

Melody touched her hand to Jeff's shoulder. "Their T-shirts," she said. "Liz always dresses Joe in green and Jeff here in blue."

Joe pointed a chubby finger at the spaghetti on his brother's plate. "Want spagettees."

"Why don't you just try a bite of your macaroni and cheese?" Melody coaxed. "It's shaped like dinosaurs."

"No!" Joe shouted. "Spagettees!"

On cue, Jeff took a huge bite of spaghetti and poked the stray strands into his already stuffed mouth with his fingers. "Mmmm," he gloated, further torturing his brother. "I lub spagettees."

Grant chuckled, and she shot him a silencing glare. "You're not helping here."

"I didn't know I was supposed to," he said.

"We agreed to keep an eye on them until their sitter arrived."

"No, you agreed," he said. "I'm on orders to relax, and if the expression on your face is any indication, baby-sitting doesn't seem to be particularly stress-relieving."

Rolling her eyes skyward, Melody wondered just how many contrary little boys she was dealing with. "Thanks for nothing," she muttered.

Melody felt a small hand tug on the edge of her shirt. "Hungry," Joe whined.

"Well, eat your macaroni, sweetie," she said. "Just try one bite.

"No!" Joe squealed at the top of his lungs. He pushed his plate away toward the center of the table.

"Spagettees!"

Melody winced. The high-pitched scream bounced off the walls before shattering her eardrums.

"Okay, sweetie. I'll make you spaghetti."

She opened the freezer and scanned the stacks of kid meals. A wave of panic washed over her. No spaghetti. There were plenty of fish sticks, chicken nuggets and corn dog entrees, and even more dreaded macaroni and cheese.

"There's got to be one in here somewhere," she

muttered. She rustled through the neatly arranged boxes and went through the cabinets, coming up empty.

She turned to Joe. His bottom lip was stuck out and his little arms were folded across his chest.

"How about fish sticks?"

"No!"

Jeff dangled a few strands of spaghetti in front of his brother before cramming them in his mouth.

"Stop it, Jeff," Melody said, and then turned to Joe. "Sorry sweetie, there isn't any more spaghetti."

"I want spagettees." Joe banged his fist against the table for emphasis. "Now!"

Jeff scooped up a handful of spaghetti and with major-league-pitcher accuracy sent it flying in the direction of his brother. It hit Joe in the forehead, the tomato sauce dripping down his little face.

She heard laughter coming from the other end of the table and shot Grant an admonishing glare.

"Sorry, Melody," he said. "But the kid did say he wanted spaghetti *now*."

She returned her attention back to the children. "Jeff! Don't throw food at your brother."

Too late. A second scoop of spaghetti flew in Joe's direction, crossing in midair with a handful of macaroni and cheese headed straight for Jeff.

"Freeze!" Melody commanded in the same no-nonsense tone that used to send everyone in her office running for cover.

The twins' eyes grew wide, and their food-filled little fists halted mid-throw. Melody had seen enough *Cosby Show* reruns while she was in the hospital to know there had to be some kind of great teaching moment here, but darned if she knew what it was.

"Now you two go wash your hands, and you can have cupcakes for lunch."

"Cupcakes!" Jeff squealed.

The microwave meals and food fight forgotten, the twins practically leaped from their chairs and hustled themselves to the bathroom.

Melody opened the cabinet to retrieve the box of chocolate cupcakes she'd spied earlier.

"Well done," Grant said from his perch on the other end of the table.

"When in doubt, bribe 'em."

Melody tossed the uneatened microwaved meals in the trash and wiped the table off. Grant rose from the table.

"You bailing out on me?" she asked.

"No, I thought I'd better check on our little friends," he said, heading off to the bathroom.

Moments later, he was back in the kitchen with a little boy in each hand. "I figured out why the boys' mother warned us about them and water," he said as the kids seated themselves. "Apparently they're convinced that the best place to get cold water is from the toilet."

Melody rolled her eyes skyward as the boys tore into the cupcakes.

"More milk!" Jeff yelled through his cupcake-crammed mouth.

"Hey man, that's no way to talk to a lady," Grant said.

"More milk, pleeeze." Jeff corrected.

Melody pulled the milk from the refrigerator. She was about to pour when her grasp weakened. The carton slipped from her hand, spilling milk all over the table and onto the floor.

"Darn it, not now," she scolded her weakened left hand. She instinctively rubbed it with her right as if that would somehow infuse it with strength.

In an instant, Grant was at her side. "Hey, it was just an accident."

While she'd dropped or spilled things in front of Joyce or Ruth and it was no big deal, this felt different somehow. She averted her eyes. "I'll just clean this mess up."

Grant eyed her curiously. "No, you have a seat. I'll take care of it."

Melody took a seat. She flexed her hand underneath the table. The boys continued to stuff their little mouths with cupcakes and didn't protest when Grant substituted apple juice for milk. For toddlers, she figured spills were everyday occurrences and they were oblivious to them.

After he'd cleaned up and the twins had scarfed down enough cupcakes, he turned his attention back to her. "The baby-sitter seems to be AWOL. How about we take these guys outside to burn off some of that sugar we fed them?"

Children's laughter filled the backyard as the twins chased the orange foam football Grant tossed at them.

Melody took in the makeshift game of toddler

football from the backyard deck. She smiled over the rim of her teacup as she watched Joe help his brother "tackle" Grant.

"Look at me, Melly," Jeff called out to her as he scampered through the grass with the ball.

"That's wonderful, sweetie."

She glanced over at Grant. Free of the confines of his tense business wardrobe and persona, he ran, jumped and tumbled through the grass with the children. The worry lines etched in his face seem to dissolve as he allowed the boys to wrestle him to the ground. For a split second he resembled the tall, lanky freshman running across Howard's campus to make it to class on time.

He'd never admit it, but she'd bet her hand-carved bamboo knitting needles he was actually enjoying himself. She allowed her eyes the luxury of watching the play of his calf muscles as he ran across the yard.

"Come play, Melly." Jeff beckoned to her with a chubby hand.

She shook her head. The tingling in her hand usually signaled the return of its strength. Still, she didn't want to chance embarrassing herself again. Especially in front of Grant.

"Yeah, play with us." Grant flashed a wicked grin.

"No, you guys enjoy yourselves." Melody felt her face grow warm and averted her eyes. Truth be told, it was more than physical weakness that kept her on the sidelines.

She feared allowing herself to join in their fun. It would be too easy to let her imagination run

103

wild. It would be easy to fantasize about what her life would be like if this was all hers. Her yard. Her rambunctious twin boys. And most of all, if Grant was her man.

She chided herself. After next week she doubted she'd ever see Grant again.

"Are you going to let them whip me?"

His voice sent a ripple of awareness down her spine. Self-conscious, she pushed an errant lock of hair from her face.

"Come play, Melly." The boys chimed in.

The phone rang and Melody went into the house to answer it. She hoped it was the sitter or the boys' mother to the rescue. This domestic scene was becoming a little too cozy for her taste.

"Hello," she said after grabbing it on the third ring.

"Geez, Melody. You really need to get a cell phone." Melody instantly recognized Joyce's voice. "I've been searching all over town for you. How'd you get roped into baby-sitting the twin terrors?"

"It's a long story," Melody said.

"I'm in the town square, and you need to get over here right away."

"I can't right now. I'm still waiting on the boys' sitter to show up."

"Okay, well, get here as soon as you can."

"What's going on?" Melody asked, the urgency in Joyce's tone piquing her curiosity. "Is it the store? Is the sign up?"

"Oh, it's up all right."

CHAPTER SEVEN

By the time she and Grant made it to the town square, a small crowd had gathered in front of Melody's shop.

The sitter, who had arrived an hour ago and couldn't quite look them in the eye as she muttered some weak excuse about car trouble, showed up just in time for the boys' naps.

"I wonder what's going on?" Melody stopped her bike on the edge of the square, opposite her shop.

Grant coasted to a halt behind her. "I'm sure everything's fine."

Dread pooled in the pit of Melody's stomach. Joyce definitely hadn't sounded like everything was okay.

Please let it be okay.

"We're not going to find out anything standing here," she said. "Let's go check it out."

In her Wall Street days problems had cropped up routinely, but they hadn't left her flustered. It was just business. However, anything involving the store seemed different, somehow more personal.

They got off their bikes and began walking across the park to the shop. Parting the throng of buzzing onlookers in front of the store, they stared up at what had captured everyone's attention.

"Oh, no!" Melody clapped a hand over her mouth.

A blinking neon sign flashed THE NITTY GRITTY in bright red letters across the front of her store. Instead of a ball of yarn, a caricature of a winking woman with a pair of the biggest blinking . . .

Melody closed her eyes and shook her head. She opened them again. No, it couldn't be. This had to be a dream or a nightmarish prank from one of those reality television shows.

The caricature winked at her, while its flashing assets continued to blink.

"This definitely isn't the sign you described to me," Grant said.

"This isn't my sign at all."

"I certainly hope not," a pinched voice said from behind her. She instantly recognized Thelma Lawrence, the pastor's wife and the last person she wanted to witness this debacle.

"Someone has obviously made a mistake," Melody said.

"Then you need to rectify it immediately." Thelma was serving her tenth consecutive term as mayor and was arguably the most powerful woman in town. "Your permit is for a retail shop, not some juke joint. I hope you aren't trying to pull something over on me, because I won't tolerate this kind of business here. Understand?"

"I assure you, this *is* a yarn shop. The only things I plan to sell here are needlework supplies," Melody said.

"Oh, get off it, Thelma." Ruth jumped into the fray.

Melody hadn't even realized she was there, but from the looks of it half the town was standing in front of her store.

"It's my job to protect the town from smut like this." Thelma wagged a finger in Ruth's face.

Ruth put her hands on her hips. "You've known Melody since she was barely tall enough to reach the candy bowl in your office. You know better than to think she'd be a part of something unseemly."

"That's right!" Joyce put in her two cents.

"Well, she was in New York a long time," Thelma stammered. "Who knows what kind of things she was into up there?"

"Thelma, this is all a big mistake," Melody said politely, hoping to smooth things over. She didn't need to make an enemy of the mayor. "I'll take care of it."

"In case you've forgotten, the festival is in a few days. People from all over the tri-county area are going to descend upon the square. What are they going to think when they see *that*?" Thelma said in a huff.

"I already told you I'd handle it." Melody looked around for the people responsible for attaching it to her building. She saw their equipment, so she knew they couldn't have left.

Ralph Woods, an old codger who made his home on one of the park's benches, rubbed a shaky hand against his gray chin whiskers. "Don't let old Thelma get you down, Melly." With the other hand he withdrew a withered dollar from his pants pocket and extended it to her. "I know you're not open for business yet, but I want to reserve my spot now."

The crowd howled with laughter.

Melody pushed Ralph's crumpled dollar out of her face. Looking over his head, she finally spotted the retreating sign hangers. Seemingly oblivious to the commotion they'd caused, she watched them casually load a ladder into the bed of their truck.

"Wait!" she shouted, maneuvering through the crowd.

She caught up to them as they were about to hop into a white pickup, the bumper of it emblazoned with beer logo stickers. "You put up the wrong sign. That's not mine."

"It's yours all right," the larger of the two men stated.

"No. I don't know what's going on here, but there's obviously been a mistake."

He reached into the cab of his truck for a clipboard and glanced through the pages. He tapped it with a pen also emblazoned with a beer brand logo. "The name of this place is 'The Nitty Gritty,' right?"

"Yes, it is, but . . ."

He interrupted. "Well, then, there's no mistake. Enjoy your sign."

"No! My store is called 'The Knitty Gritty' but the *Knitty* is with a k," Melody explained, trying her best to keep her cool. "For goodness' sakes, it's a yarn store."

"Doesn't matter to me what kind of store you're running. I just install signs."

"Well, you're going to have to take that one down immediately."

"No can do."

"Oh, yes you can. I want that vulgar sign off my premises."

"I can't help you."

"How about cutting the lady some slack, man, and getting that sign off her building?" Grant interjected.

Melody groaned. The last thing she needed was yet another person all up in her business. "This isn't your concern, Grant," she said.

"Seems to me you could use some help," he replied, his stare leveled at the workers.

"I'll handle it," she reiterated.

Grant threw his hands up in mock surrender and backed away.

Melody returned her attention to the matter at hand. "Bob," she read on the patch on his shirt. "You look like a reasonable man."

"Name's Don. My wife forgot to wash my shirt, so I had to borrow Bob's."

She willed her eyes not to roll back in her skull.

"Well, then, Don. As I was saying, you appear to be a reasonable man. And as a reasonable man, you realize a sign like that doesn't belong over a yarn store, right?"

"Makes sense."

Melody exhaled. Finally. He was actually listening to her. "So you understand why I need you and your co-worker here to take this disgusting sign off my store immediately and put up the one I ordered?"

Don took off his cap, rubbed the sweat from his brow with the back of his hand and then clamped it back on his balding head. "Yep, I sure do."

Eureka! Melody felt like throwing her arms in the air.

"Thank you," she said.

"I understand, ma'am, but I can't help you."

"Why on earth not?"

"I put them up. I don't take them down."

Don tossed the clipboard into the truck cab through the open driver's-side window. He inclined his head toward the other worker, signaling him to get inside.

"Sorry, lady," Don said as the truck's engine roared to life. "My hands are tied."

Melody leaned into the driver's-side window of the truck. "Would a six-pack untie them?"

Don licked his lips and shut off the engine. "Maybe there is something I can do."

"I want that sign removed immediately," she said. "Have the one I ordered on my building first thing tomorrow morning, and I'll have an entire case waiting for you and your buddy here."

110

"Ice-cold?"

"Of course."

Melody smiled as Don and his co-worker pulled the ladder off the back of their truck.

"What did you say to them?" Grant asked.

She shrugged. "Everyone has a hot button. I just figured out which one to push."

Grant wished he could find the button to push that would convince Melody to accept his job offer already. He'd been here almost two days and still hadn't made any headway.

Then again, he'd allowed himself to become distracted, which wasn't like him at all. The time he'd spent checking out the local minor league ball team with Dirt had been fun, but he wasn't here to enjoy himself. He should have been trying to wear Melody down.

The crowd of gawkers moved on as the workers pulled the sign down and loaded it on their truck, leaving only himself and a woman who'd jumped to Melody's defense.

Melody put her arm around the woman's shoulder. "Grant, meet my best friend, Joyce."

Joyce's eyes narrowed. If he didn't know any better, he'd think she was sizing him up. "Nice to meet you," she finally said.

"Do you guys want to come in and have a look around?" Melody asked, unlocking the door to the store.

"Sure," Grant said. He needed to have a look at what he was up against.

111

"I can't right now," Joyce said, still staring curiously up at him. "I was on my way somewhere before I stopped to see what all the hubbub was about."

"Okay, I'll give you a call later," Melody told her friend.

"Nice to meet you, Grant." Melody's friend gave him one last once-over before leaving.

A welcome blast of cool air hit Grant when he stepped into the shop. The room was a riot of color. Yarn in every imaginable color and texture was everywhere he looked. Blues, greens, reds and oranges—it was as if a jumbo box of crayons had exploded in the middle of it. Floor to ceiling cubbyholes covered three of the four walls. Yarn not jammed into them sat waiting in boxes, and what looked like brand-new furniture was shoved against a back wall.

This had gone further than he'd guessed.

He spotted a heap of old toys piled in a corner.

"Years ago this was a toy store," Melody offered. "I thought I'd use a retro toy theme. You know, Radio Flyer wagons, Raggedy Ann, Lincoln Logs, old Barbies and that kind of stuff."

"Interesting." Grant felt his developing ulcer kick up. It looked great. He should have known she'd go all out. Even back in school, she never did things halfway.

"I need to make some calls and get to the bottom of this sign business," she said.

Grant watched her as she talked on the phone behind the counter. The woman was such an intriguing mix. Tall, strong and smart, yet she also possessed an air of childlike enthusiasm and a vulnerability that was starting to get under his skin.

She looked at him and grinned. At the same time she continued to chew out whoever was on the other end of the phone.

He abruptly averted his eyes and forced himself to think about the company.

Failing was not an option. However, the more he tried to focus on business, the more his thoughts drifted to the woman in the room with him.

She hung up the phone. "The owner of the sign store got it from both barrels. Seems a strip club manager from Nashville's red light district is raising a ruckus because my sign was delivered to his place."

She heaved a sigh. "And Grant," she began, "I'm sorry for snapping at you earlier."

"Forget it."

"No. I didn't mean to be rude. I guess I'm not used to anyone coming to my rescue."

"No problem." Oh, it was a problem all right, but what else could he say? That he was becoming a sucker for golden eyes and her delectable curves made his blood run hot?

"What I don't get is why?" she asked. "Before now, all you've tried to do is talk me out of this place."

He didn't have an explanation, at least not one that made any sense. Grant shoved his hands into his pockets to ensure he kept them to himself.

She stepped closer, enveloping him in the fruity

scent of her shampoo. What was it about her that made him react like this? He'd dated his share of women, but none had elicited such feelings.

He knew she had no idea she was playing with fire. If she had an inkling of the thoughts flying through his head right now, she'd turn around and run in the opposite direction.

"Well, why did you help me?"

Weary of fighting the battle between what was best and what he wanted, Grant hauled her into his arms. Her beautiful eyes widened.

"I just can't seem to help myself," he said, seconds before lowering his mouth to hers.

Don't even think about kissing him.

Melody knew it was already too late. Willpower was no match for the magnetic pull of his lips.

She splayed her fingertips against Grant's chest, fully prepared to push him away. Instead, her hands acted on their own accord, reveling in the softness of the brushed cotton shirt covering his rock-hard chest. It was all she could do not to strip it off his back in order to feel the mahogany flesh underneath.

His scent, a heady mixture of lingering soap and masculine sex appeal, assailed her nostrils, putting every nerve ending in her body on high alert. This was the last thing she needed.

He slid his large hand from her head down to the small of her back and tugged her even closer. His touch left a trail of delicious shivers in its wake. Her knees went limp as his tongue alternately teased and tantalized, its movements stirring her to her very core. She grasped fistfuls of his shirt, clinging helplessly to him. Any notion she'd had of rebuffing him was long forgotten.

Abruptly, he broke off the kiss. "This is crazy," he whispered raggedly. "You're driving me wild."

She slowly lifted her chin and searched the depths of his deep brown eyes. Within them she saw herself as she never had. Not as a so-called money guru, but as a woman and the object of a man's desire. The newfound feminine power emboldened her, and her arms circled his neck and brought his lips crashing down to hers.

Swept away in the sweet sensations the kiss sent soaring through her, Melody wasn't sure how she wound up pinned between the wall and Grant's powerful frame. All she knew was that she couldn't get enough of him.

"I want you," he growled after they finally came up for air. The statement was bold and direct, just like the evidence of his arousal pressing against her belly. She wanted him too. Badly. More than she'd ever wanted a man in her life. It would be so easy to follow her heart, let go and give in to it.

Air couldn't have penetrated the nonexistent space between their bodies. Yet her doubts had already pried them apart. While his kisses, his slightest touch, made her want to do things she was too shy to put a voice to, she couldn't.

Her instincts had proved unreliable when it came to men and she no longer trusted the heart that had twice betrayed her.

Smoothing her hands over his broad shoulders, she brought them back to his chest. Then, summoning a strength she didn't know she possessed, she pushed firmly against him and broke off the kiss.

"I can't," she said breathlessly.

An expression as confused as the mixed signals she'd been sending out blanketed his handsome features. "Why not?"

She swallowed the lump of regret lodged in her throat. "A one-night stand isn't a good idea for either of us."

He stepped back, releasing her from his embrace. "You're right. I don't know what got into me."

The truth was this man was turning the simple life she'd created for herself upside down and shaking it. A few days ago she'd been satisfied to open her quaint store and live contentedly among her neighbors.

Then Grant Price kissed her.

Before it had been easy to brush off her attraction to him as hormones or chemistry. But now it was different.

Today she'd seen there was more to Grant than she'd thought. Beneath the surface of ultra-smooth charm and lethal good looks beat a gentle heart. He was a man who cared enough to run around a yard with two rambunctious preschoolers and go out of his way to help her, even if it wasn't in his interest to do so.

It was this Grant that both fascinated and frightened her.

"Now I need you to answer a question for me."

"And what's that?"

"Tell me why you didn't send me packing the day I arrived like everyone else who tracked you down with a job offer," he said. "Why am I *really* here?"

CHAPTER EIGHT

"I've already told you," she said.

Grant watched Melody tuck a wayward curl behind her ear, a gesture he noticed she made when she was nervous. There was a slight tremor in her voice, and her full lips were still swollen from his kisses.

This was insanity. He'd always been in complete control of his emotions, especially when it came to women. Now he was practically panting after one who didn't want him.

He had no business kissing her. It was easy enough to remember that now. Where was his common sense when she'd been in his arms driving him crazy?

Taking a step back, he cleared his throat. Too bad he couldn't clear thoughts of her kiss from his mind as easily. "Yeah, I know what you told me, but your explanation doesn't cut it."

Melody straightened her shirt and walked over to an open crate. He eyed her as she pulled out plastic bags full of yarn. "What's so terrible about me trying to pull you off the money-pursuit treadmill for a few days?" she asked, her back turned to him. "Believe it or not, I'm doing you a favor."

Grant followed her. He wanted some answers, and he wasn't going to let her brush him off again. "Plenty of overworked suits have knocked on your door pleading for your services. Again, why me?"

"Maybe I'm just sentimental. After all, we were college classmates."

"Give me a break. The only thing we did in college was compete," he said. "We did everything except challenge each other to a wrestling match."

Melody turned away from him again and began putting the yarn on the shelf. "What's the big deal, Grant? It's only a few more days. Besides, if you've changed your mind about our agreement, you're free to go at any time."

"Our agreement stands. So does my question." He stood between her and the shelf. "What does it matter to you if I work until my head explodes?"

Her yarn-filled arms froze, and her expression dimmed as if the light behind her eyes had been switched off. "That's not funny."

"Look, I'm not trying to antagonize you." Instinctively, he reached out and lightly touched her forearm.

Melody sighed and tossed the yarn back into the crate. "Okay, you're right. It is time I gave you more of an explanation," she said. "But not here. How about I treat you to ice cream?"

Grant nodded. He knew her offer was less about

ice cream and more about distancing herself from what had almost happened between them. They could both stand a little cooling off.

It wasn't like him at all to act on impulse. Yet he'd been doing just that all day.

They cut across the park in the center of the town square to the ice cream parlor. He held the door open for Melody before walking inside.

The place was was pretty much empty, except for a couple of teens occupying a corner booth.

Overwhelmed by a menu of what looked like over a hundred flavors, Grant opted for a single-scoop of plain vanilla in a cup.

"Vanilla?" Melody rolled her eyes skyward. "How exciting."

She turned to the teenager behind the counter. "I'll have two scoops of chocolate chip cookie dough. No, make it two scoops of peanut butter cup. What that heck, give me one scoop of each on a sugar cone."

Grant's eyes narrowed. "Thought you were only into healthy stuff."

She smiled sheepishly as the teen held out her cone. "For the most part, I am. However, I'm still trying to lick sweets, no pun intended." She sampled the ice cream cone and her face split into a grin. "They're my weakness."

He recalled the sweet taste of her lips. This woman was fast becoming his weakness. "I'll keep that in mind."

They took a seat at a table facing the window with a view of the square's park.

"I guess you're still looking for an explanation."

"I'm not letting you off the hook."

Grant waited patiently while she polished off the top scoop of her cone.

"Back at the shop you joked about working until your head exploded," she said. "That's exactly what I did."

Grant's mouth tightened. He had no idea what she was talking about, but decided not to interrupt. Whatever her reasoning was for blackmailing him into taking time off work, it went deep.

"Last year, my lifestyle was like yours and a lot of other hardworking black folks. I existed on fat-laden fast food and cigarettes. I didn't bother to exercise, get regular checkups or keep track of my blood pressure."

Grant shrugged. "Like you said, that description fits a lot of us."

"But the average person isn't entrusted with millions of hard-earned dollars and the stress that goes along with the responsibility. They go home at the end of the day and put work behind them. I couldn't do that, and I know you don't either," she said. "For us, Wall Street is much more than what goes on between the opening and closing bells. It's twenty-four hours a day, seven days a week."

Grant ate a spoonful of ice cream, but barely tasted it. She was right. Work was more than just a job to them. They lived and breathed it. It was what made them both so good at what they did.

"I was so busy looking at market indicators that I didn't listen to the signals my body was giving me.

I'd just pop an aspirin here, an antacid there and keep working."

Grant nodded for her to go on. He hadn't heard anything that raised a red flag; however, it did sound familiar. Only her spin on it was different. He had yet to hear something so horrible it would force a person to abandon nothing short of a phenomenal career and turn her entire life upside down.

"One morning at work it all came to a halt. I heard ringing in my ears. At first I ignored it, figuring it would stop. Then my head started to hurt. The pain was excruciating, like no headache I'd ever felt. I thought my skull was going to split wide open."

Guilt assaulted him as he observed her shoulders slump, and she heaved a wobbly sigh. Maybe he should have held off on pressing for an explanation. "If you're not up to talking about this . . ."

"No, you're entitled to know why I made this deal with you." Her voice softened. "I want you to know."

"Okay."

"I tried reaching for an aspirin, but the entire room started to spin and my left side went numb. I ended up collapsing in a heap on the floor."

Melody exhaled. "My secretary rushed in. I tried to tell her I was fine and just needed a few moments to get myself together. My words came out all slurred. It was like I was talking gibberish. Fortunately, she had the good sense to call nine-one-one."

Grant placed his hand on her forearm. The rivulets of melting ice cream dripped down her arm onto his hand. "You must have been scared out of your mind."

"I don't think I've ever been more frightened in my life."

"So what was wrong with you?" Although she seemed fine now, the thought of her going through something like that troubled him. He gently removed the melting ice cream cone from her hand and wiped her palm with a napkin.

"The doctors said I had a stroke."

"What?" Grant asked skeptically. "That doesn't make any sense. You're a young woman. Strokes happen to old people."

"I'd thought the same thing, but nearly one hundred thousand women under the age of forty-five suffer strokes every year."

Grant struggled to reconcile what she was telling him with the active and vibrant woman sitting across from him. "I don't get it. You ride a bike and do yoga. You look perfectly fine to me."

"I'll spare you a lot of the medical mumbo jumbo, but I was lucky. The hospital's emergency room had a stroke response team. The doctors made their diagnosis and quickly administered a clot-busting drug. It made the difference between long-term disability and a fast recovery. Thanks to my doctors and therapists, I have very few lingering effects from the stroke."

"Lingering effects?"

She looked down at her hands. "I still have some weakness in my left hand. It's why I dropped the carton of milk earlier."

Grant didn't know what he'd expected to hear, but it hadn't been this. A stroke. He could see how something like that would send anybody into a tailspin. No wonder she'd changed.

"Anyway, I stopped smoking, started exercising, lost thirty pounds." She looked down at the ice cream. "And for the most part, I watch my diet."

Running a hand over his close-cropped hair, he thought back to the look on her face when he'd popped open that bottle of aspirin. He nodded when the connection dawned upon him.

Melody was afraid the same thing would happen to him.

"I was blessed with a second chance. Now I see you walking in my footsteps. It's my duty to stop you," she said, confirming his thoughts.

The revelation touched him deep. He couldn't remember the last time someone had actually worried about him.

He shook his head, as if he could shake off his growing feelings for her as easily.

"Is something wrong?" Melody asked.

Everything. Wrong time. Wrong place. And most of all, she was the wrong woman. Being around Melody exacerbated the doubts he'd been having ever since the World Series had aired last year. Changing was pointless anyway. He'd made his choice years ago.

Besides, she was the one who needed to rethink her career decision, not him. "You don't have to worry about me."

"Please, Grant, don't waste this opportunity. Take this little bit of time. I'm not suggesting that you quit your job. I'm hoping that you'll see it's just that—a job. It's what you do, it's not who you are."

"I won't pretend to know the hell you've been through. Still, I find it hard to believe you can just toss your career out the window without a backward glance."

"Well, believe it." She sighed deeply. "Because when you think you're about to die, you realize the things you thought were so crucial aren't so damned important after all."

It didn't take long for Melody to figure out what Grant thought about what she'd told him. His expression said it all. He didn't get it.

Regret ate at Melody's resolve. Had she done the right thing in persuading him to take a few days off? How could she expect to teach him a lesson when she hadn't learned her own?

The kiss they'd shared earlier reminded her of a lesson poorly learned. She'd been burned twice by money-minded men. Still, she ignored the danger sign above Grant's head and kissed him with reckless abandon.

Grant's voiced snapped her out of her thoughts. "I can understand how an experience like that can cause you to make a few changes. Still, don't you think you were a bit hasty?"

Melody felt her cheeks warm. How could she explain? What could she say when she was still figuring it out herself?

"This wasn't a rash decision," she finally said. "Even before the stroke, I wasn't feeling fulfilled with work. After the stroke, I took a leave of absence and enrolled in a spiritual and yoga retreat in California."

"You're comparing a few weeks at some yoga camp with the years you've put into your career?"

"It was the first time in my life I wasn't competing or trying to prove myself. It was the perfect environment for clearing my head and healing my body," she said. "That's when I decided to quit my job and come home to live."

"So why a yarn store? Did you get some kind of mystic message while doing a downward dog?"

She smiled despite herself. "No, that came later. When I got back from the retreat, I joined a local knitting group. My grandmother had taught me how to knit when I was a little girl, and I thought picking it back up would help strengthen my hand." Melody flexed the fingers of her left hand. "I soon discovered there wasn't a place in town to buy yarn and supplies. I had to drive to Nashville. Is it starting to make sense to you now?"

"It's starting to make sense all right. It's clear to me I'm not the one who needs rescuing here. You do. Someone needs to intervene and stop you from throwing your life away."

Frustrated, she chastised herself for getting swept up in a few meaningless kisses. All Grant

Price wanted or would ever want from her was financial expertise. He just wanted her to take his stupid job.

"I've wasted enough of my life on superficial things that in the big scheme of life don't really matter."

"You act like you were in charge of fries at Mc-Donalds," he said incredulously. "Don't you miss the perks that came with you old life? The television spots? The corner office with the floor-to-ceiling windows? Being the boss?"

"Don't forget the money." She couldn't hold back the bitterness that was bubbling up in her throat. "After all, it's always about money, isn't it?"

"You say that like it's a bad thing."

Melody rolled her eyes skyward in exasperation. She'd have an easier time ramming her head against concrete, which at this point didn't seem nearly as thick as this infuriating man's skull. "This is hopeless. I'm not going to convince you to change your lifestyle any more than you can convince me to change mine." A woman seated nearby turned to look at them, and Melody lowered her voice. "So why don't we just call it a draw and move on?"

"No way," he said. "I'm holding up my end, and I expect you to do the same."

"It won't do you any good. My life is here. Walk away, Grant."

She hoped he'd take her suggestion and leave now, while she could still bear to see him go. He was the last man she should be attracted to, yet she was drawn to him like a magnet. Yes, the sooner he left, the better it would be for both of them.

"A deal's a deal, Melody. I'm not going anywhere."

When the gurgling noises coming from the coffeemaker ceased, Joyce filled her *World's Greatest Mom* mug and returned to the dining room. She sat down at the massive table, usually reserved for holiday meals and entertaining, to peruse the contents of the thick envelope containing her college acceptance letter.

She reread the letter. Her dreams of a college education were finally coming true.

Placing the letter back in the envelope, she shuffled through the remaining papers. The packet was crammed with everything from campus maps to information on special workshops to help older students make the adjustment to college life. Engrossed in reading the detailed paperwork, she was startled to glance up and find her husband standing beside her. She had no idea how long he's been there. She hadn't even heard his car pull into the garage or his key in the door.

"What's wrong?" she asked, immediately thinking the worst. Kevin rarely made it home from work on time in the evenings, let alone show up early. She looked at her watch, then up at her husband, who grinned back at her.

"There's nothing wrong."

"Then what are you doing here?"

He leaned down and kissed her cheek. "Do I need a reason to surprise my wife?"

Joyce set aside the orientation information and frowned. Despite the sweltering late-summer heat, Kevin appeared refreshingly cool in a khaki suit, sky-blue shirt and the bold blue tie she'd given him on his last birthday. He looked so good, she had to remind herself she was furious with him.

"These are for you." He pulled a large bouquet of exotic, tropical flowers from behind his back and held them out to her. "I want to make peace."

"They're beautiful." Joyce buried her face in the colorful blooms, inhaling their heady fragrance. The hurt and anger carried over from the night before slowly ebbed away. Relief washed over her. Kevin wasn't going to disappoint her after all. She should have known he wouldn't let her down. In all these years, he never had.

"I missed you last night," he said. She heard the sincerity in his voice and saw it in the depths of his dark brown eyes. "I don't like going to bed mad."

"Neither do I." Joyce recalled how large and lonely their king-sized bed seemed with them huddled on opposite ends of it. She rose from her chair. Standing on tiptoe, she wrapped her arms around her husband's neck and planted a kiss on his lips. It was meant to be a quick buss, but the familiar feel of his lips against hers was intoxicating.

He hauled her against him and deepened the kiss, lifting her off the floor as if she weighed nothing. The heated intensity of his kisses still took her

129

breath away. She moaned and felt her body relax into his powerful embrace. There wasn't another man alive who could make her feel this way.

Kevin abruptly broke off the kiss. "David home?" he whispered huskily, inclining his head toward their bedroom.

"Not yet, but he and his friends are due any moment."

Kevin drew in a ragged breath and released it. He kissed her lightly on the lips and set her back on the carpeted floor. "Let's not start something we won't be able to finish," he said. "Besides, we should talk."

Joyce agreed. While she was grateful for her husband's sudden turnaround, she was also curious as to what had brought it about. She picked up the flowers. "Give me a moment to put these in water."

"Any coffee left?" Kevin unbuttoned the top button of his shirt and yanked off his tie.

"Sure, I'll bring you a cup." Joyce practically floated into the kitchen. She smiled as she filled a crystal vase with cool water from the tap and transferred the flowers to it. She felt like a burden had been lifted from her shoulders. Kevin was already seated at the dining table when Joyce placed his coffee in front of him. He took hold of her arm and pulled her into his lap.

"I have something else for you," he said. His eyes were lit up like a kid at Christmas.

"Thought you didn't want to start anything," she teased.

Kevin chuckled. The rumble of his voice sent a flash of pleasure through her.

"Don't keep me in suspense," Joyce said.

Kevin reached into his jacket pocket, pulled out what appeared to be a travel itinerary and handed it to her.

"What's this?"

"Open it up and take a peek."

Joyce opened the folder flap. It was indeed a travel itinerary with two first-class plane tickets attached. She spotted the destination and let out a squeal. "Hawaii!" She exclaimed. "Oh, Kevin. We've been talking about going to Hawaii for years."

"That's right, I'm taking my bride on a long-awaited honeymoon. Three whole weeks. Just the two of us."

"What about David?"

"Your parents said they'd be more than happy to have their grandson stay with them." He put an arm around her waist.

Joyce closed her eyes and hugged the tickets to her chest. Three weeks alone with her husband. It would be the longest amount of time they'd ever been away together.

"This is so wonderful." She rested her head on Kevin's shoulder, then opened the folder again, just to make sure she wasn't hallucinating. She glanced over the trip itinerary. This time, the dates registered in her head.

"Wait a minute. Take a look at these dates. I can't go."

Her husband looked at her as if she'd suddenly grown an extra eye in the middle of her forehead. "What do you mean you can't go?"

"I start school in a few days. I couldn't possibly miss the first three weeks of school. I'd never catch up."

"Then put it off another semester," he said, his tone cooling. "It'll give you more time to think it through."

"I've already given it a lot of thought. We'll just have to postpone the trip."

"Postpone it? We've put off our honeymoon for twenty years. Everything else can wait."

Realization suddenly dawned on her. The flowers weren't an apology, and Kevin hadn't resigned himself to the idea of her going to school. Feeling like an idiot, she pulled herself off his lap. How could she have been so stupid? The flowers. Hawaii. Her husband coming home in the middle of the afternoon on a workday. It was all a contrived plan to make her change her mind about college.

"No," she said firmly, a thin ribbon of anger threading through her. The power in her voice startled her. She rarely told anyone no, especially her husband.

"No?" Kevin stood and glared down at her.

"That's what I said." Joyce tossed the tickets on the dining table and looked up at her husband, undeterred by the fact he was at least a foot taller than her. "I'll be in class those weeks."

"The tickets are nonrefundable."

"That's your problem!" Joyce shouted. "You should have thought about it before you came up with this lame idea to talk me out of college."

"What's the big deal about waiting a semester?"

"I've waited for years. There's no reason for me to put off my education any longer."

"I don't believe this. This ridiculous college business is more important to you than spending time alone with your husband."

"Don't go there." Joyce warned.

"Why the hell not? I think it's time you faced facts. If you start nursing school now, you'll be forty-four years old when you graduate. That's too old to be walking up and down hospital corridors for twelve hours at a time, especially when you don't have to."

Overwhelmed by fury, Joyce paused a moment, not trusting herself to speak. After a few tense moments, she spoke slowly. "That's what you don't understand. I *do* have to."

"Why?" His eyes pleaded with her. "You have plenty to do around here taking care of me and the boys."

"In case you haven't noticed, three of our boys are grown men. They don't need me to wipe their noses and hold their hands when they cross the street anymore."

"What about me?"

"What about you? You're in your office from sunrise to sunset," she said. "Besides, this isn't about you or our children. It's about me. I've spent the last two decades taking care of everyone else. What's so wrong with me pursuing something that's meaningful to me?"

Kevin shook his head. "It's obvious I'm wasting my time trying to reason with you." He grabbed his car keys from the dining table. "I might as well go back to the office."

He paused as if he hoped she might say something to stop him, then finished, "I don't understand you at all anymore." He stalked out, the back door slamming behind him.

Stunned, Joyce listened to his car start and back out of the driveway. Kevin had never walked out on her before.

CHAPTER NINE

Shielding her eyes from the morning sun with her hand, Melody looked up at the space where the offending sign once hung. The proper one was now in its place. "That should do it."

Although the store wasn't set to open for a few weeks, the sign hanging over the striped awning made it look and feel official.

"Sorry for the mix-up yesterday," Don said.

"Thanks for helping me straighten it out."

Don slid the case of beer into the cab of his truck before climbing into the driver's seat. "No. Thank you, ma'am."

Melody returned to the inside of the store where Joyce was helping her unload, sort and shelve yarn. However, instead of stocking the shelves, her friend leaned against a box with her arms folded and an expectant look on her face.

"What?" Melody asked.

"Before your sign delivery I'd asked if this deal

you struck with Grant is becoming more than you both anticipated."

Melody smoothed back a curl from her face. "I don't know, Joyce. One minute he's all business, and then the next . . ." Her voice drifted off.

"Go on."

For a moment, Melody debated whether she should say anything. "Well, don't go making a big deal out of it, but he kissed me," she finally blurted out.

"I was wondering when you were going to get around to telling me." Joyce unfolded her arms and began arranging the display of knitting needles and crochet hooks by size.

"What do you mean? It only happened yesterday."

"Please. You can spot the sparks flying off you two a mile away. It's like watching fireworks on the Fourth of July."

Melody scowled. "No. What you think you noticed was just the tension between us over this job he wants me to take."

"Mel, I don't know who you're trying to fool, me or yourself. I know sexual tension when I see it."

Melody frowned as she arranged a basket of lime and lavender skeins of cotton yarn. "Okay, I'll admit there does seem to be some kind of attraction between us."

"No kidding," Joyce said with a smirk.

"I don't know. It scares me to death. It's like I'm a different person around him. I get all flustered and tongue-tied," she explained. "I've held my own with the most powerful men in finance. What is it about this one that turns me into a glob of Jell-O?"

"Sounds to me like you're falling in love."

Caught off guard by Joyce's outrageous suggestion, Melody stared at her, speechless.

"Admit it. You're falling for him all over again."

"Don't start," Melody protested, finally finding her voice. "You're blowing this totally out of proportion. It's a little physical attraction. That's it."

Love? Melody's heart jolted. Sure, some old feelings had resurfaced. However, once she and Grant parted ways that would be the end of it.

Joyce's eyes narrowed. "Hmmmm . . . if you say so."

Melody turned from Joyce's scrutinizing gaze and delved into the bottom of a large box. "I've made two mistakes already. I'd have to be nuts to even think about falling in love again."

"Maybe you were never in love with either of them in the first place."

Melody straightened. "Of course I loved them. I accepted their proposals," she said. "What would make you say such a thing?"

"Think back to Rob and Eric."

Melody shook her head. "I don't want to rehash what happened with them."

"That's not what I mean. Do they remind you of anyone?" Joyce raised a brow. "Tall, dark-skinned, with lean builds . . ."

The hanks of purple wool Melody held slipped

from her grasp, but this time it had nothing to do with weakness in her hand. "Come on, a lot of men fit the same description."

She bent down to pick up the yarn. Images of her former fiancés came rushing back. It was the inspired music Eric made on his saxophone that had attracted her to him and his bad-boy smile. A sexy, closed-mouth grin detectable only by the up-turned corners of his mouth. A smile just like . . .

Oh, Lord, it couldn't be. Had Eric's smile merely reminded her of Grant?

Certainly it was just a coincidence. It had to be.

Then there was Rob. The physician's smile was nothing like Grant's. She exhaled a relieved sigh. Besides, it wasn't Rob's looks that had attracted her as much as his deep baritone. His rich voice had sent shivers down her spine the same way . . .

Darn it, he sounded like Grant. She turned to Joyce. A knowing look covered her friend's features.

"Honey, I've met all three men, and it's obvious," Joyce confirmed.

Stunned, Melody plopped down on a wooden crate. "All these years, have I just been chasing Grant Price?" she murmured aloud.

Joyce set her armload of crochet hooks down and put a comforting arm around her. "Don't be too hard on yourself. At least now you're dealing with the real McCoy."

Melody groaned. "Grant only wants me for his company."

"I saw the way he looked at you." Joyce shook

her head. "There were no dollar signs in his eyes. He was hungry for you."

Melody laughed. "He was probably just hungry. Ruth's got him on oatmeal."

"I know what I saw," Joyce said, picking up the crochet hooks. "He came down here about a job, but maybe his priorities have shifted."

Melody shook her head. Joyce was a hopeless romantic who still believed in white horses, handsome princes and happily ever afters. Her friend had an idyllic life with a husband who was crazy about her.

Meanwhile, Melody wondered if she would ever inspire that kind of love. She wondered if there was a man out there who would see beyond the magic she could make with money and love her simply for her?

"Grant's priorities will never change," Melody said. She rose from the box she was sitting on and cracked open a box of needlework books. "He's business first, last and always."

"I suppose he was taking care of business when you two were kissing."

Melody's eyes traveled to the wall where it had happened. She felt her face warm, while her backbone turned to jelly. If she hadn't put the brakes on it, they probably would have made love right there.

A dreamy sigh escaped her lips before she could stop it.

"If that sly smile on your face is any indication, it must have been something."

"Not to change the subject," Melody began, with

139

the intention of doing just that, "but have you and Kevin patched things up?"

Melody watched Joyce's lips thin into a firm line.

"That bad?"

Joyce nodded. "Worse. Kevin's barely said two words to me since I told him I wasn't going to Hawaii. He'd been sleeping in his study."

"Maybe he just needs time to cool off."

"We've never stayed this angry at each other this long," Joyce said. "I don't see either one of us giving in."

"Come on. There has to be some kind of middle ground."

"All of a sudden there's a language barrier between us. It's like I'm speaking Chinese, and he doesn't understand a word I say." Joyce hung the last of the crochet hooks on the display.

"To be fair, it isn't every day a woman turns down a romantic Hawaiian honeymoon," Melody countered, feeling a touch of envy.

"He bought those tickets knowing full well school starts next week," she said. "Besides, I didn't turn it down. I asked him to postpone it, to work the trip around my schedule. God knows our lives have revolved around his for years."

The fury permeating her friend's tone startled Melody. In all the years they'd know each other, she could count on the fingers of one hand how many times she'd seen Joyce mad.

"Mel, next month I turn forty years old. Forty."

"I know. I can barely wrap my lips around the word forty."

The corner of Joyce's mouth almost lifted into a smile. "It's different for you. Look at all you've accomplished. What have I done with my life? Nothing."

Melody thought about how full Joyce's life was compared to hers. Her friend's intangible accomplishments were worth more than anything she could buy.

"You couldn't be more wrong." Melody knew her words were in vain. Over the years, she'd tried repeatedly to explain that her career had been anything but glamorous.

"People think enough of what you had to say to interview you on television. How many times do you see a housewife being asked for her opinion on important issues?"

Sensing Joyce's need to vent, Melody simply listened. Knowing she couldn't make Joyce see how brief, impersonal interviews with business reporters searching for a scoop couldn't compare to a hug from your child or a goodnight kiss from your husband at the end of the day.

Joyce sighed. "Whenever we're at a function for Kevin's work, everyone there has a college degree but me." Her voiced dropped. "I feel like the dumbest person in the room."

Melody felt the pain in her friend's voice. She'd been so busy envying Joyce's life, she had inadvertently done the same thing as Kevin—not listened to her.

"Have you tried opening up to him and really explaining exactly how you feel?"

Joyce groaned. "He said I watched too much *Oprah.*"

Never having had a husband, Melody didn't feel comfortable trying to advise another woman, even her best friend, on what to do with hers. She also considered Kevin a friend, and she hated seeing both of them so miserable.

"I know you're angry with him right now, but Kevin loves you very much. Try to remember that," Melody said.

"I will." Joyce nodded. "Speaking of giving a man the benefit of the doubt, and telling a man how you feel."

Melody followed Joyce's gaze. Grant. Her heart pounded wildly in her chest.

If only she could.

Grant figured whatever Melody and her friend were talking about had something to do with him. Their animated chatter came to an abrupt halt the second he stepped through the yarn shop's door.

He said good morning to Joyce and nodded at Melody.

Glancing around the small shop, he noted it was filled with even more yarn than the day before. He couldn't help but be impressed. When had she found time to do it all?

"So what do you think?" Melody pushed a renegade curl from her face.

Grant clutched the paper bag tighter in his hand. She wore cropped white pants and a white

T-shirt, topped with a hip-skimming red linen shirt.

Her hair was down around her shoulders. He liked it that way. Every time she tried to tame those wild tresses with one of those ridiculous barrettes, his fingers itched to take it down.

"Did you knit all of this yourself?" He looked from the teddy bears modeling sweaters and dolls in ice-skating outfits to adult sweaters, caps and scarves.

She nodded. The pride in her work shone on her face.

"It must have taken quite a while."

"I started knitting practically nonstop back at the yoga retreat before I even decided to open the shop."

"I'm impressed," Grant replied. Unfortunately, he was telling the truth. He'd bought a sweater or two over the years as holiday gifts, and Melody's looked just as good.

"Thanks. Coming from you that means a lot."

Shifting his weight from one leg to the other, Grant felt like a boy gathering the courage to ask out the prettiest girl in school.

And Melody indeed looked pretty this morning. More so because she was real. She didn't bother with the hair weaves, artificial nails or surgical enhancements many women went for nowadays.

Hers was a quiet beauty that slipped under your skin and seeped into your blood. It was starting to dominate his waking thoughts and haunt his nights.

"Something smells wonderful," Joyce said.

Grant held up the paper bag in his hand. "Cinnamon rolls," he mumbled awkwardly. "Ruth sent them over."

"Nice of you to bring them." Melody took the bag and put it on the counter. Her polite tone sounded just as stilted and clumsy.

"I was coming over anyway."

Joyce looked from him to Melody, a sly smile on her lips. Although he was curious, Grant suspected it was best if he didn't know what was behind it.

"I'd better get going," Joyce said.

Melody grabbed her friend's arm. "You don't have to rush off."

"I have to go feed my kid," Joyce said, yanking her arm away. She aimed a pointed look at Grant. "Besides, it looks like you're in *very* capable hands."

Grant wanted Joyce to stay and chaperone, and at the same time he couldn't wait for her to leave. He rubbed the back of his neck with his hand. *Get a grip, man. Remember why you're here.*

He looked up, catching Melody's gaze with his own. For the life of him he couldn't think about anything but how badly he wanted to taste her sweet mouth again.

"I asked you if you wanted a roll," Melody said.

"Uh, no thanks. I'm full of oatmeal."

A hint of a smile crossed her face. "Ruth thinks her oatmeal is the answer to everything."

"I don't see *her* eating it."

Melody pressed her lips together. "Hmmm, come to think of it, I've never seen her eat it either."

They both laughed, easing the tense atmosphere.

"Go ahead, enjoy your breakfast," Grant said, knowing her penchant for sweets.

Melody shook her head. "Maybe later."

He raised an inquiring brow. "You okay?"

"I'm too excited to eat," she said. "The store doesn't officialy open for another two weeks, but I'm having a little open house to coincide with the festival."

Her expression, a mixture of excitement and vulnerability, stole a tiny piece of his heart.

The very thing that mattered most to her conflicted with what he needed from her. If she stayed here, he'd have to go home empty-handed and disappoint his father.

Melody clasped her hands together excitedly. "Since you're here, you can give me a hand with the furniture."

An hour later, Grant found himself maneuvering an overstuffed love seat into yet another spot in the room. "How's this?"

She chewed on her bottom lip before screwing her face into a frown. Grant groaned. "Oh, come on. It looks perfect here."

"I don't know. Maybe we should put the love seat over there and the chair here."

Grant resisted the urge to tell her that that was exactly where they'd been before they'd started. Instead, he plopped down on the love seat and patted the cushion beside him. "Have a seat," he said. "Let's think this through."

It wasn't until she sat down that he realized he'd made a mistake. He'd never been so aware of a woman or wanted one so badly. Everything in him wanted to ease her back onto the love seat and let nature take its course.

He glanced across the room at the spot where they had shared that searing kiss. Shifting, he crossed his legs, hoping to disguise the state of semi-arousal that the thought of her pinned between him and the wall put him in. She'd been right to put the brakes on it. If he'd followed his instincts and made love to her, he didn't know if he could walk away. Yet that's exactly what he'd have to do.

"I think it's finally right," she said, oblivious to the effect she was having on him.

"You sure this time?"

She nodded. "Thanks for being so patient. I don't mean to be difficult, but this store is a dream come true for me. I want everything to be perfect."

A tiny part of him wished her success even though the fruition of her dream meant the end of his.

"What about you? What would be your dream come true?"

"For you to say yes to my job offer."

"No, silly. Your real dream."

"I just told you."

Melody shook her head and sighed. "Let me put it another way. If you hadn't gone into the family business, what would you have done with your life? I want to know the deep down secret thing you always wanted to do."

She scooted closer to him and lightly jabbed her elbow into his ribs. "I promise not to tell a soul."

"I wanted to play ball," he mumbled.

Her eyes widened. "What kind of ball?"

"Baseball. Surprised?"

"Yeah, I am. What position did you want to play?"

"Back in Little League and high school I was an outfielder, but I didn't much care which position they put me in. I just wanted to play."

"Were you any good?"

Grant nodded. "Better than good. I was all-conference and all-state back in high school and turned down a scholarship to play in college. Even had a few scouts talk to me about trying out for minor league teams."

"Why didn't you?"

Grant's thoughts drifted back to day the university's baseball coach had come to his house to offer him a full scholarship, including a stipend for books and supplies. He still remembered handing his father the letter of intent and eagerly anticipating his reaction.

John Price had barely glanced at it. Instead he turned to the coach. "I've been saving for Grant's education since the day he came into the world. He won't need a scholarship."

The coach had looked dumbfounded. "I've seen a lot of young talent and your son here is a good ball player. He'd be a real asset to the team. We'd be pleased to pay for his studies."

Even Grant was perplexed at his father's reaction.

"Grant won't have time for baseball in college. He'll be focusing on his studies," his father said.

Then Grant's curiosity had turned to horror as his father ripped the letter and his aspirations into pieces.

Grant shrugged off the memory. He cleared his throat. "My father thought it was a waste of time."

"Any regrets?

Grant wanted to tell her how he felt a twinge of envy every time he picked up the newspaper and read that Barry Bonds or Sammy Sosa had smacked a ball out of the park.

But what still stuck in his craw was watching Frank Scott pitch a no-hitter to win the World Series, and wonder if he too could have made it in the major leagues.

He shrugged. "Who has time for regrets?"

She smiled, but her eyes remained sad. "Well, it's not on the same level as the major leagues, but some of the guys in town are playing the minor league team in an exhibition game this evening. It's a fundraiser to buy computers for the new elementary school. You should consider playing."

"Dirt mentioned it, but I don't know." He shrugged again.

"Well, it's up to you. They can always use another body."

"I'll think about it."

* * *

This was a mistake, Grant thought as the baseball whizzed by his head again.

"Strike two," he heard Ruth, who was serving as umpire, yell in the background.

At least he'd swung at the first one. The last one seemed to have vanished after leaving the pitcher's mound, and he never saw it come over the plate. What had made him think he could come out here and play ball? He hadn't picked up a bat in more than twenty years.

Shifting his weight, he relaxed his grip around the bat. The pitch. The swing. The miss.

"Strike three, and you're out!" Ruth shouted.

Grant tapped the end of the bat lightly against his forehead before tossing it aside. Damn, he thought as he retrieved his glove. He'd struck out again.

He should have left well enough alone, Grant thought. In his fantasies he was as ageless as Ricky Henderson, who'd played in the majors until he was forty-five. In his dreams, Grant was the same agile seventeen-year-old who could smack the cover off the ball.

In reality, he'd lost it.

Joyce's husband, Kevin, whom he'd met briefly before the game started, slapped him on the shoulder as they trotted to the outfield. "Don't take it so hard."

Grant shook his head in disgust. "Austin was on third. If I'd just gotten a hit, it would have brought him home and we'd have tied up the game."

"Those guys are professionals," Joe, Sr., the father of the twin boys he and Melody had baby-sat, chimed in. "We're just a bunch of weekend warriors having a little fun. So loosen up, man."

"Yeah, okay," Grant grumbled. He scanned the stands until he spotted Melody. He was too far to make out the expression on her face, which was probably for the best, he thought. The last thing he needed to see was pity in those golden eyes over the spectacle he was making of himself.

Over the next innings, he struck out his third time at bat and fouled out the next. At least he'd managed to catch a fly ball and salvage some of his tattered pride.

"Hey Grant, this is supposed to be fun," Dirt said as they sat on the bench.

Grant flashed him a halfhearted smile. "Yeah, sure."

"I know what you're thinking, but it doesn't matter what you used to be. We're not young bulls anymore. Nobody can beat Father Time," Dirt said. "But it's never too late to make the best of now."

Dirt's words hit him in a place that went beyond baseball. Was it too late for him to start making the best of now? he wondered.

Last inning of the game, and he was in the same situation as he'd been his second time at bat. The score was tied. His team already had two outs and Austin was on third.

Grant dreaded stepping up to the plate. Then something his Little League coach had said when he'd first started playing flashed in his head. *Timing is everything in hitting a baseball.*

The first ball came hurtling toward the plate. He swung—a second too late.

"Strike one!" Ruth shouted.

"Bring me home, Grant," Austin called out.

He managed to make contact with the second pitch, but it landed in foul territory.

One more chance.

Then a familiar voice called out to him from the bleachers. "You can do it, Grant!" Melody yelled.

An emotion he couldn't quite identify gripped him. It was as if she'd reached in and tugged at his heart.

The pitcher released the ball, and it spun toward him. Ignoring the impulse to swing, he hesitated for a moment, pivoted and then he brought the bat around to meet it.

Smack!

After twenty-two years, he still recognized the sound of a ball meeting a bat's sweet spot. It sailed over the centerfielder's head on its way out of the ballpark. Grant dropped the bat and began to trot around the bases.

His teammates were waiting on him as he came full circle back to home plate. He high-fived Dirt, Austin, Kevin, Joe and the other guys on the team.

"I can't believe we beat the Cosmos. They whip us every year," Joe said.

"Believe it," Dirt said. "Thanks to Grant here." He slapped Grant on the back.

As spectators in the bleachers made their way toward the field, he spotted Melody. She wore a smile that lit up her entire face. Caught up in the victory and the moment, he leaned over and planted a kiss on her cheek.

"Wow, you are good," she said.

He chuckled. "Are we talking about the same game?"

She waved her hand dismissively. "Oh, those first few times at bat were just practice," she said. "Can I treat you to another ice cream to celebrate your win?"

"Um . . . I told the guys I'd go have a beer with them," he said. "You don't mind, do you?"

"Of course not. You go ahead. I've got some knitting to do," she said. "I'll see you in the morning."

Grant smiled. He was already looking forward to it.

The bell over the door to Melody's shop chimed as she let herself in. Restless, she'd decided to organize a few things before heading home.

She tossed her keys on the counter next to the cash register and headed to the storeroom for another box to unpack. Her thoughts drifted, as they had so many times in the last few days, to Grant.

The ecstatic look on his face after he'd hit the home run soothed any doubts she'd had about the bargain they'd struck. It appeared she just might have gotten through to him, but at what cost to herself? She was as crazy about him as ever.

Spying a large box in the corner, she dragged it to the center of the sales floor and pried it open.

"How did this get in here?"

Somehow a box of things from her old office

had gotten mixed in with the ones full of knitting supplies. She started to close it, but hesitated. A photograph caught her eye. She kneeled and pulled it from the box.

She smiled. It was the framed cover of a *Time* magazine issue from three years ago. At one time it had been her prized possession. In it she wore a navy pantsuit, her arms folded as she leaned against the glass desk in her office. The bold head-line over her head asked the question, "The Greatest Investor?"

"You're darn right I was," she said, feeling the surge of the power and sense of accomplishment she'd experienced when the cover shot was taken.

"I agree," a deep voice rumbled from behind her.

Startled, she turned around. "Grant, I didn't hear you come in."

"The bell chimed and I called your name. I guess you had something on your mind."

She dropped the framed cover back in the box, but he leaned across her and retrieved it, giving her a healthy glimpse of his oh-so-sexy forearms.

"I thought you went out for a beer with the guys." she said.

"The plan fell apart after Joe got called home to watch the twins. Liz wanted to go back to the hospital to spend time with her sister and the new baby. I saw your light on so I stopped by here."

"Oh."

"Reminiscing?"

"Uh . . . no, this box got mixed up with some of the needlework supplies," she said.

"You miss it sometimes, don't you?"

She snatched the cover photo from him and tossed it back in the box. "It's all in the past, Grant. That part of my life is over."

He leaned over, and this time, he gently brushed her cheek with the back of his hand. She fought the overwhelming urge to lay her head against it.

"You can have it all back, you know."

"I don't want it back," she stammered, his nearness clouding her thoughts.

He kneeled, bringing them to eye level. She inhaled his scent, a heady mixture of fresh air, grass and sexy male. "Then tell me, what *do* you want?" he asked.

You, a voice deep within her shouted. She bit the inside of her lip to stop herself from saying it aloud.

She stood suddenly, breaking away from the warmth of his touch. "I'm going to lock up the shop and head home," she said. "I think we'd better call it a night."

Grant stood slowly, and she inched back from him. Still, the intensity of the moment remained. In a single step he closed the gap she'd created, and she braced herself for the contact her entire body craved.

Instead, he dropped a light kiss on her forehead. "I think you do know what you want, Melody. You're just afraid to admit it."

Grant's words echoed in her head the rest of the night. He was right, of course, she thought as she turned off her bedroom lamp. She was more than afraid. She was terrified.

However, her fears had nothing to do with her career choice or a job, as Grant believed. They were all over the man offering it. She wanted him, more than she ever had.

Now somehow she had to get through the next few days without making a fool out of herself by telling him.

CHAPTER TEN

"What's the matter with you?" Ruth asked.

"Nothing," Grant half-growled, half-groaned.

One or two gym visits a week had done little to prepare him for playing against men twenty years his junior. He forced himself not to wince as he walked gingerly down the staircase the next morning.

With each step his aching muscles reminded him he was too damn old for baseball. He should have taken a seat in the bleachers instead of trying to live out some decades-old fantasy.

And now he had to somehow get through yoga. He blew out a breath before tackling two more stairs. He *would* get through it.

Ruth's eyes narrowed. "How come you're walking like you're older than me?"

"I'm just a little stiff, that's all." He counted the remaining stairs. Four more to go. The way he felt, they might as well be four hundred.

"Overdid it yesterday, huh?"

"No, I didn't overdo it," Grant insisted. "I'm fine. All I need is to stretch out a few kinks."

Ruth's scrutinizing gaze was still fixed on him when he reached the bottom of the staircase. "You don't look like you're up for yoga class this morning. Why don't you go on back to bed? I'll let Melody know."

While there was nothing he'd like more than to crawl back into bed, there was no way he was going to humiliate himself by begging off. Not after Melody had watched him swagger off the field a hero last night. "That won't be necessary."

"Don't be silly. If I . . ."

"No!" Grant said, more forcefully than he intended.

"Why not?"

"So I'm a little sore. There's no reason for you to go making a big deal about it and telling Melody."

The corner of Ruth's mouth tilted into a half smile. "I thought you were only here about some job."

Grant forced himself to stand up straight. "That's right."

"Then what do you care if I tell her you can't even touch your toes this morning, let alone try to keep up with Nona?"

Grant didn't know why it mattered; it just did. He heaved a sigh. Foolish pride was the best answer he could come up with to her question, but the expression on Ruth's face confirmed she already knew.

"Okay, I won't say a word, but at least let me get you an aspirin."

His pride didn't run that deep. Grant gratefully accepted the aspirin, hoping it would kick in before Melody showed up to take him to class.

"Uh, Ruth, I apologize for being short with you."

"Don't worry about it. I'm not big on personality myself this time of morning, not until I get some coffee in my system," she said.

Grant groaned. What he wouldn't give for a cup. When he returned to Boston, a Starbucks run would be at the top of his agenda.

They heard a vehicle pull into the driveway, and Ruth went to the front door. "You'd better look alive," she said. "Your ride is here."

Ignoring the screams of protest made by his aching muscles, Grant walked out onto the porch with what he hoped was an easy gait. He was not in pain, he told himself. It was just mind over matter.

"Good morning. You ready?" Melody asked.

Despite his aches, Grant couldn't help but notice how adorable she looked. Her hair was pulled up into a lopsided ponytail, and she wore pink workout wear in a fabric that looked soft to the touch. He forced his hands to his sides to keep himself from doing just that.

He pasted a grin on his face. "Just waiting on you."

Melody gave him a curious glance. He held his breath, willing his body not to give him away. Ruth stepped out on the porch. Melody turned away, and he exhaled.

"How are you this morning, Ruth?" Melody asked.

Ruth sat down in one of the porch's high-back rockers and took a sip from the cup of coffee she'd acquired. "Now that I have my coffee, I'm good," she said. "I thought I'd show Grant mercy and wait until he was out of the house."

Grant managed to keep the smile glued to his face. The scent of coffee wafted under his nose. "Who needs coffee to start the day, when I've got yoga to look forward to?" he said smoothly. If he had been Geppetto's wooden puppet, his nose would have surely grown.

"I'm baking an apple pie for the church scholarship fund committee meeting tonight, Melody," Ruth said. "I can make an extra one for you."

Melody chewed at her bottom lip, then shook her head. "I'd better pass this time. I've been eating way too many sweets lately."

Grant's jaw dropped. He turned to Ruth, who looked just as surprised.

"You're turning down pie?" he asked.

"I'm trying to exercise a little willpower," she said, walking to her SUV. "Now let's get going before I can change my mind."

Grant caught a glimpse of Ruth out of the corner of his eye as he hobbled down the three porch stairs. The older woman frowned and muttered something about idiotic, macho pride.

She could call it whatever she wanted. It was all he had this morning, and he had every intention of hanging on to it.

"You're in a good mood," Melody said as she backed the SUV out of the driveway.

With her attention on the road, Grant dropped the bogus smile. "Maybe my new routine is growing on me."

"Glad to hear it," she said, "because it really is for your own good."

"Speaking of realizing things for our own good, have you thought any more about last night?"

"What about it?"

He watched her visibly stiffen as she clutched the steering wheel. "Melody, I saw the look on your face when you were looking through your old work things."

"I already told you those boxes were at the shop by accident. I wasn't reminiscing. I was looking for circular knitting needles."

Stifling a moan, Grant twisted in his seat in a vain attempt to get more comfortable. "Just admit it—you miss your old career sometimes. If you can't say it to me, at least be honest with yourself."

"So what if I miss it once in a while?" she said. "It won't change anything. I enjoy what I'm doing right now."

Grant let the subject drop. For now, her defensive tone was enough for him. It let him know she was thinking about everything she'd given up.

Wrapped up in his impending victory, he was surprised to look up and see Melody stopping the Explorer in her driveway.

"Did you forget something?"

"No," she said simply before getting out of the

SUV. She came around to the passenger's side and opened the door. "Can you get out on your own or do you need help?"

"What are you talking about?" Grant stammered. "Of course I don't need any help."

Melody rested her hand on her hip. The expression on her heart-shaped face matched the one Ruth had worn when she grumbled about macho pride.

"The ruse is up. I know you're hurting."

Grant swallowed the lump of pride lodged in his throat. Ruth had agreed not to tell, and he'd been with her the entire time. How had she managed to out him to Melody? he wondered.

"I can get out on my own," he said finally.

"Okay." She sounded skeptical, but grabbed her yoga mat from the back and started for the house.

He pulled himself to his feet and followed her. He'd been in town a few days now, but this was the first time he'd been inside her home.

He glanced around the living room. The furnishings, like Melody herself, perplexed him. Two overstuffed chairs sat adjacent to a cream leather sofa. Sleek onyx vases and modern sculptures sat on polished cherry wood tables covered with lace doilies. Floral wallpaper covered three walls, while the fourth held a fireplace and several large bookcases.

Void of books, the floor-to-ceiling bookcases were crammed with yarn in every conceivable color and texture.

"Have a seat." She gestured to the leather sofa,

and then shook her head. "On second thought, maybe you'd better stand. You'll only have to get right back up again."

"Interesting décor," Grant said, still trying to figure out the strange mix of styles. Somehow it came off as cozy and oddly charming.

It contrasted sharply with his ex-girlfriend Celeste's home, which was museumlike in its perfection.

Melody dropped her yoga mat on one of the overstuffed chairs. "My grandmother left this house to me. Most of the things are hers, but I added a few of mine." She smiled as she surveyed the room. "I'm still working on getting just the right blend, but I'm sure you don't want to hear my decorating woes."

Grant continued to survey his surroundings. "What do you have planned for me?"

"Well, I'm going to start off by giving you the best back massage you ever had," she said.

Images of Melody running her hands along his back, kneading, rubbing and touching assailed him. He might be sore from playing weekend warrior, but he was still a man. "Are you sure that's such a good idea?" he asked.

Melody pushed the cocktail table from the center of the room and rolled up the rug. "Of course it is," she said, unfurling her yoga mat in the middle of the living-room floor.

Grant didn't think so, but the more he entertained the notion of her hands all over him, the more he liked it.

"Excuse me a moment; I need to look for something in the back," she said.

Grant took the time to survey the row of photos on the fireplace mantel. All were of Melody and an older woman he assumed was her grandmother. In the first one, her grandmother held her as a baby. In the last, the smiling older woman was holding up a copy of the issue of *Time* on which Melody graced the cover.

He heard Melody enter the room. "She sure seemed proud of you," he said.

"I'd like to think so."

"Look at that big smile on her face at your college graduation and on the photo of her holding that magazine," he said. "I'll bet she worked hard to make sure your college tuition was paid and to buy all those books."

Melody sighed. "Give it a rest and get down on the floor."

"Floor?" He looked curiously at the two cans of tennis balls in her hands.

Following her instructions, he eased his achy body down onto the yoga mat. He didn't know exactly what she was up to, but he wasn't in the mood or position to protest.

"Now tell me where it hurts," Melody said, kneeling beside him.

He did, and she positioned a tennis ball at that particular spot between him and the yoga mat. "Are you sure you know what you're doing?" he asked.

"Of course, I know what I'm doing," she began.

"Well, I kind of know. I learned about it at the yoga retreat."

"You took some kind of class?"

"Not exactly," she said, her voice unsure.

"What does that mean?"

"Okay, I read about it in a magazine article."

"An article?" Grant shifted and a tennis ball rolled from underneath him.

She retrieved it and stuck it back in place. "It was all about do-it-yourself massage."

"So you're using me as a guinea pig?"

"Oh, come on."

He was just about to get off the ridiculous tennis balls and the floor when she smiled at him.

"Please."

The combination of her smiling down at him and the magic word were too potent. At that moment, he wouldn't have been able to deny her anything.

He exhaled. "Okay, what now?"

"First, relax," she said. "Now slowly roll up and down, then from side to side for a while."

He knew he looked absurd, but Grant had to admit it wasn't half bad. It wasn't the sensual massage he'd initially imagined, but it felt surprisingly okay.

"Tell me if it hurts and we'll stop," she said.

"I'm curious," he said, as he rolled on top of the tennis balls. "How did Ruth manage to let you know I was sore?"

"She didn't."

"Well, how did you know?"

Melody chuckled. "Your good mood tipped me off that something wasn't quite right," she said. "Then when you didn't complain about missing out on coffee, I just knew."

He continued to roll along the tennis balls. "There's something else I want you to know," he said.

"What's that?"

"Actually, I want us to be clear on what happened the other day."

Melody rolled her eye. "How many times do I have to tell you, I was only looking through those boxes for circular . . ."

He managed to reach out and touch her arm without losing his precarious balance on the balls. "Not that," he said. "I mean the other day, when I kissed you."

She averted her eyes. "You know, the magazine article said this massage technique is good for tension. You might want to keep a few old tennis balls in your office."

"Why don't you want to talk about it? What are you afraid of?

She glared at him before pushing herself off the floor. "I'm going to make some tea."

Melody opened the kitchen cabinet over the sink and three skeins of red yarn tumbled down on her head. She stuffed them back into the cabinet and slammed it shut.

This man had her so shook up, she couldn't remember her own kitchen. She retrieved a box of tea bags from the pantry and placed it on the counter.

Melody didn't have to turn around to know Grant was standing behind her. His presence filled the small kitchen.

"Every time our conversation takes an intimate turn, you run from me. Why?"

"I do not," she said, her back still turned to him. She picked up the box of tea bags, but her hand was trembling so badly she put it back on the counter.

She closed her eyes, took a deep breath and slowly released it. Turning around, she forced herself to meet Grant's stare. "Furthermore, there isn't anything intimate between us."

"Then what do you call what happened at your store the other day?"

"I call it you using any means to get me to change my mind about your offer."

He braced his hands on the counter, trapping her between his arms. "That's exactly what we need to talk about, and this time you're not going to run."

Her anger didn't dilute her reaction to him. Despite telling herself she was too upset to notice the scent of soap that still clung to his skin or feel the warmth of his breath on her face, she did.

"When we kissed, that job was the last thing on my mind."

"Yeah, right," she said, as memories of the kiss replayed in her head.

"All I could think about was you."

"Why now?" she blurted out. "You never gave me the time of day in school. Why am I all of a sudden so damned irresistible?"

Grant pushed off the counter and began pacing the small kitchen. "Don't you think I've asked myself the very same question at least a dozen times in the last three days?"

"Well?"

"Honestly, I don't know." He stopped in his tracks and rubbed a hand over his short-cropped hair. "I can't explain it. All I know is that I care about you. Very much."

She wanted to believe him. However, his real reason for being here, what kept him here was still business—not her.

He stared at her a moment. "You don't believe me, do you?"

"I . . ." she started, and then paused in search of the right words.

He continued. "Back in college, we were fierce competitors, and I did everything in my power to beat you. Sometimes I did. Sometimes I didn't," he said. "But think back, Melody; have I ever once lied to you?"

Melody racked her brain for an instance when he hadn't been truthful with her and couldn't come up with a single one. Even when they'd run against each other in a hotly contested race for student government president, he'd run an honest campaign.

"No, you haven't. Not yet."

"Until I do, I think I deserve the benefit of the doubt," he said. "Do you think you can give me that much?"

"I can try."

He took her hand in his and squeezed it lightly. "That's a start."

Joyce stripped the plastic bag from Kevin's suits and hung them up in his closet. He was still barely speaking to her, but the fact didn't stop her from picking up his dry cleaning.

She mentally went down the list of errands she'd run. Even in a small town, trips to the bank, post office, cleaners and grocery store could eat up an afternoon. Not to mention she'd spent the morning driving her parents to the eye doctor for exams and new glasses.

After tonight's church scholarship fund meeting, she planned to soak her tired bones in a tub full of bubbles and turn in early. Joyce put the groceries away and plopped down in a kitchen chair. No matter how tired she felt, she wouldn't get much sleep tonight, she thought. Not with Kevin still angry with her.

The phone rang. She spotted Kevin's office number on the Caller ID, and for a moment, she considered letting it go to voice mail. The last thing either of them needed was to get into yet another argument.

"Hello," she said finally.

"Good, you're there," Kevin said. He actually sounded relieved. Maybe he was as sick of this tension between them as she was.

"I can't talk long. I'm due in court in twenty minutes," he said. "I called to tell you Paul Wilson swung back through town on his way home, and he wants to take us to dinner tonight. You can meet me at the office."

"But the church scholarship fund meeting is tonight."

"You'll just have to skip it," he said firmly. "Paul is expecting us, and his business is very important."

"I can't skip it. I'm chairing the committee, and we're meeting here," she said.

"Well, postpone or cancel it. I don't care how you handle it; just be at the office at six sharp."

Any other time Joyce wouldn't have thought twice about doing as he asked. Only this time he hadn't asked, she thought. He'd issued a command, as if she were a subordinate at work.

Anger welled up in her, but she maintained her cool. "I'm sorry, but I can't make it tonight."

She heard a sharp intake of breath on the other end of the phone. The scholarship fund was important too. Kevin should know that, seeing as how he had once been a recipient.

"What in the hell has gotten into you lately?" he huffed. "Look, I don't have time to get into it with you right now. Meet me at six. I'm counting on you, Joyce."

A click sounded in her ear, and she hung up the

phone. She picked it back up to call the other ladies on the committee to cancel, paused and then hung up again.

Two hours later, the meeting was in full swing, but Joyce's mind kept drifting. She sat at her dining-room table surrounded by Ruth, Liz, Edith and Thelma. She glanced at her watch. It was after seven. By now, Kevin must know she wasn't coming. The phone had rung an hour ago, but she'd let it go to voice mail.

Edith Riley was on the committee. She liked Edith well enough, but the woman could spread gossip faster than the speed of sound. The last thing she wanted was to get into an argument with Kevin with her around.

"Did you get that?" Thelma asked. "Joyce?"

Startled by the pastor's wife calling her name, Joyce looked up from the yellow legal pad. She hadn't heard a word they'd said. Instead of taking notes, she'd been doodling and thinking about her problems.

"I'm sorry. Could you repeat it?" she asked. "I'm a little distracted tonight."

"Liz suggested that we come up with some fundraising alternatives to the annual rummage sale," Thelma said.

Joyce nodded absently. "That sounds fine."

"Is everything all right, dear?" Edith asked, nostrils flaring as if she were physically sniffing out something amiss.

"I'm fine, just a bit tired."

"Your brow has been furrowed since we arrived.

Are you sure there isn't something bothering you?" Edith persisted.

"Oh, give it a rest, Edith. She said she was fine," Ruth said from the other end of the table. "Let's try to stay on topic."

"I was thinking we could have a fish fry or sell cakes or something. Anything involving food is a surefire moneymaker," Liz said.

Joyce tapped the end of her pen against her cheek. "Sounds good, but keep in mind we wanted to increase the amount of money we award the recipients. Tuition and fees have increased dramatically. If we want our scholarships to be more than a token award, we have to keep up."

Ruth shrugged. "I don't know if that's going to be possible. We're all aware of the treasury report."

"Maybe we could appeal to the pastor to . . ." Edith began, but stopped when she saw Thelma shake her head.

"We'll have to get in line. Nearly every church committee is appealing for more funds," she said.

Joyce snapped her fingers. "I got it," she said. "We can send out letters to our former scholarship recipients, asking them to contribute to the fund. The majority of them graduated from college years ago and have moved on to successful careers."

"That's a wonderful idea," Thelma said.

"I'm sure they'd be happy to help the fund assist other students," Ruth chimed in.

"I'll draft the letter and bring it by for your approval," Edith volunteered.

Joyce noted everything on her pad. It seemed like sitting around thinking about Kevin had done some good after all.

"Well, we accomplished a lot tonight," Liz said.

"I agree," Joyce said, "and if there isn't anything else, we can adjourn."

Ruth stood. "Oh, I almost forgot, I brought an apple pie. I left it in the car."

"What are you waiting on? Go get it," Thelma said. "I'm starved."

"I could use some pie myself," Edith chirped.

Joyce signed. Pie certainly sounded better than sitting around moping. She pushed the legal pad aside and stood. "I'll put on a pot of coffee."

The pie looked delicious, but Joyce could only pick at it. She was physically sitting at the table, but her head was a million miles away. Had she been wrong not to meet Kevin for dinner? she wondered. She thought back to the way he'd ordered her to be there and shook her head.

"Joyce, didn't you hear Liz talking to you?" Joyce felt Edith touch her on the arm.

"Oh, I'm sorry," Joyce said.

"Are you sure everything is all right?" Edith asked.

Joyce pasted a smile on her face. "I'm fine."

Edith inclined her head toward her plate. "You've barely touched your pie."

"Get off her back," Ruth said. "I swear, Edith, you're always looking for something to shake up the rumor mill."

"Then I guess none of you wants to hear the latest," Edith huffed, crossing her arms.

The women glanced around the table at each other, until Liz broke the silence. "I want to hear it," she said.

They all leaned in as Edith launched into a story that even Joyce found herself laughing at. In fact, they were all laughing so hard, she didn't hear Kevin come in.

"Good evening, ladies," he said. Joyce looked past his patented courtroom smile to the coldness radiating from his eyes.

"Help yourself to some pie," Ruth offered.

"No, thank you." He leveled a stare at Joyce. "I just came from dinner."

"Well, I'd better be going," Thelma said.

"Don't rush on my account," Kevin said, the easy smile still glued to his face. "You ladies were having such a good time, I could hear you laughing from outside. I don't want to be responsible for breaking up the party."

Joyce gritted her teeth. It was just like him to make it seem like they were just playing around. Maybe they were gabbing when he walked in, but they had gotten a lot of business accomplished. "We weren't partying, sweetheart. We'd finished our business so we were chatting and enjoying this delicious dessert Ruth made."

"It is getting late," Liz said. "I'm sure the twins are driving Joe crazy by now."

Kevin stalked off to his study while Joyce told her

guests goodnight. She didn't think they'd suspected the tension between them. A lawyer for years, Kevin was too schooled in controlling his emotions.

Edith still looked suspicious. Not even Kevin was smooth enough to get past her nosy meter.

Joyce's gaze wandered to Kevin's closed study door as she cleared the dining-room table. As much as she wanted to put an end to their disagreement, she knew trying to talk to him now would only result in yet another argument. She was glad David was spending the night at a friend's house.

She rinsed the dishes and loaded them into the dishwasher. Satisfied both the kitchen and dining room were straight, she went up to bed. Maybe tonight she was tired enough to drop off to sleep instead of worrying about what her decision to go to college would do to her marriage.

The more Kevin thought about the embarrassment he'd suffered tonight, the angrier he became. To top it off he came home to find Joyce laughing like she didn't have a care in the world.

He turned on his CD player, but the smooth jazz notes coming from the speakers didn't soothe his frustration. His wife acted totally oblivious to the havoc this school business was bringing to their lives, he thought.

Opening his briefcase, he pulled out some contracts he needed to look over. After reading the same line over and over again, he gave up and left his study to go up to bed.

The house was quiet, and he assumed Joyce was probably asleep by now. Sleeping was the only thing they could do lately without getting into it, he thought.

Their bedroom was dark, but he didn't bother turning on the lights. He stripped down to his underwear and slipped into bed. They alternated tossing and turning until they rolled into each other in the middle of the king-sized bed.

Kevin heaved a sigh before turning on the bedside lamp. "Since neither of us can sleep, we might as well get this out in the open," he said.

Joyce sat up and ran a hand through her short-cropped curls. She was wearing a lavender nightgown—his favorite. It was just plain cotton, but the color made her look even more beautiful. Looking at her softened the hard edge of his anger, but didn't make him forget it.

"How could you let me down tonight?" he asked. "I wouldn't have asked you if it weren't important for you to be there too."

"First of all, you didn't ask me. You ordered me like I was some underling."

"Excuse me if I was on my way to court and didn't have time to beg you," he said. "So you thought you'd get back at me by standing me up in front of a client."

Joyce threw up her hands. "I told you I couldn't make it. Besides, you've known about the scholarship fund meeting for over a week."

As much as he loved his wife, for the life of him he didn't understand her logic. How could she compare what looked to him like a hen party to dinner with an important client? he wondered.

"Don't look at me like that," Joyce said. "I've been with you long enough to know what you're thinking. My meeting was important too."

This back and forth was getting them nowhere. His sweet, accommodating wife was turning into someone he barely recognized, and he didn't know what the hell to do about it. He reached out and switched off the lamp. "The bottom line is I needed you, and you weren't there."

He thought the subject was closed for the night until he heard Joyce's angry voice in the darkness. "Now you know how it feels."

Chapter Eleven

Only one day left.

Grant stood under the shower spray the next morning trying to figure out how he'd managed to bungle everything so badly.

So far he was a two-for-two loser. Melody didn't trust him, and he didn't feel any closer to bringing the *USA Today* All-Star mutual fund manager to Price.

He thought he'd made real progress the other night when he'd caught her with that old cover photo of *Time*. The spark in her eye and the pride-infused tone of her voice had given him a glimmer of hope.

Two days later, he was right back where he started.

Grant grumbled as the steam rose from the shower. Maybe if he'd spent more time talking up the job and less time kissing her, he would have completed his mission.

He blew out a heavy breath. His attraction to her

had blindsided him, he thought. Caring for her hadn't been part of his plan, nor had being drawn into this town with its damned homey atmosphere.

"Neither excuse is going to cut it with Dad," he muttered aloud.

But tomorrow the second half of their bargain began. He hoped returning to Boston would clear his head and help him regain his lost focus. There he would be on his home turf. Melody would be in his territory, and he'd have a week to really show her what she was missing.

"Once I get you home, you'll forget all about this place," he said aloud. He wouldn't give up. He'd never failed his father, and he wasn't about to start now.

Pivoting, Grant allowed the hot water to pummel the muscles in his back. He twisted to one side, then the other.

No pain.

The ache he'd carried in his back like a set of luggage was strangely absent. He bent to the side, and then reached his arms over his head. Not a twinge. Grant shrugged. Maybe he would pick up a few canisters of tennis balls for his office.

Rubbing the bar of soap between his palms, he spread the lather over his broad chest. In his mind he relived the weight of Melody's full breasts crushed against him, as her lush curves molded to his body. His thoughts drifted to fantasies of her joining him beneath the spray.

He could almost smell the tantalizing scent of her apple shampoo.

This was madness.

Turning the cold water on full blast, Grant ducked his head under the icy droplets. The water cooled his ardor and snapped him back into reality.

No wonder he hadn't made any progress in persuading her to accept his offer. "You should be thinking about her wearing a suit in an office, not in the shower naked," he muttered.

Fortunately, today was the day of the festival everybody in town was so excited about, so he and Melody wouldn't be alone together. And this chemistry, attraction or whatever it was between them wouldn't have an opportunity to crop up and muddle his thinking.

He shut off the water. Grabbing a towel from the rack, he wrapped it around his waist.

Exhaling sharply, he forced himself to remember that his father and Price Investments were depending on him. Today he would keep them foremost in his mind. He would keep both his hands and his lips off Melody.

"This is business," he admonished himself. "There's no place for personal sentiment in business."

Yet this morning the mantra didn't fire him up. It left him feeling oddly hollow.

"Breakfast!" he heard Ruth yell from the base of the stairs.

Oatmeal. His stomach rumbled in revolt.

Suddenly one day seemed like forever.

* * *

Hours later the town square and The Knitty Gritty were alive with the sounds of adult conversation and children's laughter.

The bell above Melody's door sounded and Liz walked into the shop with the twins in tow.

"We want puppets," Jeff said.

"Me too!" Joe demanded, then added, "Please."

"They saw another kid with one and practically dragged me across the street," Liz explained.

Melody was pleasantly surprised to find her finger puppets had been a smash hit with the children in town and their parents. Then again, who didn't love a freebie?

She only had two puppets left. Thank goodness they were both the same. Melody plucked two horses from the table that earlier today had held a nearly a hundred hand-knitted finger puppets.

"Here's a horse for each of you," she said, handing them to the twins.

At Liz's prompting, the boys thanked her and rewarded her with hugs. A pang of envy hit Melody as they wrapped their little arms around her.

Grant was wrong, she thought. She didn't want her old life back. Maybe if she hadn't devoted herself to growing other people's money, she'd have a family of her own by now.

"These are cute, Melody," Liz said, looking at the sweaters on display. She held one up. "I wish I could make something like this for the boys and my new baby niece."

"They're easy to knit," Melody said.

Liz put the sweater back on the display table. "Really?"

"I'll be teaching knitting classes in the evenings," Melody said. "You should give it a try."

"I don't know. The boys really zap my energy."

"It only meets once a week."

Liz fingered the sweater again. "I think I will," she said. "It won't kill Joe to watch his sons one night a week."

Liz enrolled in the beginner's class. So far, her adult classes were nearly full, and she was going to have to add a second junior knitting class to the schedule. Melody was thrilled, considering the shop didn't officially open for another two weeks.

A few more people poked their heads in after Liz left, but the traffic into the shop had slowed considerably. Most of the kids were playing the games set up in the park in the middle of the square, while the adults roamed through the various booths and exhibits.

Melody looked out the window and spotted Grant standing under a magnolia tree talking to Dirk. He didn't seem to mind Liz's twins yanking at his pant leg to get his attention, while their mother took a well-deserved break on a nearby bench.

She wondered if he ever missed having children, or if he had repressed any feelings on the subject, just like he'd done his desire to play baseball.

After Dirk left and Liz managed to corral the boys, Melody decided to close the shop and join Grant.

After locking the door, she turned around and her jaw dropped. The female cop manning the D.A.R.E. booth had abandoned her post and sidled up to Grant.

The police officer removed her hat and a cascade of brown curls tumbled down her back in perfect order. No hat hair. Not a strand out of place. Melody thought of her own kinky mop and exhaled in defeat.

She guessed the woman was twenty, twenty-two tops. There was no way she could compete with a woman who looked like that.

Melody fumed as she watched the officer undo the top two buttons of her shirt. It was a small gesture, but it seemed to transform the standard-issue uniform into something found in a Victoria's Secret catalogue. She should be ashamed of herself, Melody thought. She could see the woman's ample cleavage from yards away.

"Grant is free to do as he pleases, and I am not jealous," Melody repeated through clenched teeth as her feet strode toward them on their own accord.

Then she saw him look at her over Officer Sexpot's shoulder. His dark eyes seemed to light up as she walked toward him, and the intensity of his gaze made her feel warm all over. When Grant looked at her, it was if she was the only woman on the planet.

"Hey, stranger," he said, causing the good officer to turn around.

To be fair, Melody could understand why the

younger woman had practically draped herself over Grant. Beyond being gorgeous, he had a commanding presence that drew women to him like magnets.

"Hi, yourself," she replied.

"Melody, I'm sure you already know Blair."

"Actually, I don't." Melody extended her hand and introduced herself.

"Well, that's a first in this town," Grant said.

Ignoring Melody's outstretched hand, Blair looped her arm around Grant's and rested her red fingernails on his bicep. "Nice meeting you, *Melanie,*" she said. There was a smile on her lips, but her eyes remained cold and hard. "Any other time, I'd love to chat, but Grant and I were having a private conversation."

Grant's brows furrowed. "We were only talking about drug prevention."

"Well, I just thought that maybe you'd like to talk." She paused and winked. "Alone."

"There's nothing you and I have to say to each other Melody can't hear too."

Blair shot Melody a withering glance. "Suit yourself." Releasing her grip on Grant's arm, she flounced back to her booth.

Melody was taken aback to see Grant's attention wasn't directed at the pretty cop. He was looking at her.

"I looked in on you at the store a few times, but you looked busy," he said.

She smiled. "I know. Who would have thought those finger puppets would be so popular?"

He caressed her bare arm, causing her knees to quiver. Grant must have felt something too, because he drew back his hand as if he'd touched fire.

For a long moment, they simply stared at each other. Melody averted her eyes and broke the awkward silence.

"So what have you been up to?" They'd only been apart a few hours, but she realized she'd missed him.

"I got drafted into helping with the hit-the-teachers-in-the-face-with-a-pie booths," he said. "They needed someone to help keep up with the pie demand. Apparently the pies are actually aluminum pie tins covered in Redi-Whip."

"It was nice of you to lend them a hand."

"I don't mind. They were swamped." He paused. "But there's something I don't understand. It seems the only one anybody wants to hit is Austin. His line snaked around the square. He's even more popular than the principal."

"How many times did they hit him?"

Grant shook his head. "When I left they'd gone through seventy cream pies and hadn't landed one."

"That's too bad."

"I thought you liked him."

"I do—now," she said. "He's a nice guy, but a tough teacher. He gave me a C in chemistry."

She watched Grant's jaw drop. "You got a C in a class?" he asked incredulously.

She had to admit; it still niggled at her. The grade had ruined what was otherwise a perfect straight-A transcript. "It's the lowest grade I ever received in any class. He said he was holding me to a higher standard because I was smarter, but it seems to me I was penalized for being above average."

A wicked smile spread across Grant's face. "Maybe you should take a shot at him."

Melody felt the corners of her mouth tilt upwards at the thought of Mr. Gise wearing a face full of aerosol cream. She shook off the delicious image.

"No, that's okay." Back in high school she'd spent two weeks' allowance buying pies to hit him with and had missed every time. She'd even cornered her grandmother at the quilting exhibit to ask for an advance.

She wasn't alone. For weeks after the festival, most of the kids were broke because they'd spent their allowance hoping to cream the teacher they all loved to hate.

"Come on, you know you want to. Besides, it's for a good cause," he said.

"No."

Grant held his hands up in mock surrender. "Okay, I'll drop it. If you don't want to extract a little revenge, I won't bring it up again."

Melody rolled her eyes skyward. "I thought the subject was already dropped."

"It is. I was just standing here wondering how that high-school transcript of yours looks with all those As"—he leaned in closer—"and one big, fat C."

He'd known just what to say to shatter her resolve. "On second thought, I believe I will give it a whirl."

At the pie booth, they found Mr. Gise taunting one of his current students. The kid had a pie in his hand and a determined look on his face.

"Missed again," he shouted out after the kid's pie landed about a foot short. From the looks of it, most of the pies had landed in the grass around the teacher and a lucky few had grazed his pant leg.

The kid and his buddy started to walk off. "Hey, you're not giving up, are you?" Austin called after them.

"I'm not spending all my money on you again this year," the kid waved him off.

"Suit yourself. I'll see you for Chemistry II next week, then," he said.

Melody plucked down five dollars for three pies. Fifteen pies later, she was out thirty bucks and hadn't come close to hitting him.

"I thought I had him that last time," she grumbled, feeling as defeated as she had back in high school.

"Why don't you try a few with your eyes closed, Melody? You may have better luck," Austin taunted as he stroked his beard.

"That does it," Melody said, digging through her pockets for another five. "Get ready to eat a face full of pie!"

She paid for another three pies and threw them with all her might. Each fell short of its target.

Melody heaved a weary sigh. Maybe she'd work on her aim and try again at next year's festival. She glanced over at Grant. "I'm going to call it quits."

He looked as if he was about to comment, but stopped short.

"What?" she asked.

He shook his head. "Last time I tried to help, you jumped down my throat."

"I already apologized," she said. "So if you have any ideas, speak up now because I'm down to my last five dollars."

Grant reached into his wallet and pulled out a five. "This round is my treat."

"You back for more, Melody?" Austin called out. "Too bad you didn't work this hard when you were in my class."

Melody scooped up a pie. "I'm going to bean him good."

"Easy now," Grant said, resting a restraining hand on her arm. "Don't let him bait you."

"But did you hear what he said?"

Grant chuckled. "I heard him," he said. "Block him out and listen to me."

"Okay, what do you want me to do?"

Melody shivered as he leaned in and whispered against her ear, "You took golf back in college, right?"

"Yes, but what does that have to do with throwing a pie?"

"Notice how he baits everyone, so they'll throw as hard as they can," he said. "Remember how we'd all try to hit the ball as hard as we could?"

Melody smiled as it dawned on her what he was trying to tell her. "The harder we tried to hit it, the more frustrated we got."

Grant nodded. "The pie tins are too light to be thrown so hard from this distance. They just end up floating to the ground."

He released her arm. "Now this time, don't throw it," he said. "Just focus on your target and give it a nice, slow, underhand toss."

Melody chewed on her bottom lip as she took aim and did exactly what Grant had told her. The pie sailed through the air and landed right on top of Austin's head.

"Bull's-eye!" she shouted.

"I see you're still holding a grudge about that C you got in chemistry," Austin said, shaking the whipped cream from his hair.

"Don't bother wiping it off," Melody said. "You've got more coming!"

CHAPTER TWELVE

"You smell that rain?"

"I didn't know rain had a scent." Grant looked up at the clear night sky. Not only did he fail to smell any precipitation, he didn't see or feel any either.

"Well, it does," Melody insisted, as they strolled down the street leading to her house. The festival had ended earlier. After he'd practically dragged Melody from the pie booth, they'd enjoyed a concert in the square followed by a fireworks display.

Soothing sounds of chirping crickets echoed in the darkness, while the rustle of leaves, stirred by the occasional warm breeze, filled the evening air. The same noises had nearly driven him nuts his first night in town.

Grant wasn't sure when his ears had made the adjustment from city noise. His loft back in Boston didn't insulate him from a siren blast or other city sounds.

"So tell me, how does rain smell?" He leaned

closer to her. One thing he knew for sure, whatever rained smelled like, no scent could compare to the alluring fragrance of apple shampoo still clinging to her hair. He closed his eyes for a millisecond and treated himself to the momentary pleasure of inhaling it.

Reluctantly, he turned away, successfully defeating the overwhelming urge to run his fingers through the wild curls. Still, his hands itched to tame the renegade mane. Melody pushed her hair off her shoulders, inadvertently giving him another whiff of the fruity shampoo.

Goodness, the woman would have him craving apples until the day he died.

"It's a dampness. You can almost feel the moisture in the air."

"I don't feel anything. Besides, damp isn't a smell," Grant teased.

"Hmmm, I guess it smells a bit like a freshly mown lawn and a little like . . . oh, I can't really describe it. I just know when I smell it." She shrugged her shapely shoulders. "It's going to rain."

"Your Doppler Radar must be off. It's a clear night," he said, scanning the horizon.

She opened her mouth to say something, then apparently decided against doing so and promptly closed it. They continued walking, their pace slowing as they reached the edge of her driveway.

Thunder rumbled in the distance. Grant peered up into the night sky at the electric sizzle of lightning that followed it. He spared a glance at Melody. Her brow was arched at an I-told-you-so angle.

"I apologize for doubting you. That nose of yours is more reliable than the weather forecast."

A stronger blast of thunder sounded, closer this time, sending a fierce tremor through the ground beneath them.

"Looks like it's going to get pretty intense," Grant said, as the first raindrops began to fall. They climbed the porch stairs and ducked under the cover of the wraparound porch.

"I'll say goodnight and let you get inside."

Melody took a seat on the porch swing. "No, I think I'll sit out here a while."

"Really?"

The porch light flicked on, bathing the area in a soft glow.

"They're motion-activated," Melody explained.

He watched as she sat on the porch swing and slowly began to rock, her magnificent golden eyes fixed upon the sky. The rain picked up, filling her gaze with wonder and expectation. It was like the stormy skies had cast a spell over her. In turn, she must have woven some kind of magic over him. He couldn't take his eyes off her.

God, she was gorgeous.

Still staring into the heavens, Melody abruptly halted the wooden swing's back-and-forth motion with her heels.

"Have a seat," she said, patting the space beside her.

Grant sat down, and the swing resumed rocking. "Are you sure you don't want to go inside?"

Melody shook her head no. The porch light

shut off. For a while they rocked in companionable silence, the lull in conversation filled in by the steady drumbeat of the summer rain.

"How old were you when your mother died?" she asked, breaking the silence.

His eyes widened, her question catching him off guard. It wasn't one he was asked often. As a child he'd quickly learned that bringing up his mother only deepened his father's somber expression. The loss of his wife was a hurt unhealed by the passing of time for the elder Price.

Grant cleared his throat. "Six."

"Do you remember her?"

He shrugged slightly. "Bits and pieces. Her smile. Her laugh. I guess my most vivid memory of her was holding my hand on my first day of kindergarten."

"You're lucky to have your father and brother."

Grant nodded, remembering she had lost both her parents. "Thomas is a good guy." He smiled. "And of course, there isn't anything I wouldn't do for my dad."

A pang of guilt sliced through him. He hadn't thought all day of the vow he'd made to his father or Price Investments. At the moment, neither seemed important. His promise and the business had taken a backseat to the amazing woman at his side.

The past few days had made him doubt his initial stance that she was wasting her life in this town. She was so happy here. He'd come to secure the services of the financial wizard with the so-called Midas Touch. Now he knew it was the woman, not the Wall Street legend, who was the true treasure.

How could he ask her to leave?

"Grant, are you okay?"

Her voice broke into his thoughts. "Yeah, I'm fine."

"I hope I didn't make you too uncomfortable asking about your mother."

"I guess it just feels a little strange," he said.

"How so?"

"My father looked so sad anytime Thomas and I mentioned her that I guess we learned not to." His voice dropped off, and he stared out toward the falling rain.

"That's too bad," Melody said.

Grant heaved a sigh. "Yeah, it is. Over the years, there have been times I've wanted to ask him about her, but I don't want to rip open the wound for him."

"You're a good son," she said.

Grant glanced down at his hand, which Melody had reached over and covered with her palm. The pure sweetness of the gesture tugged at his heart, and he entwined his fingers through her long, slender ones.

He stole a glimpse at Melody, who continued to be fascinated by the storm. The sweetest half smile graced her lips.

"How old were you when your parents died?" he asked.

"Four. They died in a plane crash. My mother had a concert in Paris. They took an earlier flight back to the States so they wouldn't miss my birthday, but they never made it."

"What do you remember about them?"

Thunder clapped noisily while lightning flashed from the heavens, illuminating the night. Heavy rain continued to pummel the earth.

"I only have faint recollections of my father, but I do remember how Mother loved storms." The smile spread into a full-fledged grin.

Grant looked up at the curtain of rain. "Apparently, her daughter does too." Now he understood why she'd insisted on staying outside.

She nodded. "After all these years, every time it storms I think of her. I remember sitting on her lap watching them. Sometimes she'd sing to me," Melody said, resting her head on his shoulder.

"Your mother had a beautiful voice." Grant wrapped his arm around her and she scooted closer.

She lifted her head. "How do you know?"

"My father has all of her albums," Grant said, gently pushing her head back onto his shoulder. "He actually saw her Metropolitan Opera debut."

"Really?"

"Dad says she brought the house down with her rendition of Bizet's *Carmen*." He rested his chin atop Melody's head.

"That was before I was born, but my grandmother spoke of that night often. I think it was one of her proudest moments."

"Do you sing?"

"Not a note," she said emphatically. "My father

was a music professor, and my mother might have been one of the greatest mezzo-sopranos ever, but their daughter can't carry a tune."

"I'll bet you're just being modest. You probably sing like an angel."

Melody chuckled lightly. "My poor grandmother tried putting me in voice lessons, then piano, flute and finally guitar in an effort to unearth my musical talent," she said. "Nobody wanted to believe a child with my background named Melody had absolutely no musical talent."

Her admission surprised him. "You're kidding, right?"

She shook her head. "Oh, no. Not you too. What is it about a big-boned sister that makes everybody think she can sing?"

"It's not that. You're so good at everything, I'm astonished there's something you can't do." Grant straightened his shoulder, lifting Melody's head. With his fingertip, he tilted her chin toward him. "What you call big bones, I call feminine curves. There's nothing wrong with looking like a real woman, sweetheart."

Tears shimmered in her golden eyes. She blinked them back and turned away. "Thank you for saying that."

"It's true. For someone so smart, I can't believe you can't see your own beauty."

"Look, I know this job is important to you, but . . ."

"This doesn't have a damn thing to do with a job," he growled. "This is about me and you."

"There is no us, Grant."

"There could be." The words slipped out before he could stop them. Yet now that they were said, he was glad. His head warned him the idea of him and Melody together didn't make sense. The old power- and money-driven Melody would have been a perfect match. That Melody, he understood.

Too bad he didn't want the old Melody. It was this enchanting woman, with her yoga, yarn and sinfully sexy apple-scented hair who kept him up all night fantasizing about how it would feel to touch her, to kiss her, to taste her. She made him do what no other woman had—question his bachelorhood and wonder what it would be like to wake up next to her every morning.

Fed up with speculating, he reached out to seek an answer to at least one of his burning questions. He tugged at the ribbon securing her hair and sent a cascade of curls tumbling down around her shoulders.

"Perfect," he said hoarsely. He threaded his fingers through the thick tresses, luxuriating in their softness. Gently cupping her face in his hands, he pulled her toward him and finally kissed the lush lips that had tantalized him all day.

The intensity of the fierce storm raging around them paled in comparison to the explosive impact of his mouth brushing against hers. The brief contact sent a jolt of pure pleasure through him.

Unprepared for the powerful surge, Grant broke off the kiss. He smoothed back her hair with his hand and rested his forehead against hers.

"Melody." His voice came out as a ragged whisper.

One glance into her magnetic eyes and he knew. It hadn't been his imagination. What had just happened between them was more than a simple kiss. She'd felt it too.

A soft sigh escaped her parted lips and his self-control was shattered. He deepened the kiss, drinking in her sweetness. She tasted of sweet tea and cotton candy.

When they finally parted, he could feel her trembling. He stroked her bare arms with his hands.

He detected the same tremor in her voice, as she stood and held out her hand to him. "Stay with me tonight?"

He looked up into her golden eyes, and for the first time he saw more than beauty. They gave him a glimpse into her very soul. Summoning the self-control that had deserted him moments ago, he gave her the only answer he could.

"No."

Melody flinched.

No.

The word reverberated in her head as if he'd shouted it from a mountain peak. She'd held her heart out to him, and he'd crushed it beneath his heel like a discarded cigarette butt.

All that raving about how attracted he was to her had just been an act. She had to hand it to him. His performance had been flawless. She'd hung on every word falling from his smooth-talking lips.

Melody exhaled, releasing the air trapped in her lungs. She'd fallen for the same old game. But it appeared even Grant had his limits. He was desperate for her to work for him, but not enough to bring himself to make love to her.

The ache of his rejection was compounded by an aftershock of utter humiliation.

How could she be such a fool?

The hand she held out to him curled into a fist. She turned toward the front door. She had to get as far away from him as she could.

"Melody, please." He rose from the swing. "Just hear me out."

"You've already told me everything I need to know."

Grant grasped her arm, turning her toward him. "No, I haven't," he said. "I've got something to say, and you're going to listen."

Anger warmed her face as she struggled for control. Why didn't he just go and leave her in peace?

"I care about you, Melody." His voice softened. "Very much."

"Yeah, right. I'm not stupid."

"You're sassy, sexy and stubborn as hell, but we both know you're not stupid."

Melody raised her hands in protest, breaking his grasp on her arms. She wished she could turn off her feelings for him as easily.

"Believe me, Melody, there's nothing I'd like to do more than haul you off to your bedroom and make love to every inch of you," he said. "It's taking all the self-control I can muster not to do just that."

"But you said . . ." Her voice trailed off. It hurt too much to repeat.

"I know what I said, and I meant it." He reached out and caressed her cheek. "I won't sleep with you, because you're not ready. Not yet."

Melody averted his gaze. She couldn't look at him. If she did, she'd fall right back into his trap.

He lifted her chin with his fingertip. "You're scared and you're unsure. As much as I want you, I can't take advantage of your vulnerability. When we make love—and we will—I want you to give yourself to me without any doubts."

"I don't believe you."

"Well, believe this." He advanced on her, pulling her into his arms. Melody gasped. The hesitancy and gentleness of his previous embraces was lost, replaced by a fierce possessiveness no man had ever shown toward her.

Earsplitting thunder sounded along with the warning bells in her head. Her common sense told her to extricate herself from his powerful arms, run into the house and shut the door behind her. Instead the magnetic heat from his body pulled her even closer. God help her, but it felt good to be in his arms.

Without preamble, he crushed his lips to hers. Like his embrace, this kiss was commanding, as if he wanted to brand her as his.

The more they kissed, the more she wanted to kiss him. Why couldn't she get enough of this man?

"We'd better stop before things get out of hand," he finally said.

Embarrassed by her reaction to him, Melody nodded slightly.

"Sit with me." He motioned toward the swing. "We don't want a good storm like this to go to waste."

They seated themselves on the swing. He draped his arm over her shoulder. Slipping off her sandals, she curled her feet up under her and snuggled into the crook of his arm.

"Now talk to me," he said as they rocked.

Melody shrugged. "We've been talking all night."

"No, I mean really talk to me. Tell me who hurt you so badly that you're afraid to trust again."

Her head snapped up. She squirmed in the seat, suddenly uncomfortable. A few moments ago, she had been more than willing to give herself to him. Yet the thought of sharing the hurtful details of her past romances, if you could call them that, seemed daunting and somehow incredibly more intimate.

She chewed on her bottom lip. Would his opinion of her change if he knew how foolish she'd been, not once, but twice?

"Don't be afraid." He lifted his arm from around her shoulder and rested his large hand over her smaller one.

Her heart turned a somersault in her chest. "I'm not scared," she said aloud. It was a lie. One she hoped her clammy palms didn't reveal. Trusting him made her nervous; trusting her heart again terrified her.

"I've been engaged before," she began slowly, "twice." She paused, searching his face for disapproval, but his expression remained impassive.

Heaving a heavy sigh, she continued. "To make a long story short, both of my former fiancés were handsome and extremely charming."

Grant nodded. "Yet you didn't marry either?"

"I couldn't."

"Why not?"

"Because they didn't love me." *Because they weren't you.* The thought started her.

"They both were obviously smitten enough to ask you to be their wife."

"They were smitten all right—with money." She shook her head slightly. "What they really wanted was the Wall Street legend, the stock market guru. They wanted me to make them money."

She figured by now Grant was probably sorry he'd asked. Still, she'd started, so she might as well get it out in the open. "You never gave me a second glance in college; now one minute you're talking to me about a job and the next you're calling me beautiful."

He leaned over, smoothing her hair off her face with his hand and causing her pulse to skitter. "Which makes it even harder for you to trust me in particular."

She nodded.

He stared deep into her eyes. "I'm not some green college kid, and I'm not your former fiancés, Melody. I genuinely care about you, and I think you feel the same way about me. Don't make us both pay for what other people did in the past."

"I've made the same mistake not once, but two times already," she said. "I'm not sure what you're really after."

"When I knocked on your door, it was definitely only about a job. Now I'm not sure either."

"About the job?"

"I haven't thought about work or anything to do with it all day."

Melody's eyes widened. "So how does it feel?"

He paused, and then his mouth spread into a wide grin. "Pretty good," he admitted. "But don't change the subject. We were talking trust."

"Which works both ways. I've told you everything, but I don't know anything about your life beyond your work," she said.

"There isn't much more to tell."

Melody doubted it. He was much too attractive to not have a love life. "Ever been married?"

"No."

"Ever come close?"

She heard a telltale hitch in his voice before he said no again. "Are you sure?"

He sighed. "I had been seeing someone, but we broke up last year."

"How long were you together?"

"Five years."

"She must have been pretty special if you were with her for so long."

Grant nodded. "Celeste is a wonderful woman.

We probably would have stayed together if her sister hadn't gotten married."

"Did she meet someone else at her sister's wedding?"

He shook his head. "Nothing like that," he said. "Her sister's ten years younger than Celeste. So from the moment her sister announced her engagement and on through the wedding reception, Celeste endured all kinds of questions and comments about not having landed a husband."

Melody didn't want to feel sorry for the woman who'd had Grant for all those years. Yet as a single woman now almost in her forties, she could certainly empathize.

"After the wedding, Celeste changed. Her focus shifted from her very successful interior design business to getting me in a tuxedo and in front of a minister," he said. "Our comfortable relationship was all of a sudden tense and difficult. We argued about it all the time. I felt like I was in some kind of pressure cooker."

She watched as he ran his finger along the inside of his shirt collar as if it were suddenly choking him.

"You have something against marriage?" Melody asked.

"Not really. It's just, as much as I cared about Celeste, I knew I couldn't marry her," he said. "I didn't love her enough."

"Have you ever been in love?" Melody covered her mouth with her fist to stifle a yawn.

"That's enough questions for now, sleepyhead."

She yawned again. "Now who's running when the conversation takes an intimate turn?"

Her head dropped onto his shoulder as her questions remained unanswered. Fighting off another yawn, she struggled to keep her eyes open. She'd allowed herself to get too used to this man. She couldn't bring herself to think about how lonely she'd feel after they parted ways.

When she opened her eyes again, the rain had stopped and the telltale orange of the sunrise rimmed the darkness. Startled, she blinked. She was still on the porch swing, a throw pillow from her living-room sofa was propped under her head and a crocheted afghan covered her legs. However, Grant was nowhere in sight.

She stretched her arms over her head. The last thing she remembered was curling up next to him.

"Breakfast is almost ready, sleepyhead."

She turned to see Grant standing in her doorway. Even slightly rumpled, he looked delicious. Her hand immediately shot to her unruly hair. She didn't need to see a mirror to figure she was a mess. "Breakfast?"

He pushed opened the screen door and handed her a mug, which she gratefully accepted.

"Did you know your kitchen cabinets are stuffed with yarn?" he asked.

"I ran out of places to put it," she said, sniffing the curl of steam wafting up from the cup. "Mmmm, strawberry-kiwi. Thanks."

The telephone's ring shattered the early morning quiet. "I'd better get that," Melody said.

"What if you just let it ring?"

"It might be important."

"I can't think of anything more important than sharing a quiet breakfast together," he said. "After all, weren't you the one telling me to stop being a slave to communication devices?"

Melody nodded and took a sip of her tea. "You're right. I guess I can stand to take some of my own advice," she said, not quite ready to let the outside world intrude on the tenuous bond they'd formed last night. If there was ever a time to stay in and enjoy the moment, this was it.

The intrusive ringing stopped.

"So what's for breakfast?"

"My special omelets. The vegetables are already cut up and the eggs are beaten. All I'm waiting on is you."

"Well, I'd better get going. I'm starved." Melody bounded off the swing. She handed the cup of tea to him and headed for the bathroom.

A quick shower later, she sat at the kitchen table watching Grant put together their morning meal. It was the first time a man had ever cooked for her. She liked it.

"You seem pretty comfortable in a kitchen," she said.

"Some nights by the time I leave the office, even McDonald's is closed, so I learned a few basics." He slid the vegetable-filled eggs from the skillet onto her plate. "Omelets are my specialty."

"It looks delicious."

He kissed the top of her forehead. "So do you."

"Breakfast and compliments, I could get used to this." But she knew better. Grant would be leaving soon. After she spent next week in Boston, she'd never see him again.

Melody took a bite of omelet. She wondered how many women he'd fixed breakfast for after an exhausting night of lovemaking. The mere thought made the eggs turn to rubber in her mouth. A good-looking man like him, she knew he'd had more than his share of eager lovers. It was only natural.

Besides, this attraction between them was just that, an attraction. She had no claims on him, and they'd made no promises to each other.

"So what do you think?"

"Huh? Oh, the omelet," she said. "It's terrific."

The phone rang again.

"You must be pretty popular. It's barely dawn and your phone's been ringing off the hook."

"I'd better answer it this time. I'll make it quick, so we can enjoy the rest of the morning in peace."

She grabbed the kitchen phone. A few moments later, she handed it to Grant. "It's Barbara from your office. She says your father has been driving everyone nuts since you left, and either you come back immediately or she's quitting."

Melody picked at her omelet while Grant talked in the other room. Their time here had been nice, but it was done anyway. The call from his office merely made it official.

Now it was time for her to uphold her end of the bargain.

206

CHAPTER THIRTEEN

"What's the matter? I thought you'd be chomping at the bit to get these back," Melody said.

Grant looked down at his cell phone, Blackberry and laptop, and made no moves toward the high-tech gadgets on the kitchen table. He didn't want their constant beeps and chimes reminding him of his real life and what he should be doing.

A few days ago he could hardly wait to get them back, as well as contact the office. Now all he wanted was more time with Melody.

Grant was tired of thinking about duty and obligation. Usually he welcomed them, but right now they and these assorted gadgets felt like two-ton weights strapped to his ankles dragging him underwater.

He left them in the off position. There would be plenty of time to be accountable to the assortment of chirping gizmos later. He didn't want to look beyond the present and spending time with Melody.

He wanted to listen to her laugh, gaze into

those magnificent eyes and experience smiles that reminded him of the sun bursting through the clouds after the rain.

"We need to talk about our deal," he said, pacing the kitchen floor.

"What about it?"

He stopped and rubbed the back of his neck with his hand before letting out a weary sigh. "I'm letting you off the hook. The deal is off. You don't have to come to Boston to review our fund's holdings or hold workshops," he said.

Melody stared up at him, dumbfounded. He couldn't blame her. After all, the only reason he'd stayed this week was in order to get her to come back with him.

He walked over to the chair she was sitting in, grasped her hand and pulled her to her feet. "However, I do want you to accompany me to Boston," he paused, "but not for work. I'd like to you do it for me—for us."

"The store opens in two weeks, and there's still so much to do." Her words were hesitant, but her eyes told him it was just fear talking.

"You agreed to come with me anyway as part of our old deal, so time shouldn't be an issue," he said, not wanting to accept no for an answer.

She shook her head. "That was different. Besides, I didn't really expect you to hold up your end of the bargain. I thought you would have hightailed it out of here days ago."

"Okay, if not for the entire week, then for a few days."

She pulled her hand from his and turned away briefly before facing him again. "Why do this? Your life is there, mine is here. Dragging this out only delays the inevitable."

"I'm not ready to say good-bye just yet."

"Then stay a while longer," she said softly.

He took her hand in his again, this time holding it tighter. "Come home with me, Melody. Let me wine and dine you, take you out on a real date. Let me spoil you."

Tears shimmered in her eyes. "I don't remember a man ever wanting to spoil me," she said.

"Then let me be the first."

Melody exhaled heavily and pinned him with a tentative gaze. Again, he saw the vulnerability that never failed to pull at his heartstrings.

"You were right about me before. I want to, but I'm afraid." Her voice dropped an octave. "I'm scared to trust you, and more so, I'm terrified of trusting myself. I've been wrong before. I don't want to open myself up only to get hurt again."

Grant smoothed back her hair and caressed her sweet face. He'd walk through fire before he'd hurt her. "You've got to take this chance. We both do. If you don't we'll both spend the rest of our lives wondering if we let fear cheat us out of the best thing that could have ever happened to us. I think we'll both regret it."

He held up his hand, forestalling the rejection he saw stamped all over her face.

"Please, Melody. Say yes."

* * *

A flat tire, speeding ticket and spilled gas station coffee were not bad omens.

"There's no such thing," Joyce whispered as she speed walked from the parking lot to the school of nursing building. But it sure did feel like the powers that be were conspiring against her this morning.

She was late. What a way to start the first day of her college career. She glanced down at the huge brown stain on the front of her pale blue blouse. She hoped it would soon dry into a less noticeable big brown stain.

After stopping to ask directions twice, she finally stumbled upon the small auditorium where the orientation was being held. She slid into the first open seat she could find.

A heavyset man, who appeared to be running things, handed her a sheaf of papers. He smiled, instantly putting Joyce at ease. "We just got started, so you haven't missed anything. I'd just asked everyone to tell me a little about themselves and why they're here."

He motioned to a woman sitting in the front row. She had long, and from the looks of her flawless walnut-hued skin, prematurely gray hair. Joyce wondered if she too was a housewife returning to school.

"Go ahead, Ms. Johnson."

"As I was saying," the woman began, "I have a master's in Communications and have taught high-school journalism for the last ten years."

Joyce clasped her hands to stop her fingers from

fidgeting. Turned out Ms. Johnson wasn't the only one with impressive credentials. Student after student rattled off degrees and work histories that Joyce found both awe-inspiring and intimidating.

Teachers, downsized stockbrokers and even an engineer explained for what reason or another they were returning to school and looking to start new careers in medicine. Not a housewife in the bunch—except for her.

Doubt inched down her spine and her voice trembled slightly as she introduced herself. Everyone was polite and appeared interested. Still, she couldn't silence the voice inside her head. The one telling her she was the dumbest person in the room.

Melody questioned her decision to accompany Grant, even as a member of the private plane's flight crew advised her the plane was about to land.

Experience had taught her following her heart resulted in pain and betrayal. Yet she couldn't resist his heartfelt plea. Who was she fooling? One look into those dark chocolate eyes of his, and she'd do anything he asked.

Grant had excused himself shortly after the private jet took off from Nashville, saying he had to make some calls.

He'd checked in periodically, but was mostly scarce for the three-hour flight. The plane's small crew had been very attentive and provided her with refreshments and reading material. However, it wasn't their attention she sought.

Grant had been away from the office for a week,

and she understood there were probably dozens of matters that required his attention. Still, she couldn't help feeling abandoned after he'd talked so much about them spending time together.

She hadn't expected the week in Tennessee to change him completely, but she did hope his priorities had begun to shift.

"Sorry about that," he said, reentering the cabin. "I had some calls to make. I didn't expect them to take so long."

"I'm sure you had pressing business," she said coolly.

"Yes, but it's all taken care of now."

"So how are things at the office?"

A puzzled look crossed his chiseled features. "I have no idea."

"You've been on the phone a while; it must be in real chaos." She tried to keep her disappointment out of her voice, but even to her own ears she sounded like a jealous fishwife.

All they'd shared was a few kisses. That didn't give her the right to act territorial.

"I haven't checked in with the office. Like I told you, this time is reserved for us."

Now it was her turn to feel confused. Then it dawned upon her that he was more than likely checking in with a woman. He'd mentioned his old girlfriend, Celeste, but hadn't said much more about his love life. What made her assume he was unattached? A handsome man like him wouldn't lack for female companionship. Melody bit the inside of her lip. She was doing it again, being jealous over a man on whom she had no logical claim.

Then again, hearts weren't logical.

Stop it! she silently reprimanded herself. He'd asked her to trust him, and although trust didn't come easy for her, she would try.

He held his hand out to her, pulling her out of her seat and into his strong arms. "I only have a few days to convince you to let me into your heart, and I don't have another second to waste. Let's get going."

"Not so fast," Melody said, enjoying the feel of his arms holding her firmly against him. Inhaling the sexy scent of his cologne, it was all she could do not to swoon. "Mind telling me where we are? Because this certainly isn't Boston."

"We rarely fly into Logan—too much congestion," he said. "It's more convenient to use Manchester's airport. Southern New Hampshire is practically a Boston suburb."

"So we're driving down to Boston."

"Eventually."

"But I thought . . ."

"All I want you to think about is this." He lowered his lips to hers in a kiss that made her toes curl, and like his previous kisses, it left her panting for more.

Before she knew it they were zooming along the interstate in Grant's Mercedes. Even in the last week of August, New England's summer breeze felt cool against her skin compared to the Tennessee heat.

"You have absolutely no intention of telling me where we're going, do you?"

"No."

Melody eased back into the leather passenger seat. Allowing her eyes a long, lazy look at Grant, she noted everything from his dreamy dark eyes to those impossibly sexy forearms of his. She wanted to memorize everything about him in the few short days they had together.

The next thing she remembered was waking up.

"Welcome back, sleepyhead."

Melody blinked and straightened in her seat, surprised to find them following a ribbon of two-lane road winding through lush green countryside instead of in the midst of a Boston traffic snarl.

She peered out the car window at a sign welcoming them to Maine.

"Maine?" She arched a brow. "I thought you had to get back home."

"I do, but not before I treat you to one of the best lunches on the planet."

Melody cringed inwardly. They'd already passed several restaurants with bright red lobster claws adorning the buildings.

"I don't know how to tell you this, but I'm allergic to shellfish."

He flashed her a grin. "Who said anything about seafood?"

"Maine is synonymous with lobster. It's a natural assumption."

"It's also a wrong one."

"Am I correct in assuming you're not going to tell me?"

"Yep."

"How about a hint?"

His face looked impassive until she added the word *please,* then he exhaled. "No hints, but I will give you a warning."

"A warning?"

"Absolutely nothing healthy allowed. The key words for the next few days are fun, decadence and junk food."

"I don't know if I like the sound of that," Melody said cautiously.

A thick carpet of greenery gave way to rocky coastline edging the choppy waters of the Atlantic. She's seen the ocean from the vantage points of Florida and the outer banks of North Carolina. Neither compared to this spectacular view.

Melody let down her window to soak it in, taking in a big gulp of fresh air. Bold colors surrounded her, making her long for yarn in the same vibrant green of the dense brush or in the brown of the rocky cliffs that separated it from the ocean. But especially, she wished she could knit up something in the same deep blue as the ocean. Melody didn't think she'd ever seen the inky blue shade in nature. The water glittered like sapphires.

A few minutes later, they turned into a narrow lot in front of a small, gray, ocean-weathered shack. The crooked sign on the front of it looked like the kids from the old black and white *Our Gang* comedies has tacked it up.

On the side of the building, shaded by trees, were four picnic tables, just as weathered as the building.

Melody raised a curious brow. "Hot dogs?"

"Not just hot dogs, sweetheart, but a Jo's steamed hot dog. The best food you ever put in your mouth."

They walked up to the pick-up window.

"How many?" A croaky voice barked. Melody assumed it was attached to the heavily tattooed man whose arm dangled out of a sliding glass window.

"Two," Grant said.

"Doesn't he need to know what we want on them?" Melody asked.

"He knows," Grant said. "It would be a sin to eat them any way other than with Jo's secret sauce."

Fortunately, they did get a choice of drinks. She opted for bottled iced tea, while Grant ordered a soda and a bag of Maine Coast potato chips.

"You come here often?" Melody asked, after they seated themselves at one of the picnic tables.

"I reserve this exclusively for special occasions and special people."

"I'll bet you bring all your women here," she said cautiously.

"Actually, you're the first I've ever invited."

"I'm honored, Mr. Price." She hesitantly unwrapped the paper from her hot dog.

"Go ahead and try it," Grant coaxed. "One bite and you'll be hooked."

"I doubt I'd drive all the way from Tennessee for a hot dog."

Grant smiled. "Who knows? Maybe you won't be that far away."

"You're not going to start up with that job thing," Melody said. "I thought we had an understanding."

"Who said I'm talking about the job?"

"Then what?"

"I brought you here to show you a good time, and that's exactly what we're going to have."

After eating what she had to agree was the best hot dog she'd ever tasted, Melody felt her guard begin to come down. "It was delicious. Thanks for bringing me."

"So what would you like to do next? A walk along the beach?"

"Maybe later. Right now, I'm dying to get into some of those antique shops we saw down the road."

They made the short drive back to the row of wood-framed stores. Aged and softly faded by the ocean's salty breeze, the buildings looked like they had been plucked from the pages of an early American history book. The row of stores extended nearly two blocks and Melody hoped to hit every one of them.

They walked hand-in-hand as they browsed the various shops. Melody wasn't sure who had reached for the other's hand first. All she knew was, it felt good and as natural as breathing.

Passersby assumed they were a couple and treated them as such. Melody didn't bother correcting them, and she noticed Grant didn't either. The strangers were off base; still, she couldn't help but wonder what it would be like if they really were a couple.

She forced herself to snap out of it and face the truth. They weren't a couple. Not really. A few kisses weren't a commitment. At the most, all they were to each other was good friends.

She glanced over at Grant to find him smiling at her.

"What are you grinning at?"

"You look like a kid in a row of candy stores."

Melody chuckled. That was exactly how she felt. The shops were crammed full of exquisite pieces of eighteenth- and nineteenth-century furniture, wood-burning stoves, silver, quilts and a host of other collectibles.

She made a mental note that if she ever came back she'd bring a U-Haul to fill with these spectacular finds.

"What about you, see anything you like?"

Grant shrugged. "It looks like a bunch of old junk to me."

Melody was about to tell him about how the craftsmanship that went into creating these pieces was almost nonexistent in today's pre-fab, cookie-cutter world, when something caught her eye and she did a double take.

"Oh my goodness. It's perfect." Melody crouched down to take a closer look at the vintage toy fire truck. The old pedal truck was a little before her time, but she remembered seeing them in her beginning readers as a child. Her mind spun with the endless possibilities for yarn displays.

Grant frowned. "That rusty thing?"

"It'll look absolutely perfect in my store. What a find!"

She inspected the other side of the antique toy. The once bright red paint had faded, and the bell on the hood was missing, along with one of the ladders. However, there were no dings and most of the original accessories appeared to be intact.

Basically all it needed was a coat of paint and a few tweaks, and it would be as good as new.

"Aren't you curious about what I want to do with it?"

Grant shrugged again. "I've been in your shop. I figure you're going to cram it full of yarn like everything else in there."

"I may even knit up a toy Dalmatian to go with it."

"I've been hanging out with you too much. That actually sounds like a good idea."

"Just wait until you see it," she said, then realized he wouldn't.

He shrugged. "You can always send me a picture or something."

For a second she thought she'd detected a hint of sadness in his voice, or maybe she was merely projecting her own feelings onto him.

The portly shop owner, who'd greeted them when they walked in, ambled over. Melody had caught him staring at her a few times, but hadn't thought anything of it.

"Don't I know you from somewhere?" He scratched his balding head.

Melody smiled politely. "I don't think so."

"Your face looks awfully familiar."

"I'm interested in the toy fire truck," she said, changing the subject.

"Oh, an elderly lady in Portland found it while cleaning out her attic." The man stopped and squinted at her before continuing. "She said she used trading stamps to get it back in 1955 for her son's third birth—" He stopped mid-sentence. "Hey, I know where I know you from. You're the stock lady. Melody Mason, right?"

Melody nodded. "Back to the truck, do the pedals and steering wheel still work?"

"I thought so. I can't believe you're actually in my store."

The shopkeeper gripped her hand and pumped it in a hearty handshake. "What brings you to Maine?" he asked, an awestruck expression on his face.

"Hot dogs." Melody turned and winked at Grant.

"I'm Craig Martin," he said. Then yelled out for his wife, who came from a back room to join them. "This is my wife, Candy."

"Nice to meet you both," Melody said. She tried introducing Grant, but Craig Martin's attention was focused solely on her.

"Don't you remember her, honey?" Craig asked his wife.

Melody groaned inwardly, feeling a bit like one of the pieces they had on display.

Recognition lit up in Candy Martin's eyes. "Ohhhhh, I do know you! You're the lady who used to write us all those nice letters."

"Letters?" Melody asked, searching her brain to figure out if and when she'd met the Martins, and when on earth she had written to them. She didn't think the stroke had affected her memory.

Craig put his arm around his wife's shoulder. "My Candy here is talking about your letter to shareholders in the semi-annual reports for our mutual fund."

"Oh," Melody said, relieved there wasn't a previously undetected gap in her memory.

"We started investing in that mutual fund about twelve years ago," he said. "Sometimes when the market looked rocky, we'd think about pulling out. Then we'd get our report and see a letter from you explaining your strategy and advising us to stay the course."

Candy smiled at her husband, then at Melody. "Thanks to you, we were able to retire early and buy this shop."

Melody's heart swelled with pride. She'd always been aware of the tremendous weight she carried, being responsible for other people's money. However, her job interaction was mostly with corporation CEOs, co-workers and of course, the numbers.

Meeting the Martins gave it a human face. It

made her feel good. It topped what she had thought was her crowning moment—the *Time* magazine article on her.

"You made our dreams come true," Craig said.

Melody smiled and shook her head. "No, you two made your own dreams come true by diligently saving."

"Anyway, if you want that fire truck, it's yours. Take it as our gift," he said.

"I couldn't." She dug into her purse and pulled out her wallet. "I insist on paying."

Melody and the couple went back and forth. Her ethics wouldn't allow her to take the truck without paying, and they didn't want to take her money.

She heard Grant clear his throat. "I'll take care of the bill for the fire truck," he told Craig. "You wouldn't want to take away my chance to impress the lady, would you?"

Grant closed the trunk of his car.

"I can't believe I let you talk me into putting that rusty piece of tin into the trunk of my Mercedes," he said. "Craig offered to ship it to you."

He walked around to the passenger's side to open the door for Melody. She touched the side of his face with her palm. "I know, but I just had to have it now."

"Okay," he groused playfully. "I brought you up here to spoil you rotten, and that's exactly what I'm going to do."

"Don't you owe me a walk on the beach?"

Of the three nearby beaches, Grant opted for the horseshoe-shaped one bordered by cliffs and the harbor. Since the tiny public beach didn't have bathhouses, shops or restaurants in close proximity, it didn't attract the summer crowds.

Grant parked next to the only other car in the small lot. He'd barely shut off the engine before Melody was out of the car and looking out at the water. She pushed her sunglasses up on her head. "It's so beautiful here," she said.

Grant watched her with a mix of amazement and admiration. She could have just about anything she wanted, yet she appreciated the simple things.

Each moment he spent with Melody, he uncovered a different layer of her multifaceted personality. Each one pulled him closer to the magnetic, fascinating woman underneath.

What man wouldn't find himself falling for a woman who treated a hot dog and a walk along the beach like afternoon tea at Buckingham Palace?

He sneaked a peek at her as they walked along the beach. Being with Melody was refreshing, like sunshine breaking through the clouds after a week of rain.

He felt himself smile. She just made him feel good.

Grant reached down, picked up a broken shell from the sand and tossed it back into the ocean.

"I don't believe it," Melody said, as they walked along the sands. "You actually look like you're relaxed and enjoying yourself."

She was right, he realized. He was having a good time. "I guess I am feeling pretty mellow."

She threw up her hands. "I tried just about everything to get you to chill out last week and nothing worked. So much for my stress-relief boot camp."

Grant chuckled. She really had tried, and unlike him, her motives had been pure. She'd had no ulterior motive. She'd freely given of her time and put up with his cantankerous attitude only because she'd wanted to help him. In return, he'd fought her every step of the way.

"If it weren't for you, it never would have occurred to me to take any time off," he said. "I'd say that made your boot camp a success."

She beamed; her gorgeous smile was a reward in itself. He felt her nudge him with her elbow. "I'll race you up that hill," she said.

Grant followed her eyes to the top of the craggy cliff. "And if I win?"

Melody arched a brow. "You won't."

"We'll see about that."

"Okay, on your mark, get set." She hesitated a moment before he heard her yell, "Go!"

He took off with every intention of whipping her good, but the closer he got to the top of the hill, the less important winning became. Melody ran past him. She wore the same determined look on her face he remembered from their school days. Her hair had come loose from its ribbon and it flew in the breeze. Again, he wondered why it had taken him so long to see how truly beautiful she was.

He made it to the top of the rocks a few minutes after her.

"I won!" she shouted.

Grant couldn't help laughing when she did a short victory dance.

"Who's the competitive one now?" he asked.

She flashed him a sheepish grin. "I must have had some kind of college flashback, or maybe you just bring it out in me."

She sat down on a large rock and hugged her knees to her chest.

"We do have a knack for bringing out the competitor in each other." He seated himself beside her. "You drove me crazy back then."

"Me?" Melody asked, clearly surprised. "We barely said two words to each other over the entire four years."

"That probably made it worse. Whenever we crossed paths, I was trying to figure out what you were up to."

"I thought you were too busy being the center of cheerleader and sorority girl attention to even care about me."

"They weren't the ones who swiped the student government presidency right from under me."

"Swipe?" Melody's eyes widened. "I beg your pardon, but I earned that. Do you know how many hours I put into campaigning? And I didn't have the advantage of being popular like you did."

"I was shocked they announced your name instead of mine. I felt like I had just taken a blow from Mike Tyson."

"Oh come on, you're exaggerating. It couldn't have been that bad."

"No, the bad part came when I broke the news to my father, after I had assured him it was in the bag."

Melody eyed him quizzically. "After all the awards and accolades you won, I can't imagine him being angry."

"No, he didn't exactly get mad, but he never let me forget it, either." Grant shook his head. Too bad he couldn't shake off the memories of his dad's profound disappointment in him that day. It was as if the things he'd accomplished had vanished. All his father cared about was the one he'd lost.

John Price wasn't a man who tolerated failure. Not from himself and certainly not from his sons.

Grant exhaled sharply. "Dad just had very high expectations of me. He still does."

He thought back to the displeasure he'd heard in his father's voice, and how it had cut him to the bone. It had always been that way for him. One utterance of displeasure from his father was worse than a beating.

Since then Grant had made sure he never let the old man down again. And he hadn't, until now.

He felt a light touch on his arm.

"Where were you just now?"

"Someplace I'd rather not be," he said, shaking off the thoughts.

"You okay?"

He nodded and placed his hand over her smaller one.

"You know you can talk to me," she offered.

"There's a lighthouse nearby. Would you like take a look at it?" he asked, not-so-smoothly changing the subject.

"Yeah, sure."

"Good," he said. "And later I have a surprise for you."

CHAPTER FOURTEEN

Kevin pulled into the garage, surprised to see Joyce's car in its usual space. With all the recent college hubbub, he'd half expected her to be out at some sorority rush.

He parked his car alongside hers and grabbed his briefcase. Okay, maybe he was exaggerating. But what was he supposed to think? What kind of wife turns up her nose at a Hawaiian honeymoon and doesn't show up at an important dinner with a client?

"One who doesn't give a damn about her husband," he muttered, slamming his car door closed.

The scent of baking bread greeted him when he walked through the door, his anger abating in favor of his appetite.

Joyce was seated at the kitchen table behind two towering stacks of textbooks. If he hadn't known better, he would have sworn she'd been the victim of an encyclopedia salesman. She closed the book she'd been thumbing through and looked up at him. For a moment, he almost forgot about being angry.

"Hi," she said softly. Her eyes held the same expectant expression he'd seen all week. They silently asked when this growing rift between them would end, and what it would take for them to reach a compromise.

Hell, he wished he knew. He didn't relish seeing disappointment blanket his wife's features, and even worse, he hated knowing he was responsible for it.

He swallowed the lump lodged in his throat before mumbling a greeting in her direction. Her hopeful expression faded, and his heart sunk as if lead anchors weighed it down.

It was Joyce who made the first chip at the wall of silence erecting itself between them. She got up from the chair and began clearing the books from the table.

"I got an e-mail from the twins this morning. They're both overdrawn and want us to deposit money into their accounts," she said. He detected the slight tremor in her voice as she struggled to keep it even. "David is going out for burgers with his friends, so it's just me and you for dinner tonight."

Shrugging off his suit jacket, Kevin draped it across a kitchen chair. She'd stuck to talking about the kids, a safe topic. "What are we having?"

She stopped and eyed him curiously. "Sandwiches. The bread should be ready in a few minutes."

Kevin released a heavy sigh and plopped down

into one of the bar-style stools in front of the kitchen counter. "Is this a preview of things to come? I come home after a hard day's work to lunch meat."

Like she hadn't heard a word he'd said, Joyce walked over to the sink, washed her hands, then checked the timer on the bread machine.

Since Kevin was already annoyed, his wife's cool manner irked him even more. He was spoiling for a fight, and it looked like she wasn't going to give him the satisfaction. He crossed his arms and leaned them against the counter. "Are you going to answer me or what?"

Joyce huffed out a breath before she turned to him. Eyes that had been filled with expectation, then sadness, flashed with anger. "It's sandwich night, and it has been for ten years," she said, her tone slow and deliberate. "In all this time, you've never objected to it once. Why now?"

Because everything is changing, he wanted to say. *You're changing. I feel like I'm losing you.* Instead, he continued to grumble over the prospect of a cold dinner, when he knew darn well she was right. He knew it was sandwich night, an idea he had come up with years ago.

"First and foremost, you are a wife and a mother. I don't want our family taking a backseat to this," he said, gesturing toward the stacks of books on the baker's rack. "You've already demonstrated by skipping dinner the other night that you have too much on your plate."

As an attorney, he knew his argument wasn't logical, but he wasn't in the mood for logic. School hadn't officially started and he was already tired of it. He wanted his wife back. He wanted their old life back.

Joyce drew in a deep, ragged breath and released it. He had been with her long enough to know she was silently counting to ten and praying for patience.

"I've had a tough day, and I don't want to argue with you, Kevin. Let's just sit down and eat, okay?"

Let it go, the warning voice in his head advised, but he ignored it, instead giving over to the urge to keep pushing the issue. "I think the peanut butter and juice box will hold," he said in the condescending tone he knew she disliked. "I want to talk about what this college bug you've got is going to mean to our lives. I don't think you've actually sat down and thought it through. The upheaval, the inconvenience, the . . ."

"The sacrifice?" Joyce said. Her voice quivered with unspoken fury and her eyes shot daggers in his direction. "Like the sacrifices we made so you could get your education?"

"Yes, and now I make a good enough living to make any further sacrifices unnecessary."

"You mean any sacrifices on *your* part unnecessary," she said, pointing her finger at him. "What about our plan, Kevin? You were going to go to school, then me."

"Oh, come on," he said with a humorless chuckle. "Don't start that again. That was twenty years ago. We were kids."

Joyce sighed and looked down at the floor. "Maybe I should have gone first. Then I wouldn't find myself standing here justifying wanting an education."

As hard as he tried to understand where his wife was coming from, for the life of him he didn't. "To go to work? For what?"

He walked around the counter and gently placed his hands on her arms. "It's a tough world out there, baby," he said, softening his tone. "Why get into the rat race when you don't have to?"

She pulled away from him. "For growth, personal satisfaction. I need to do this for me, and it has nothing to do with money."

"Is this you or Oprah talking?"

"Don't be insulting. It's beneath you."

"Well, what am I supposed to think?" Kevin asked, his frustration mounting. Every time they attempted to talk this out, the conversation went around in circles and left them right where they'd started. "Things were going along great. The boys are practically grown, my practice is going well, the house is almost paid for . . ."

"Our sons, you, the house. What's missing from that checklist?"

Kevin closed his eyes and squeezed the bridge of his nose with his fingertips. He slowly opened them and shook his head. "I have no idea what you're talking about."

"The idyllic picture of the storybook life you just painted is missing something—me," she said, her voice trailing off.

"Oh, don't be so touchy. You know what I meant."

"I've been so wrapped up in being the good wife and the perfect mother that I've slipped into the background," she said. "No wonder you didn't bother mentioning me."

"That's what this is all about?" Realization began to dawn upon him. "Look honey, I'm sorry if I don't say it often enough, but the boys and I appreciate everything you do for us. You are an amazing wife and even better mother."

Guilt seized Kevin as he observed sadness overtaking the fury in his wife's eyes. He averted his gaze. He'd give anything to put a smile back on her face, but he couldn't help feeling the way he did.

"Is that what you think?" she asked.

Kevin rubbed the back of his neck with his hand. Just when he thought they'd taken a step forward, they ended up two steps back.

"All I'm saying is you're needed right here. You don't have to go out for recognition. The boys and I appreciate everything you do."

Joyce threw her hands up. "I'm not a puppy looking for a pat on the head. I was hoping for—no, expecting—a little emotional support and encouragement from my husband. And I don't understand why I have to beg for what I've always given you freely."

Again hope flickered briefly in her eyes. He knew what she wanted. All he had to do was tell her to go for it and he was there for her no matter what. On the surface it seemed like a small task: just grit his teeth and lie right through them.

Instead, he shrugged. "I don't know what to tell you."

Joyce felt herself flinch as if she'd been slapped. Turning away from Kevin, she walked out of the kitchen. To hell with it, she thought.

"Where are you going?"

"To bed," she said, not breaking her stride.

She heard Kevin's footsteps coming up behind her. "We weren't done talking," he said.

Numb with anger, Joyce stopped but kept her back to him. "What you mean is *you* weren't done talking. Did you hear me when I told you I'd had a hard day or did you just not care?"

"I . . ." Kevin stammered.

She shook her head. "It doesn't matter. Either way you were too wrapped up in your needs to care about mine," she said, climbing the staircase.

"Don't try to turn the tables; I'm not the one trying to change everything," he said.

"Let it go for now, Kevin," she said. "Before we both say something we'll regret."

"Oh, come on. You know you want to. It'll make you feel so much better."

Grant looked at the infectious grin on Melody's face and couldn't hold back his own. "I keep telling you, it's a surprise."

"Give me a hint?"

Grant chuckled. She had been trying to wheedle it out of him for most of the hour and a half drive from southern Maine down to Boston. "No."

"Can you at least tell me where we are?"

"The front door of my condo," he said. "Close your eyes, keep them closed and stop asking so many questions."

"I hate surprises." She pulled her full lips into a faux pout.

"No, you don't. You love them."

Melody giggled. "You're right. I do," she conceded. "Now hurry up and open the door. The suspense is killing me."

Her enthusiasm was contagious, and Grant couldn't help but smile. To the world, Melody Mason's name was synonymous with financial wizardry. To him she was the perfect mix of beauty, brains, strength and vulnerability. Everything he could want in a woman, and nobody could have been more blindsided by it than him.

"Keep your eyes shut. No peeking."

She did as she was told. He unlocked the door to the loft and a quick glance revealed that his instructions had been followed to the letter.

"Can I open them?"

"Not yet." He led her through the open door. "Okay, you can look."

Her eyes blinked, then widened in delight. "Oh, Grant!" she squealed.

Clear helium balloons bounced against gold Mylar ones shaped like stars, transforming what was normally a dining room into an ethereal slice of the heavens. A shimmering silk tablecloth covered a round table bearing tiered golden trays filled with mini versions of Melody's favorite desserts. A phone call to Ruth had insured he didn't miss a one.

In the center sat a crystal vase of white roses and champagne on ice.

She peered around the room. Her eyes sparkled in amazement. "My God. Look at this."

"You approve?"

"It's beautiful." Her voice cracked on the last word.

Grasping her hand, he brought it to his lips, turned it over and pressed a kiss to her palm. He felt her hand tremble as he kissed it.

"Dessert is your weakness," he said. "Melody Mason, you are mine."

Tears filled her eyes before one rolled down a perfect cheek. Grant brushed it away with his thumb. "Don't cry. I did this to make you happy."

She swiped at another tear with the back of her hand. "Can't you see?" She smiled through the tears brimming her golden eyes. "I am happy."

"I love to see you smile."

"For the first time in my life, I'm overwhelmed. I don't know what to say."

"Then don't talk." He inclined his head toward the dessert-laden table. "Why don't you sample your treats instead? I ordered all your favorites."

He watched her eyes go wide as she surveyed the trays. "What can I tempt you with?"

"Wow, peach cobbler, an apple tart, orange cheesecake."

"What do you want to try first?"

"I don't know how to tell you this."

Grant kissed the tip of her nose. "You can tell me anything."

"I'm not hungry."

"You're not? I don't get it. I made sure we skipped dinner. You should be ravenous."

"Let me put this another way: I'm hungry all right, but not for food."

Grant's heart turned over in his chest as he grasped her meaning. Then she spelled it out to him in no uncertain terms.

"I want you," she said. Then she clasped the collar of his shirt and pulled him toward her lush mouth.

A second before their lips met, he thought he heard her whisper ever so softly, "I love you."

Melody's pulse pounded in her ears as an obviously startled Grant suddenly pulled away. She couldn't blame him. The words had simply slipped out, leaving her as surprised as he no doubt felt.

Embarrassed, she averted her eyes, afraid of his reaction. Her mouth went dry as she searched for a way to save face.

"Maybe I shouldn't have said . . ." she began.

He placed his forefinger over her lips, silencing her. Then he removed his finger and touched his lips lightly to hers in a heart-melting kiss so sweet it nearly took her breath away. "I've wanted you from the moment you stepped out on your porch. I've tried everything, but I can't get you out of my head."

He groaned raggedly before bringing his mouth

down on hers again, the gentleness replaced by need and longing. His tongue explored her mouth, while his hands set her body on fire. The taste and feel of him dominated her senses.

She heard herself gasp when they finally came up for air. Their gazes connected, holding for one electric moment. Pure desire radiated from the depths of his deep brown eyes.

"Don't be afraid to trust your heart. I know this is a lot to ask, but I want you to put your faith in me." He took a step toward the bedroom, stopped and held his hand out to her. "Let me love all the hurt away."

She nodded slowly and placed her hand in his. With the simple gesture, she broke the restraints of past hurts crippling her spirit and allowed herself to live in the moment.

The earth shifted beneath Melody's feet as Grant scooped her up into his lean, muscular arms. His embrace was powerful and at the same time achingly tender. Within it her nearly six-foot body felt downright diminutive. What was it about this man that made her feel as if she truly were the most beautiful woman in the world?

"You *are* stunning," he whispered against her ear, as if he'd read her thoughts. The deep timbre of his voice sent a tremor down her spine. "I've never wanted any woman the way I want you."

He kissed her slow and hard. The passionate kiss dreamily transported her from his arms to the center of his king-sized bed. There he proceeded to slowly unbutton her top, not stopping until he'd stripped away every stitch of clothing separating her skin from his.

Insecurity niggled at her. She didn't have the body of a twenty-year-old, and even at that age she'd been nothing to brag about. If he saw the imperfections of time and gravity, would he still want her?

Instinctively, she covered her bare breasts with one arm and reached with the other to turn off the bedside lamp.

He rolled off the bed and stopped her. "Don't hide from me, baby," he demanded huskily, flicking the light back on. "I want to see you."

The sight of him, naked and fully aroused, made her blood run hot in anticipation. His lean physique gave her a new appreciation for the male anatomy. She swallowed hard. *Damn, he looks good.* She took a deep breath and willed her runaway heartbeat to slow.

The evidence was undeniable. This man wanted her.

Her fears allayed, she dropped the arm covering her breasts. Her skin grew warm beneath the bold scrutiny of his gaze.

"You're more exquisite than I imagined," he murmured.

The mattress dipped as he rejoined her on the bed, covering her body with his. Her inhibitions vanished as she melted into him like warmed chocolate over a ripe strawberry. His scent, the feel of his hands on her body, the sheer maleness of him made her yearn for more. So much more.

She wanted all of him.

"Are you sure?" he asked, his breath labored. "If we don't stop now, I'm not sure I'll be able to."

"I don't ever want you to stop."

He kissed her softly and reached for the foil packet in the nightstand drawer for protection. Words were no longer necessary. Melody opened her heart to him, uniting their souls in the age-old ritual that transforms friends into lovers.

Melody awoke at dawn to the sound of Grant's humming.

Slowly stretching her arms over her head, she greeted the morning with a yawn. She felt magnificent, and if the sound of the off-key tune coming from the other room was any indication, so did he.

She rolled over and opened her eyes. The other side of the bed was rumpled and there was a dent left in the pillow. Melody smiled. She hadn't dreamt it.

Grant had indeed made love to her last night. Sweet, slow, delicious love to every inch of her, and she'd drifted off to sleep cocooned in his protective embrace. His masculine scent mingled with his sexy cologne still clung to her skin.

Throwing back the covers, she wrapped herself in Grant's robe and padded barefoot into the kitchen. Any morning-after awkwardness she may have felt evaporated the moment he looked at her. His smile was warm and intimate. A lover's smile.

He wore black silk pajama bottoms that rode low on his narrow hips and made him look good enough to do all the things she'd done to him last night all over again.

"About time you got up," he said. "I've already squeezed in a dozen Sun Salutations."

Melody's eyes narrowed with skepticism. "You did not."

Taking a seat on one of the counter stools, she propped her elbows on the black granite counter and rested her chin in her hands.

"I brought your suitcase up. It's in the living room." He placed a bowl of sliced apples, bananas and pineapple in front of her, accompanied by a glass of orange juice.

"I thought we were living a life of wanton decadence," she said, surveying her plate. "This looks pretty healthy to me."

"Well, after last night, I didn't want to lead you completely down the path to ruin."

"I recall being a more than willing participant."

"You were insatiable," he growled into her ear, then lightly bit the lobe.

Melody giggled. "Hmmm, breakfast and kisses. A girl could get used to this."

"I intend to see to it that you do."

Grant poured himself a cup of coffee and sat down next to her. He took a sip and closed his eyes briefly. An expression of absolute pleasure crossed his face. "My first shot of joe in a week."

"Oh, it wasn't that bad."

"I'll never take coffee for granted again."

Melody laughed. She scanned her surroundings, noticing his living space for the first time.

The rooms were set in a palette of soothing earth tones and accented with African art and sculptures. For a man who spent the majority of his time at work, she found his place surprisingly comfortable and inviting. "You have a nice place. It's not at all what I expected."

"So what, you thought I lived in a dump?"

"No, just more of a bachelor pad."

This time Grant laughed. The deep, rich sound made her tingle right down to her toes. "Oh, empty except for a recliner and wide-screen television, or maybe just a cot and a computer."

"I didn't think it would be so warm and elegant," Melody said, still in awe. She ran her hand over the granite countertop. "There's so much attention to detail."

Grant shrugged. "Well, I can't take credit for it. I gave a decorator free reign, and I have a housekeeper come in a couple days a week."

"Have you lived here long?"

"About ten years. This building used to be a warehouse, but it was gutted out and turned into lofts."

He took another sip of coffee and grabbed a slice of apple from her plate. "I have to make a brief stop by the office," he said. "I'll be done by one or so. How about meeting me for lunch?"

"Are you sure? You've been away for over a week. I know you have a lot of work to catch up on."

"Lunch at noon," he reiterated. "The rest of the day is ours."

"If you say so."

In one swift motion, he pulled her from the stool into his arms. She braced her hands against his bare chest.

"I say so." He lifted her off the ground and kissed her hungrily.

Melody felt her knees weaken. If he hadn't been holding her, they would have buckled for sure.

"Now let me get dressed, woman, before I don't get dressed at all."

Moments later, she smiled to herself as the sound of Grant's singing drifted from the shower. She wrapped her arms around herself. Last night, he'd told her how much he wanted and cherished her and went on to make her feel just that.

There was one thing he hadn't said. He never mentioned love.

It doesn't matter, she told herself. He had already given her a night she'd remember for the rest of her life.

Even if she never heard from him again after she returned home, she'd carry this feeling with her forever.

Meanwhile, she'd put what she'd learned at the yoga retreat into practice and just live in the moment. She fully intended to enjoy every one of them.

While Grant showered, she reached for the phone book and the cordless phone.

As long as she was here, she might as well take advantage of it. Thanks to a last-minute cancellation, she was able to snag an appointment for the works at Olive's Beauty Salon and Spa. The trip to Roxbury would be well worth it.

She felt like a new woman. Maybe she could look like one too.

"Mel," she heard Grant call out to her from the bathroom. "It's lonely in here."

She smiled to herself. A shower sounded like a good idea. Untying the robe, she let it slip off her shoulders and drop to the floor.

The jewelry store saleswoman pulled out a third tray of bracelets.

"Your girlfriend must really be something special," she said, holding out a diamond-encrusted tennis bracelet.

Scenes from his and Melody's romp in the shower replayed in Grant's head as he nodded in agreement. She was special, all right. He'd never met a woman quite like her. He'd gone after Melody to offer her a job, and she'd walked away with his heart.

"How about his one?"

"Too fussy. I'm looking for something simple, classy and elegant."

The clerk held up another bracelet. "This one is beautiful."

"Too plain."

Next she showed him a two-carat, marquise-shaped diamond pendant with a platinum setting. Again, he shook his head.

"How about a pair of earrings, sir?" the clerk suggested. "We have a fabulous selection."

"I'm not sure exactly what I'm looking for, but I'll know it when I see it. I want it to be special."

After examining and rejecting at least two dozen more pieces, Grant was about to give up. Then a flash of amber light caught the corner of his eye.

Abandoning the earrings, he followed the flash to another glass jewelry case and looked down at yellow stone. The glittering rock matched Melody's eyes.

The salesclerk pulled the tray bearing the ring from the case. "This is a two-karat yellow diamond set in eighteen-karat white gold. Stunning, isn't it?"

Get a grip, man, he silently cautioned himself as he shook off the thoughts running through his mind. The woman had only been in his life a week. He needed to take more time before even considering such a big step.

Yet the banished notion haunted him. It didn't matter if it had been a few days or a few years. He loved her.

His gaze wandered back to the yellow diamond, before he forced himself to turn away.

He finally decided on a gold bracelet and, with the salesclerk's assistance, added two gold charms. One of a tiny golden knitting basket and another of a ball of yarn.

He smiled as he envisioned Melody's reaction.

"Will there be anything else?"

He opened his mouth to say no, then looked at the ring again. Oh, what the hell, he thought. "Yes." He cleared his throat. "I'll also take the ring."

The salesclerk pulled it from the case. "So when are you going to propose?" she asked.

His gaze lingered on the glittering yellow diamond that reminded him so much of Melody's fiery gaze. "Soon."

CHAPTER FIFTEEN

Joyce pulled the phone away from her ear and stared at it. "You did what?" she asked, putting it back to her ear.

"I cut my hair," Melody repeated.

"That's what I thought you said."

"Well, aren't you going to say anything? You've been after me to go short for years."

"Why don't you describe the cut, while I try to digest the fact you actually let a beautician armed with scissors near your head."

Joyce heard a giggle. Giggle? Melody hadn't even giggled when they were teenagers. It was a side to her friend Joyce wasn't accustomed to. She listened as her friend animatedly gave her the details on the short, feathery style.

She could hear the happiness in Melody's voice. It practically emitted through the phone. Joyce glanced down at the textbook she'd been reading before the phone rang. At least one of them had something to be glad about.

Her first morning of school had been over-whelming. Every professor had hit her with a deluge of reading and assignments. They each acted as if she were only taking their class.

"Do you think Grant will like it?"

"Of course he will. It sounds fabulous," Joyce said, truly thrilled for her. Pushing her own troubles aside, she focused her attention on Melody. "Are you having fun up there?"

"I'm having the best time."

Joyce tried to keep up as Melody filled her in on a whirlwind of antiquing, hot dogs in Maine and the special desserts Grant had arranged for her. However, the unbridled excitement in Melody's tone told her there was more to it than she was saying. A lot more.

"I'll bet he provided dessert," Joyce said. "So when are you going to tell me what you two are *really* doing?"

"Like you didn't guess two seconds after you picked up the phone."

Joyce laughed. "I knew it! I told you that man was crazy about you."

"Believe it or not, I mentioned love last night."

"Whoa!" Joyce knew how hard it must have been for Melody to drop her guard. However, she'd seen the two of them together and every instinct told her Grant felt the same way about Melody. They belonged together.

"So what did he say?"

Joyce strained to make out a garbled reply.

"Sorry, I just drove through a tunnel," Melody said.

"Since when do you have a cell phone?"

"Grant loaned it to me. I was going to take the T to run a few errands, but he insisted I drive his car. I want to check out a yarn store before meeting him later for lunch," she said. "What were you asking before?"

"Never mind. I already have my answer." Joyce smiled knowingly.

She'd been married for years and Kevin's eye twitched anytime she went near his car. No man gave up his car keys to a woman he didn't care for. Not without a fight or even worse, a laundry list of instructions on how to drive it.

"How'd class go today?" Melody asked.

"Just fine." Joyce hoped her upbeat tone didn't sound too fake. She knew better than anyone how much Melody deserved this slice of happiness. There was no way she was going to ruin it whining about her school and marital woes.

After they'd hung up, Joyce looked down at the second chapter of her chemistry textbook. She'd barely comprehended a word of chapter one. Exhaling wearily, she flipped back to the beginning of the book.

Grant felt the weight of the ring in his pocket as he rode the elevator to the top floor of the Price building. He didn't know when he'd give it to her or bring up the possibility of marriage.

Right now all he wanted to do was clear his slate for the day, so he could spend it with her.

"Morning, Barbara." Grant stopped at his assistant's desk.

"Mr. Price," she said, startled. "I wasn't expecting you back today."

"Officially, I'm not. I just came to take care of a few things. I'll be leaving at lunchtime and so are you."

Barbara's eyes widened. "You're giving me the afternoon off?" Disbelief laced her tone.

"And a week at that spa in Arizona. You know, the one in the brochures you peek at when you think I'm not looking."

Excitement flickered in her eyes briefly, and then her lips twisted into a skeptical frown. "What's the catch?"

"No catch. Make that two weeks off with pay, and I'll spring for the trip."

"Are you feeling okay?"

"Never better." Grant found himself humming as he strolled through the door connecting Barbara's office with his. He set his briefcase on his desk and picked up the pile of pink message slips that had stacked up while he was away. He flipped through them, noting most had the urgent box checked.

Within a few minutes, Barbara stood over his desk with two aspirin and a mug of black coffee. Usually he gratefully accepted the daily offering, but today he waved her off.

"Thanks, but I'll pass," he mumbled, as he began sorting out the messages that truly were important.

"What about your back?"

"Back's fine."

"Headache?"

"Nope."

Barbara plunked the coffee mug down with a thump, causing some of the hot brew to slosh over the rim. "Okay, what's wrong?"

"Nothing." Grant pushed the pile of non-urgent messages aside so he could concentrate on the others. "Nothing at all. In fact, I feel great."

Barbara grunted. "You on medication?"

He thought she was joking until he spotted the furrows creasing her forehead. "Of course not. You know better."

"It's either that or aliens abducted the real Grant Price and left you in his place."

Grant chuckled. "What's so strange about me sitting at my desk looking over messages?"

"I'll tell you what's so strange. What am I supposed to think when you waltz in here talking about an afternoon off and a vacation?" She paused only to take a breath. "I haven't had an afternoon off in twelve years. Hmmph! When I had my gallbladder taken out last year, I was barely out of the operating room before you were asking if I felt well enough to return."

Grant grimaced. Had he really been that bad?

If Barbara had told him that a week ago, before Melody, he would have asked her if she was trying to make a point. However, everything was different now. He was different.

He opened his mouth to apologize, but Barbara was on a roll. Realizing what an abysmal boss he'd been, he listened. It was the least he could do. He owed her that much and more.

"Then all of a sudden, after I don't know how many years of you practically snatching coffee and aspirins out of my hand every morning, you claim not to need either." She slapped her palms down on his desk and leaned forward. "Well, don't make me hound you to death. Tell me what happened to you down there!"

Grant patted her arm. "Calm down, Barbara. I promise to fill you in, but I need to speak with my father first."

As if on cue, the elder Price strode into the office. A broad grin covered the older man's features. The kind of smile Grant hadn't seen on his father's face in ages, if ever.

"I heard Miss Mason came back with you yesterday. I knew you'd pull it off," he bellowed. "I'm proud of you, son."

Grant closed his eyes briefly. The undeserved show of approval stabbed at his conscience. He cleared the lump of dread caught in his throat, knowing what he had to say would wipe the joy off his father's face.

"So where's our Miss Mason?" John Price rubbed his palms together and glanced around the room. "We have a lot to discuss."

"Have a seat, Dad. We need to talk."

Grant watched Barbara's glance flicker from father to son before she made a quick exit.

"I'll stand." The smile dropped off the elder Price's face. "So what's going on? She did return to Boston with you, didn't she?"

"Yes, she's here, but it's not what you think."

"What are you talking about?"

"Melody turned down our offer. I wasn't able to change her mind." The admission left Grant feeling like a concrete weight had been lifted from his shoulders. His sense of relief lasted only seconds before he shrugged on the even heavier burden of guilt over failing his father.

John Price sighed heavily and eased himself into the chair facing Grant's desk. The lines etching his face seemed more prominent than they had moments ago when he'd walked through the door.

"You okay, Dad?"

"Damn! I thought you had this in the bag."

"I did everything I could. I gave it my best effort."

"Your best would have convinced her to join our team." John Price shook his head in disgust.

"We can't force her to work for us."

"Well, if she won't take the job, what's she doing here?"

"She's here with me."

It didn't take long for his father's confused expression to give way to a sly grin. "Why didn't you say so in the first place?" he said. "Sorry for doubting you, son. I should have known you'd do *anything* to get her up here."

* * *

Melody could barely suppress the shivers of nervous anticipation trickling down her back as she stepped off the elevator. Out of habit, she reached up to push a wayward curl off her face, only to realize it wasn't there. She ran her hand across her freshly-shorn locks. After a lifetime of long, thick hair, the chin-length cut would take some getting used too.

The stylists at the salon had oohed and aahed over her transformation as she left the shop, and already she liked how much lighter the chic cut made her feel.

She walked through the door with Grant's nameplate on it, which turned out to be a suite of offices. She stopped at the receptionist's desk. The young woman manning the phones acknowledged her with a nod and motioned for her to wait.

"Sorry about that. Mr. Price's assistant has the afternoon off, and I'm the only one on phone duty."

"Melody Mason, here to see Grant Price. I believe he's expecting me."

The receptionist squinted. "I've seen you on magazine covers in Mr. Price's office, but you look so different in person. Much prettier."

"Thank you," Melody replied. She didn't feel like the same person either. It seemed like those photo shoots had taken place a lifetime ago.

The phones lines started ringing again.

"You can just go on back," the harried receptionist said. "His office is straight through the glass doors and down the hall to your left."

The rumble of male voices on the other side of

the glass doors met her. She had every intention of making her presence known, but what she heard stopped her in her tracks.

"I should have known you'd do anything, even romance that homely gal for the good of the company," a deep voice rumbled. "Grant, you've shown me over and over again where your heart is. How could I have ever doubted your loyalty, son?"

His words sucked the air from Melody's lungs. She clutched at her chest as she waited for Grant's reply. *Tell him, Grant. Tell him how you feel about me. How we feel about each other.*

Then it hit her, like the sting of a slap to her cheek. She was the one in love.

Not once had Grant uttered the word.

The only thing she knew for sure was that his family's business meant everything to him and there wasn't anything he wouldn't do for it.

"No! It's not like that, Dad."

Melody finally allowed herself to breathe, but it was no sign of relief. The forcefulness of Grant's denial had done little to ease the old insecurities his father's words had excavated.

She knew she should knock, clear her throat, anything to let them know she was there, before she found out something she didn't want to know.

"Well, what else could it be?"

"I care deeply for her, Dad."

Again, Grant's words didn't soothe her. Neither did memories of last night's magic. Doubt had already crept into her head, pushing aside the feel of Grant's touch and the passion of his kisses.

The older man laughed. "Don't get me wrong. I appreciate you going all out for the sake of the company and giving this your all, but don't think you can pull one over on your old man."

"Melody and I happen to enjoy each other's company. What's so hard to believe about that?"

"Son, I've seen the kind of women you date. Celeste was a former Miss Massachusetts," the man said. "Let's face it, that Miss Mason may be a money magnet, but she's no beauty queen."

Melody reached up to smooth her nonexistent hair off her face. All morning, she'd been hoping to wow Grant with her new look. Ha! What a joke. It would take more than a haircut and a little bit of makeup to turn her into the kind of woman Grant truly desired.

"She's *my* beauty queen." She heard Grant come to her defense, but paid little attention to what he said to his father.

Only John Price's words echoed in her ears. They hurt, but the truth always did.

He'd simply voiced what she already knew. It was about money. And even if it wasn't, where Grant was concerned, she could never be sure.

It would best for both of them if she just ended this thing between them, before she got hurt any more than she already was.

Summoning her strength, she willed the tears welling in her eyes not to fall. She pasted on the deadpan mask, which had served her well in the business world.

"Good afternoon, gentlemen," Melody said

loudly, in a voice void of the turmoil swirling around inside her. She boldly strolled into the office, willing herself to keep her emotions in check.

The startled look on Grant's and his father's faces questioned whether she'd overheard their conversation.

"Melody! How long have you been standing there?" Grant glanced at his watch.

Long enough. "I just got here." Her voice sounded cool and unattached, when she was anything but. "I hope I'm not interrupting anything important."

Then Grant smiled at her, and her outwardly cool facade nearly melted into a puddle of want.

"You cut your hair." He smiled. "It looks good. You look good."

Melody felt herself flinch. Yeah, she looked good to him all right. Like a million . . . no, millions of bucks.

"Miss Mason, I'm John Price." The older, distinguished version of Grant extended his hand and Melody automatically shook it. "Grant's explained to me that you're here for personal reasons, but I was hoping we could talk a little business."

"Like I explained to your son repeatedly over the past week, I'm not interested."

"What harm could it do to talk?" He looked down at his watch. "It's nearly noon; we could all go out to lunch."

"Dad, Melody is here strictly as my guest, and the two of us already have plans for lunch— alone," Grant interjected.

"Well, after lunch then," John Price said.

Melody bit the inside of her lip. It was easy to see where Grant got his persistence, as well as his inability to take no for an answer. Like father, like son.

Today they'd both learn that when she said no, she meant it.

"Dad, we have plans," Grant said.

"Well, how about dinner tonight then?" John Price persisted.

"I won't be here tonight." Melody stared directly at Grant.

A look of surprise mingled with disappointment crossed Grant's handsome face. He turned to his father. "Melody and I need to talk, alone."

The older man's eyes traveled from Grant to her and back to Grant again. If faces were newspapers, the headline emblazoned across his forehead would have read, "Get her in line."

Out of respect for Grant, Melody refrained from telling the old man she'd take a job in hell and work alongside the devil before she'd work for him. Besides, she shouldn't hold a grudge against John Price. If anything, she should be grateful.

His harsh words had shaken her out of this romantic fantasy world and back into reality. He'd reminded her to watch her back and, more importantly, to protect her heart.

"What's this about you leaving?" Grant asked, after the elder Price left, closing the door behind him.

"This has been nice, but it's time to get back to the real world," she said with a nonchalance she didn't feel.

"So that's what you're calling what went down between us last night—'nice'?"

Melody felt her cheeks warm. No, nice didn't begin to describe what they'd shared. He'd made her feel cherished, like the most beautiful woman in the world. Making love with him had been one of the most wonderful experiences of her life.

But she was awake now and it was time to face reality. There was no future for them.

"We made love last night," Grant said. "Now you're going to up and leave like it meant nothing."

"It was very special," she admitted.

"Then why are you walking out?"

"It's just not going to work between us. We're too different. Your life is here and mine is back in Tennessee."

"I thought we'd already decided to give it a chance and see what develops."

She shook her head. "I'm not interested in a long-distance relationship."

Grant's puzzled expression hardened. "That's bull."

Melody flinched, taken aback by his angry tone. "It's for the best," she warbled.

"Get off it, Melody. The least you could do is tell me the real reason you're so anxious to hightail it out of here."

"I've already explained it to you. It's the truth. If you can't accept it . . ."

"You still don't trust me."

Melody felt her shoulders slump as she released a deep sigh. She shook her head. "No. I don't," she said softly. But more than him, it was herself and her own traitorous heart she didn't trust.

"What I want from you has nothing to do with money."

His eyes brimmed with sincerity. She quickly averted hers before she fell under his spell.

John Price's words echoed in her ears. *"You've shown me over and over again where your heart is . . ."* And the bottom line was she could never trust that his heart was truly with her. Money would always be first and foremost with Grant.

It was the same old story; only the main characters had changed.

"I'm sorry, but I just can't take the risk. I've got to go."

"By now you should know how I feel about you," he said. "I won't beg you to give me the benefit of the doubt." His tone was brusque, but his expression pleaded with her not to go.

Her aching heart echoed his urgent plea. Yet she couldn't trust it any more than she trusted him.

Grant thrust his hands into his pants pockets to keep himself from reaching out to Melody's retreating form. His fingers grazed against the velvet jeweler's box just as the door clicked shut behind her.

Don't let her leave. Go after her. Tell her you love her. Make her see that she is the most captivating, maddeningly stubborn and sexy woman you've ever met. Tell her you want to make her your wife.

260

Grant yanked his hands from his pockets and made a dash for the door. He stopped just short. He shook his head. What was the point?

If she didn't trust him now, she never would.

CHAPTER SIXTEEN

For a woman who'd just taken steps to ensure she wasn't making a fool of herself a third time, Melody didn't feel relieved.

Instead her battered heart felt like it had suffered its harshest blow yet.

Melody leaned back into the seat of the commercial airplane and stared blankly out the window. She'd fled Grant's office and his life like the devil himself had been on her heels. He hadn't come after her. Not that she'd expected him to. There was nothing left for them to say. The expression on his face when she'd admitted she didn't trust him, had said it all.

She waved away the flight attendant's offer of a beverage. She'd done the right thing. Spending more time with Grant would have only made it worse. Facing the truth about their doomed relationship and moving on with their lives was best.

For both of them.

* * *

The doorbell chime roused Joyce out of a deep sleep.

She lifted her head off the pillow and glanced at the clock. Ten o'clock. She rubbed at her eyes, unable to believe she'd slept so long. An early riser, she rarely slept past seven. Automatically, she glanced over at Kevin's side of the bed. She'd forgotten he hadn't slept there. He'd spent another night on the sofa in his study.

The doorbell sounded again. Pushing herself off the bed, she shrugged on her robe and headed toward the back door.

"Coming," she mumbled sleepily.

Opening the door, she was glad to see Melody on the other side of it. It felt good to look at a friendly face. Things had been so tense around the house lately. She felt like she was walking on eggshells.

"You okay?" Melody's eyes widened. "If you were sleeping, I can come back later."

"What are you doing back so soon? I thought you were still in Boston."

Melody shook her head. "I've been back for a few days now. I needed some time to myself to think."

"So Grant didn't come back with you?"

"It didn't work out between us," Melody said.

"Hon, what happened?"

"Long story. But I don't want to get into it right now," she said. "I'd rather hear what's going on with you. You look like hell."

"I feel even worse." Joyce pushed open the screen

door and gestured for Melody to come inside. Her friend didn't look much better than she did.

Joyce was concerned about what had gone down between Melody and Grant, but she didn't want to push. Melody would fill her in when she was ready. "Why don't you start the coffee, while I take a quick shower. Then we can get this pity party started."

Ten minutes later, Joyce gratefully accepted a mug of hot coffee from her friend. "I thought you were going to foist tea on me, until I got out of the shower and smelled the java brewing."

"This morning you looked like you could really use the coffee," Melody said. She poured hot water over a teabag.

Joyce added a packet of artificial sweetener to her cup. "Flunking tests and being on the outs with your husband is exhausting."

"Tests? It's only your first week."

Joyce shrugged, sipped her coffee and set the mug back on the table. "Actually it was a pop quiz in chemistry, and I missed four of the five questions," Joyce said. "Then later my math professor called on me for an algebra problem, and I couldn't make heads or tails of the equation."

"It happens to the best of us. Just study hard and do better next time."

Joyce felt her shoulders slump as she exhaled. "I guess."

Melody's eyes narrowed over her teacup. "What aren't you telling me?"

"It's nothing." Joyce pushed away from the table and began bustling about in the kitchen. "I've got blueberry muffins. They're not homemade, but still pretty good."

"I'll take the muffin—make it two—then I want you to sit down and talk to me."

"Want me to nuke them?"

"No, thanks."

Joyce plunked two muffins on a saucer and slid it in front of her friend. She hated wearing out Melody's ears with more of her problems. It seemed all she did lately was whine and moan about her troubles. She was sick of them herself.

"I'm going to sit here and stuff my face with muffins until you talk."

Joyce blew out a breath as she plopped down in her chair. "Okay, here it goes. I'm thinking about dropping out."

"You mean quit school?" Melody stammered, sounding like she was about to choke on her tea.

Moving quickly, Joyce went over and patted her on the back. "You okay, hon?"

Melody nodded and cleared her throat. "Fine. My tea just went down the wrong pipe." She cleared her throat again. "Now did I hear you right? Did you just tell me you were considering dropping out?"

Joyce took a gulp of her cooling coffee. "Maybe Kevin's right, and I didn't really understand what I was getting into."

"Honey, at some time or another everyone has

screwed up on a test or frozen in class. I remember being a freshman and mumbling like an idiot whenever a professor asked me a question," she said. "It's first-week jitters, that's all."

"Oh, Mel. I'm surrounded all day by people who are smarter or younger than me, or both. I feel like I don't belong there. It's like I'm the dumbest person in the room," Joyce confided.

"I'll bet they're just as nervous as you are. Just give yourself some time to adjust."

Joyce nodded. "Okay. I guess I'm afraid I'll come out of this with no degree or marriage."

"Kevin still hasn't come around?"

"We alternate between fighting and giving each other the silent treatment. The tension is so thick around here you can almost see it."

"I'm surprised. That's so unlike you two."

"I know. Over two decades together and we've never once gone to bed angry until now."

"You have to know you two will get past this."

"I don't know how much more of it I can take. Something has to give." Frustration welled up in Joyce as she ran her fingers through her hair. "Is school really worth ruining my marriage over?"

"Only you can answer that. All I can tell you is I'll be here if you need me."

"Same here. I'm not sure what happened in Boston, but I do know that man is crazy about you. I hope you two can work out your differences."

Joyce drained the last of her coffee. A few weeks ago, her biggest problem was what kind of cookies to bake for the church bake sale. Now she was facing flunking out of school and losing her husband.

Despite Melody's pep talk, doubts filled Joyce's head. She couldn't help but wonder if her attempt to improve her life had screwed it up for good.

CHAPTER SEVENTEEN

Grant was engrossed in the figures scrolling across his computer monitor when Barbara tapped on his door. Since Melody had walked out on him a month ago, he'd thrown himself back into work with a vengeance.

This time it wasn't about money, ambition or family loyalty. Like a drunk seeking solace in the bottom of a bottle, Grant drowned himself in work. He needed to forget.

"I'm headed out to yoga class," Barbara said. "I'm stopping by the deli for a sandwich on the way back. Do you want me to bring you something?"

"No, thanks. Enjoy your class."

He glanced up moments later, surprised to see her still standing in the doorway. "Was there something else?"

"No. I'm just wondering when my real boss is coming back. The one who never misses a chance to tell me how yoga class is a big waste of my time or grouses if I take as much as a bathroom break."

"You're exaggerating."

Barbara made a grunting sound in her throat and crossed her arms across her chest. "So maybe you're okay about an occasional bathroom break. Still, nobody, especially a man, changes this much unless they're in . . ."

She stopped mid-sentence and her face took on its *Barbara knows all* expression. "You're in love, aren't you?"

Grant felt himself flinch. Denying it would have been futile. Barbara could read him like a book.

"I thought you were on your way out?" He turned back to his computer monitor, but his mind refused to focus. Every time he pushed Melody from his thoughts, her image popped back into his head. He missed her smile, her laugh, and the funny feeling he got in his stomach when she looked at him.

"I knew something was going on with you. It's Miss Mason, isn't it?" Barbara asked, then proceeded to answer her own question. "Of course it is. You've been acting like a stranger ever since you got back from Tennessee."

Grant frowned. "Do I need to remind you this is a business? My private life is not up for discussion."

"Until now, your love life wasn't worth a mention. You and Celeste seemed more like business partners than lovers."

"I am not having this conversation. If you're not taking a lunch hour, you can get back to work."

"Okay, I'm going. I'm going," Barbara said, retreating. "But for the record, Miss Mason must be pretty special. She's had quite an effect on you."

Grant sighed as Barbara finally left. Melody had had an effect on him, all right. He'd flown down there to convince her to take a job. Instead she'd made a place for herself in his heart.

He'd lost out on both counts. He couldn't persuade her to take the job and even worse, he didn't have her.

No sooner did Barbara leave than his father showed up. It wasn't like he was getting much done anyway; the numbers on his computer screen might as well have been hieroglyphics.

"What can I do for you?" Grant swiveled his chair around to face his father.

"Don't look so thrilled to see me."

Usually he was glad to see the old man, but today, like every day since Melody had left, he wasn't much in the mood to see anyone. He'd do better grabbing his laptop and working from home.

"Don't take it personally, Dad. I've got a lot of things to catch up on around here."

"Well, what I have to say should wipe the scowl right off your face."

Grant didn't foresee that happening anytime soon. "Go ahead."

"I've decided you'll be the one who takes over when I step down later this year."

At last, the words Grant had spent most of his adult life hoping to hear. The job was his. He paused, waiting for the feelings of joy that came along with victory to wash over him.

Nothing.

Inside he felt as hollow as he had moments before.

"What's the matter, son? I expected more enthusiasm than this," John Price said.

"I'm thrilled," Grant said, trying to convince himself as much as his father. "You just caught me by surprise."

"Good. For a moment you had me worried you were still stewing over Miss Mason."

"That's over." Melody had made it abundantly clear. She didn't trust him, and she never would.

"I wanted her too, but you did all you could," John Price said.

Grant rose from his desk and walked over to the window. Had he done everything he could? Would it have made a difference if he'd told her how he felt? That he was in love with her?

He felt his father's hand on his shoulder.

"Grant, I know you're disappointed, but Price Investments will thrive with or without Melody Mason," John Price said. "She would have been a tremendous asset, but we'll survive."

Grant had no doubt the business would survive, but would he? He'd been with the woman a little over a week. Now, a month later, everything he saw, heard or did brought Melody to mind.

He should be lifting a flute of champagne in celebration, but the last thing he felt was festive. His father had just handed him everything he'd ever wanted and all he could think of was what he'd lost.

His father patted him on the shoulder. "Just let it go, son."

Grant nodded. His father was right. It was time he stopped moping and moved on. He had a job to do.

Joyce's feet felt like lead as she trudged out of the crowded classroom.

"Man, this class is a lot tougher than I anticipated," a woman she recognized from orientation as the former schoolteacher said.

"Amen to that." But so were all of her other classes. Joyce adjusted the book-laden backpack on her shoulders.

The woman frowned. "I studied my tail off and still only got a B on the exam."

"I stayed up all night reading." For all the good it did her. Joyce's mind flashed to the returned test paper emblazoned with a big red D-minus.

She'd gone from flunking to barely passing.

"Well, I'd better head over to the library and hit the books. We've got that algebra test day after tomorrow," the woman said. "You want to come along?"

"Maybe another time. I've got to get home." Joyce groaned inwardly as she walked across the courtyard of the bustling campus. Between preparing for this last exam and the ongoing battle with Kevin, the upcoming algebra test had totally slipped her mind. This evening would be another night of black coffee and cramming.

Maybe she could avoid yet another scrimmage with her husband.

Popping the lock on her car with the remote, she slid into the driver's seat and turned the air conditioner on full blast. She reached into her book bag and pulled out her test paper.

"Damn," she whispered, before crumpling it into a ball and shoving it back into her bag. She tossed the heavy book bag into the backseat and opened her purse.

Automatically, she grabbed her cell phone and turned it on. She kept it off during classes, but like most mothers she preferred to keep it on at other times in case one of her children needed her—despite the fact that her little boys were all grown up and nowadays their calls were usually about lack of food or money.

A series of loud chirps signaled she had an urgent message, sending her mother's instincts into red alert.

Joyce felt her heart free fall to her gut as she returned the call. "This is Joyce Holden," she said to the man who answered. She recognized the voice of her son's football coach.

"I'm at the hospital emergency room with David," he said.

"Oh my God, is he hurt? How bad? What happened?" Joyce hammered the coach with a barrage of questions.

"He took a hard hit at practice today, fell awkwardly and hurt his arm."

"How bad is it?"

"I'm not sure, but he was in a lot of pain. Doc Gallagher is taking a look at him now."

"I'm in Nashville, but I just got on I-65. I'm on my way."

"When I couldn't get a hold of you, I called Kevin. I'll stay until one of you gets here," he said.

Joyce ended the call, and pressed the gas pedal a few miles per hour beyond the speed limit. Her son needed her. Nothing else mattered.

Perspiration dotted Kevin's brow as he half walked, half ran into the emergency room. The half hour drive from Nashville had only fueled his fears, and to top it off he hadn't been able to get in touch with Joyce.

"Ray!" he called down the hallway to the retreating figure wearing a scrub top and khakis.

Ray Gallagher, the small community hospital's emergency medicine physician and a regular in Kevin's Sunday golf foursome, stopped in his tracks and turned an about-face.

"He's okay, man," he said before Kevin could utter a word.

Kevin took a moment to let the words sink in. "What happened? His coach said he took a hit at football practice."

"David's arm has a hairline fracture. I put a cast on it that'll have to stay on for roughly four weeks, maybe less. Kids tend to heal quickly."

Kevin released the breath he'd been holding ever since he'd received the coach's call. Still, he

wouldn't be okay until he looked at David for himself. "I need to see him. Where is he?"

"Relax, man." Ray patted him on the shoulder,
and then directed him to the emergency room.
"Joyce is helping him get dressed. I'll be over to
talk to the three of you in a few minutes."

Kevin rushed into the cubicle to find Joyce helping their youngest into his shirt. David had thirty
pounds on Kevin and was nearly as tall, but when
Kevin looked at his son, all he saw was his baby boy.

"How are you feeling, son?"

"Okay, I guess." David winced as Joyce helped
him slide his other arm into his shirt.

Dwarfed by their offspring, Kevin noted how his
wife handled David as easily as she had when he
was a newborn. He couldn't help but be touched
by the gentle care she displayed.

Their eyes met and she acknowledged his presence with a nod and a tentative smile. He nodded
and felt the corners of his mouth lift into a smile
of his own.

"You didn't have to leave work, Dad," David
said. "Mom's here."

Guilt pricked his conscience as he watched her.
Just days ago he'd blasted her for putting school
first and not being there for her family. Now here
she was, doing what she always did.

For the first time since his wife had sought an interest outside of their family and close-knit community, Kevin doubted himself and the lack of
support he'd shown her.

Ray came in with instructions and wrote a prescription for a painkiller. Not long afterwards, they managed to get their son home and settled on the sofa in the den, where David fell asleep with the remote control clutched in his hand.

"Think we should wake him up and send him to bed?" Kevin asked. It was the first thing he'd said to his wife in weeks that wasn't laced with anger.

"No, he's had a tough day." Removing the remote from her son's grip, Joyce turned off the television and covered their son with a light blanket. "Let's not disturb him until it's time for a pain pill."

"We need to talk."

"It's been a long day," she said, shaking her head. "I'm not up for a fight."

"No arguing. Just conversation."

Joyce blew out a weary breath.

"Promise," he said.

"Coffee?" she offered.

"Have a seat. I'll make it."

Moments later he poured two cups. He added cream and sweetener to one and slid it across the kitchen table to his wife. "I don't like what's been going on between us lately."

"And you think I do?"

Kevin understood the defensiveness that laced his wife's tone. Who could blame her? Every time she'd tried to reach out to him, to reassure him, he'd emotionally smacked her down.

"I know you don't like it," he said.

"Look, like I said before, I don't need to get into

another knock down, drag out. Not tonight." She rose from her seat.

Kevin reached across the table and gently grasped her arm. "Don't walk away," he said.

"Why not? You did."

He knew he deserved whatever she dished out. "I know, and I apologize," he said. "I want us to get past this, get our lives and our marriage back on track."

Relief washed over him as Joyce sat back down.

"How?" she asked softly. "We've both made our positions clear."

"I can't say I've completely changed my view on this school thing, but I'm willing to make an effort. It's important to you, and I love you."

His wife exhaled wearily and slowly shook her head. "I appreciate you telling me all of this, but it may be too late."

Panic hit Kevin—hard. "We've been together since we were kids; how can you give up on our marriage?"

"No, it's not that." She averted her eyes.

"Then what? What's the matter, baby?"

"I'm flunking. I haven't passed a quiz or test since school started."

Her admission surprised him, but it shouldn't have. How could she study when their home had turned into an armed camp?

Back when he'd had to spend every waking moment studying, she had carried their family on her back. She'd done all she could to protect his study time.

He reached out and placed her small hand in his. "We'll get you a tutor, one for every subject if we have to. I'll give you a refresher on how to study myself. We'll figure this out," he reassured her.

She looked up at him. "Why now? What changed?"

"I watched you with David today. Like I have so many times with the other kids. You're the warmest, most caring person I know. It's unfair of me to cheat the world out of that kind of nurse."

Her lips eased into a hint of a smile.

It had been far too long since one had graced the face of his beautiful wife.

Grant tried typing on his computer keyboard again. He stared at the flat-panel monitor. Nothing. The damned thing had frozen up on him again. Frustrated, he slammed the mouse against his desk.

A knock sounded at his door. Hadn't he made it clear he didn't want to be disturbed? He pinched the bridge of his nose with his fingertips. Nothing around here was working the way it was supposed to this afternoon, including the employees they paid to man the outer offices.

"What?" he called out.

The door creaked as it slowly opened. "Sounds like your dad was right and you could use some cheering up."

Grant looked up at the sound of the familiar voice. "Celeste."

Wearing a pale peach suit and balancing on impossibly high heels, she walked in looking every bit a former Miss Massachusetts. As always, her weaved-in hair and her makeup were pageant perfect. He stood and walked around his desk. Despite the bitter note they'd ended on, it was nice seeing her again. He really did care about her.

She leaned in and kissed him lightly on the cheek. "It's good to see you again, Grant."

"You too." He motioned toward the chair facing his desk. "Have a seat."

Celeste dropped her peach suede handbag in the chair. "Actually, I've come to get you out of here for a while. I thought I'd treat you to an early dinner."

Grant shoved his hands into his pants pockets and walked to the other side of his desk. "Today isn't a good day," he said. Hearing the words aloud reminded him, he hadn't had a good day since Melody left. "I'm really swamped."

"It's never a good day for you to leave work, and you're always busy."

"How about a rain check? I'll give you a call one day next week."

"No, you won't." She crossed her arms, her four-inch heels digging firmly into the carpet.

"Celeste, I don't think . . ." he started.

She relaxed her stance. "At least have coffee with me. I've been thinking about the way things ended between us, and I'd really like to talk."

Grant glanced down at his frozen computer monitor. He wasn't getting much done anyway, he thought.

"Okay." He rolled down his shirt sleeves and buttoned the cuffs. "Let's go."

Grant had dated Celeste for five years and hadn't laid eyes on her in months. She was a sensational-looking woman. Seeing her again should have rekindled something, he thought. Yet as they walked the two blocks to Starbucks, his head and his heart remained firmly in small-town Tennessee.

With a woman who doesn't want or trust you.

He ordered a cup of the strongest blend brewing and a slice of cake, the dessert case reminding him that he hadn't eaten all day. Celeste requested a nonfat, whipped concoction.

He took a sip of coffee and sighed appreciatively, savoring the caffeine jolt.

Celeste raised a perfectly arched brow. "I don't remember you liking coffee so much."

Grant took another sip. "Let's just say I've learned not to take it for granted." He put the cup down. "So how've you been?"

She nodded. "It was hard for a while, but it's going better."

He glanced down at his coffee and back to her. "Look, Celeste, I never meant to hurt you."

She waved a manicured hand. "I shouldn't have tried to force you to do something you weren't ready for," she said. "I can't explain it. Between watching my baby sister walking down the aisle like a fairy-tale princess and fielding questions on why it wasn't me, I caught wedding fever."

"You were under a lot of pressure yourself. I re-

member your relatives being pretty relentless, especially your aunt."

Celeste dropped her sophisticated facade, threw
her head back and really laughed. "My great-aunt
Kay," she said. "Can you believe she asked me if I
was gay?"

"And your sister practically torpedoed you when
it came time to toss her bouquet." He chuckled,
relieved they could find humor in a situation that
had once created only strain between them.

Celeste's expression grew solemn. She reached
across the table and covered his hand with hers.
"Seriously, I needed to tell you how sorry I am for
letting it come between us and ruin what we had."

Grant wasn't sure where she was headed with
this, but he knew for him there was no going back.

"Maybe it was time." He pulled his hand from
underneath hers. He patted her hand lightly before resting his in his lap.

"I'm not following you."

Grant didn't want to hurt Celeste any more than
he already had, but he had to be honest. He owed
her that much.

"Our relationship was routine, comfortable and
convenient. We understood about each other's
work. We didn't make demands. We never argued.
On the surface it seemed great," he said. "But even
you have to admit there was something missing."

"Love."

"I . . ." Grant started, but wasn't quite sure how
to word it.

"Neither one of us was in love." She said it for him.

"It's why I couldn't marry you."

Celeste nodded slowly. "I didn't understand it then, but I do now. You see, I got engaged three months after our breakup," she said.

Grant's eyes widened. For the first time, Grant noticed the diamond solitaire on her ring finger. Although it was a different cut and color, it reminded him of the one he'd bought for Melody. His gut twisted at the memory.

"Congratulations. Dad didn't mention you were getting married."

"It's a long story," she said.

Grant took a sip of coffee. "I'm listening."

"Well, at first I was ecstatic. I had a diamond on my finger and a man who couldn't wait to waltz me down the aisle," she said. "However, as the planning ensued I began to resent the time it was taking away from my decorating business."

Grant took another sip of his cooling coffee. He knew how wrapped up Celeste was in her business.

"I pushed the date back a few times. Then my fiancé suggested we elope. . . ." Her voice trailed off before it picked up again. "I began to feel as pressured as I must have made you feel."

"So where do you two stand now?"

"I broke it off with him last month," she said.

"Sorry to hear it," Grant said. His gaze dropped to the large diamond on her finger.

"Oh, the ring," she said, extending her hand. "I returned the one he gave me and replaced it with this one. I decided I didn't need someone else to put a ring on my finger, and I bought my own."

"Good for you." Grant smiled, relieved Celeste no longer resented him. Their breakup had been hard, but in the end it had been the best thing for both of them.

He picked up a fork and dug into his cake. It couldn't compare to one of Ruth's desserts, but it wasn't like he'd be sitting at her table anytime soon.

"That looks good," Celeste said.

"I'll go up and get you a slice."

"I'd better not." Although she shook her head no, her eyes said yes. "I can't eat cake and expect to stay a size four."

Again, Grant's thoughts drifted to Melody. He wouldn't have had to offer her cake twice, he thought, and felt the corners of his mouth tug into a smile.

"So what about you, are you seeing anyone?" Celeste asked.

"No." Grant had been single before, but somehow now it left him feeling hollow.

"Why do I get the impression there's more to it?"

"You're imagining things."

Celeste picked up his fork and helped herself to a bite of his cake. "Why don't I believe you?"

CHAPTER EIGHTEEN

Melody taught several knitting classes, but this evening's was her favorite by far.

Each week she looked forward to the pack of preteen girls crowding into the shop. Their giggles, whispered secrets and clumsy fingers made her forget how utterly miserable the last month had been.

Now class was winding down, leaving her back where she'd started.

This was crazy. Her knitting classes were full, and the shop was doing a brisk business, even better than she'd expected.

She should be out celebrating. Instead she was mooning over a man who at this very moment was probably getting reacquainted with Celeste, of whom his father thought so highly.

Melody groaned inwardly. He'd only been here a week, but nearly every place in town reminded her of him. Again she wondered what it was going to take to get Grant Price out of her system.

"Am I doing it right?" A small voice staved off a wave of melancholy.

Melody looked down at the little girl, whose purple beads on the ends of her braids clicked every time she moved her head.

Focusing her mind on work, Melody examined the child's project. The rows of purple knit stitches were straight and even. Soon the garter stitches would begin to look more like a scarf. Gradually the girls would advance to making flower-shaped throw pillows and matching rugs to decorate their bedrooms.

"It looks great." She patted the child's shoulder.

Reassured, the girl turned her attention back to her knitting while she waited on her mother to pick her up.

The bell over the front door chimed several times as parents came to retrieve their children. Soon the shop was cleared and all that was left to do was tidy up and close for the night.

Melody was about to turn the sign in the window over to CLOSED when Joyce tapped on the door. Her friend had been hitting the books hard, and they hadn't seen much of each other in weeks.

"Hey stranger. I thought you met with your tutor today," Melody said.

"We're done for the day. So I thought I'd stop by and see how you were doing. We haven't talked in ages."

"You're just in time to help me clean up."

Joyce let her purse drop from her shoulder. She

scrunched up her nose at the broom Melody foisted on her.

"You're looking good," Melody said. "School must agree with you." Joyce practically glowed. Joy and contentment radiated from her pretty face.

"Thanks. It's tough, but Kevin and the tutors he got me have helped a lot."

"He really did a turnaround and came through for you."

Joyce stopped sweeping for a moment and smiled. "Things are better than ever between us. The other night, he even cooked dinner. Chicken and dumplings."

"Kevin?" The dust cloth Melody was holding fell to the floor, and she bent over to pick it up.

"I know. He hasn't touched a pot or pan since we got married."

"How was it?"

Joyce scrunched up her face. "Don't ask. David took one look and pulled a pack of hot dogs from the fridge."

Melody drifted to the last time she'd had hot dogs, and her time with Grant in Maine. It had been a perfect day and an even better night. Then reality had caught up with them. She'd thought they'd had something truly special, but in the end it wasn't strong enough to withstand the real world.

"I'm sorry, Mel. Here I am going on and on, and I haven't even asked how you're doing."

"Oh, I'm fine," Melody said a bit too quickly,

straightening a bin of yarn. Since she'd returned from Boston, she'd felt like the walking wounded.

Joyce pinned her with a skeptical gaze. "Are you sure, hon?"

"Of course I'm sure. The shop is doing great."

Her friend leaned the broom against the wall and crossed the hardwood floor. "I'm not talking about the shop and you know it. What's going on with Grant? Have you heard from him?"

Melody pressed her lips together and shook her head, afraid her voice might give away her feelings.

"I still can't believe you walked out on him because of something his father said. How can you hold what someone else said against the man?"

"His father was right."

"Grant didn't think so."

"Maybe Grant's father knows him better than he knows himself," Melody said, busying herself with rearranging skeins of yarn that were already in their proper places.

"You could have given him a chance," Joyce said softly.

Melody stopped and turned to her friend. "Get it through your head, Joyce. He only wanted me to take his job. When it comes to me and men, it's always about money."

She didn't mean to take her misery out on her friend, but she might as well face facts.

Joyce wasn't deterred. "I find that hard to believe, Mel. I saw the way Grant was with you. He clearly adored you."

"You're a hopeless romantic, who happens to be married to the man of her dreams. I think it's wonderful, but it doesn't mean love and romance are in the cards for everybody."

Joyce snatched the skein of yarn from Melody's hand and tossed it in the bin. "When Kevin and I were having our problems, I considered leaving him."

Surprised by her friend's revelation, Melody pulled her attention from the yarn bins. "You were going to leave Kevin?"

Joyce nodded slightly and Melody knew from the look in her eyes that she was serious. "The reasons I stayed weren't about love or romance as much as they were about faith and trust."

"I don't understand," Melody said.

Sadness replaced the seriousness in Joyce's eyes. "I know you don't," she said softly. "I stayed because no matter how bad things seemed, I believed Kevin would eventually come around. I trusted him." Joyce reached out and took both of Melody's hands in hers. "You see, more than love, Kevin needed my faith and trust." She released Melody's hands. "You say you love Grant, but maybe what he really needs is your trust."

Melody knew where Joyce was coming from. Yet deep down, she didn't know if she was capable of trusting him. It would be devastating to put her heart on the line again, only to discover later it was all about the job and money.

She shrugged it off. "I can't sit around moping."

She grabbed the broom and started sweeping vigorously. "I have my hands full with the shop."

"You need more in your life than this shop. It's not enough."

"For now, it's going to have to be," Melody said. "I've wasted too much time and energy already. Now can we *please* change the subject and forget about Grant Price."

As the words left her mouth, Melody questioned if she or her heart could ever forget.

Grant leaned forward in his office chair and rubbed at the ache plaguing his back. It had returned with a vengeance. Maybe he should have listened to Melody and gotten those tennis balls.

He glanced up at the clock. Time had gotten away from him again. He'd said goodbye to Celeste earlier and had worked right into the night. No wonder his back was acting up.

His stiff muscles protested as he rose from the chair. He grabbed his jacket, but opted to leave his briefcase. After a few hours of sleep, he'd end up right back here anyway.

Not that he minded. Working to the point of exhaustion kept thoughts of Melody at bay. Still, once in a while they crept to the forefront, and he'd find himself grinning like an idiot over some quirky thing she'd said or done.

God help him. He missed her.

Mentally shaking off thoughts of Melody, he shut off the light and closed the door to his office.

Too bad he couldn't get the woman out of his system as easily.

He spotted a light coming from underneath the door of his father's office as he walked past. The old man put in long hours, but he rarely stayed this late. Grant knocked and pushed open the door at the same time.

"What are you still doing here?" father and son asked simultaneously, then both chuckled.

John Price pulled off his bifocals and squeezed the bridge of his nose with fingertips. For the first time, Grant noticed that his youthful, vibrant father appeared tired. The lines around his eyes etched deeper. He looked old.

"How did it go with Celeste?" His father's eyes brightened.

"Fine." Grant leaned against the doorjamb. "It was nice seeing her again."

"Nice? Is that all? A knockout like her pays you a visit and that's the best you can do?"

"I know you meant well, but you shouldn't have called her over."

His father put his glasses back on. "But you said you two had a nice visit."

"We did, but that doesn't mean I like you interfering in my life," Grant said. "Just so you know, your plan didn't work. There is nothing romantic between me and Celeste."

"Son, I'm sure if you just reconsider . . ."

"Enough about me. You never said why you were still here."

"I had a backlog of paperwork on my desk to get caught up on," John Price said.

"I could have taken care of it. There's no need for you to have to stay here all night."

"It's okay. I wanted to," he said.

A sadness Grant hadn't expected shadowed his father's eyes; then the reason behind it dawned upon him.

"You wanted to stay or you didn't want to go home?"

His father put his glasses back on and looked up at him. "Do you know what today is?"

"Mom's birthday," Grant replied, having remembered only moments earlier.

"Yeah, if she were here she would be sixty-nine today and we would have had forty-seven years together." A wistful expression flickered across his father's weary face. "It's funny; she's been dead for more years than we were married, but sometimes when I get home I still expect her to greet me at the door."

Grant tossed his suit jacket on the sofa across from his dad's desk and sat down on the other end. He tried to conceal his surprise. Since his mother's death, his father rarely, if ever, talked about her. "You still miss her."

John Price nodded. "Every day. She was the light of my life."

Grant listened, seeing for the first time a glimpse into the intense bond his parents had shared.

"I know you're too young to remember much about her, but your mother was an incredible woman. We met on the first day of the first grade," he said, then paused and looked at him. "Did you know that?"

Grant shook his head.

"Back then there wasn't any kindergarten," his father said wistfully. "I snatched a red crayon out of her hand, and she knocked me on my behind."

Grant smiled. It was hard to imagine his father as a boy. He found it even harder to think of another kid overpowering the man everyone found so intimidating.

"Then what happened?"

Grant observed his father trembling as the old man released a worn sigh. "That was the moment I fell in love. I've loved your mother since I was five years old, and if I live to be a hundred and five, I'll still be in love with her."

Grant couldn't help but be touched by his father's total devotion to his mother's memory. Yet over the decades he'd watched his father be plagued by another feeling, loneliness. John Price would never admit it, but it was obvious. And in all that time he'd never seen the old man even go out on a date.

"Mom passed away a long time ago, and you never . . . well . . ." Grant paused to choose his words carefully.

"You're wondering why I never moved on, found someone new and remarried?"

Grant nodded. "I know how much you loved

Mom, and what you had together was special. Still, I know you get lonely."

His father's eyes narrowed and his face took on the seriousness reserved for when he had something important to say. "Over the years, I've managed to catch the eye of a lady or two. Some of them quite beautiful," he said. "But when you've had what your mother and I shared . . . that kind of love never leaves you. It's more than enough to last a lifetime."

This was a side of his father he hadn't seen before. Not accustomed to hearing his father reveal something so personal, Grant leaned forward.

"If you're lucky enough to ever have anything even close, cherish every moment. If I had known my time with your mother would be cut short, I would have spent less time working. Now it doesn't matter how long I'm at the office. Nobody's waiting for me at home."

His father's words sank in as Grant took a long look at the older version of himself—a glimpse into a desolate future devoid of love and companionship. Grant could almost see himself thirty years from now, sitting in that same chair, filled with remorse and wondering how he let Melody get away.

Grant rose to his feet. Clearing his throat, he put his brain on pause and simply let his heart do the talking.

"I can't do this anymore."

"Do what?" his father asked.

"This." Grant threw his hands in the air and

looked around his father's office, then looked his father in the eyes. "I've never wanted Price Investments. Not really."

His father dismissed Grant's words with a wave of his hand. "You're talking out of your head, son. Why don't you go home and get some sleep?"

"Listen to me, Dad. All my life, I've strived to please you, to make you proud of me." He paused and shook his head. "I'm forty years old. I think it's time I did something for me."

"I'm turning over the company to you. What else could you want?" his father asked, still clearly perplexed.

"Did you ever think about what I wanted?" Grant asked. "I put aside baseball and my dreams for you and this company."

His father's voice rose. "Are you blaming me for making sure my sons had good educations to fall back on?"

"No, Dad. I'm not laying blame."

"Because I don't regret any decision I made on your behalf. No, I didn't want you out there chasing some sports pipe dream without a degree to fall back on," he said.

"I was good, Dad, really good."

"So were a lot of boys, and most of them didn't make it to the major leagues. Instead, they ended up selling sneakers in the mall. I wanted more for you."

Grant heaved a sigh. What was he doing arguing about the past with a man who, whether Grant agreed or not, had done his best? He shrugged it off. "It doesn't matter now."

"Then what is this all about?"

"I want out, Dad," Grant said, slowly and clearly so there would be no misunderstanding. "I'm resigning from Price Investments."

"We're both tired, it's late and I don't have time for games," John Price huffed.

"This is no joke. My resignation is effective immediately. I apologize for the short notice, but there's nothing going on you or Thomas can't handle."

His father looked at him as if he'd lost his mind. "You're serious, aren't you?"

Grant nodded.

"I don't understand you. Hell, I've been grooming you to take over since you were a little boy."

"Up until a short time ago, I thought it was what I wanted too. I suppressed my doubts—what I wanted—to make you happy. But the time I spent in Tennessee with Melody brought it all to the surface."

His father stared back at him open-mouthed. "Oh, come on. You're not still upset over not being able to convince that woman to work for us. I'm disappointed too, but we've got to move on."

"My feelings for Melody extend beyond a job. I'm in love with her." It was the first time he'd uttered the words aloud. It felt good.

John Price's brow buckled and his lips contorted into a frown. "I don't believe what I'm hearing." His deep baritone was laced with anger and confusion. "I'm waiting for you to tell me this is all a mistake."

"That's not going to happen, Dad. My mind is made up."

"You're going to throw away what we've taken a lifetime to build—over her? Do you know how idiotic that sounds?"

"After everything you just told me, you of all people should understand." Grant ran his hand over his short-cropped hair. "Melody makes me feel the way Mom made you feel. When I'm with her I feel like a better man."

His father's chest rose and fell as he released a defeated sigh. "Why quit? Can't you be in love and work?"

"Melody's convinced the company is all that matters to me, and that my only interest in her is business."

His father's eyes narrowed. "You're standing here willing to put aside everything for her. How does she feel about you?"

"I believe she feels the same way."

"You're willing to risk it all for a woman you might not ever have?" John Price's brow lifted.

"Yes."

"And if you're wrong, and she doesn't want anything to do with you? What then?"

Grant shrugged. "If she rejects me, then I'll deal with it and move on. But I'll know I did everything I could," he said. "Either way I won't be coming back to Price Investments. It's time I made my own way. I have to start living my own life, Dad. Not yours."

Sadness shone in his father's eyes. "I can't force you to stay."

Grant walked around the desk and laid a hand on his father's shoulder. "I appreciate everything you've done and all the sacrifices you've made."

Grant's step felt lighter as walked out of his father's office and away from Price Investments.

Finally, he'd shrugged off the burdens of guilt and responsibility he'd shouldered all of his adult life. From here on out his life was his own, he thought.

Now all he had to do was convince a certain stubborn woman down in Tennessee to share it with him.

CHAPTER NINETEEN

Kevin took the stairs two at a time to the third floor of Nashville's main library. Spotting his wife immediately, he paused at the entryway and simply stared.

His chest tightened as a burst of love swelled within it. Joyce's beauty never failed to take his breath away.

Again he wondered what he'd done to deserve having this wonderful woman in his corner. Thank God he'd come to his senses. If he hadn't bent his rigid stance on the college issue, he might have broken his marriage beyond repair.

Joyce hadn't noticed him yet. Her lovely brow was furrowed in concentration, and her attention focused solely on the open textbook in front of her. Poor baby, Kevin thought. She'd spent every waking moment studying.

Feeling silly for standing around ogling his own wife, Kevin finally strode over to the table where she was seated.

"Hey, pretty lady."

She smiled up at him. The gesture made him feel like he was holding a million dollars.

"Sorry I'm late. I got hung up in a deposition," he said, sitting down in the chair next to her.

It had become their weekday routine to skip lunch and instead meet at the downtown branch of the Nashville library. It was walking distance from his office and a short drive from campus.

An hour spent helping his wife with algebra was preferable to gobbling down a sandwich at his desk.

"No problem, hon. It gave me time to squeeze in a chapter of psychology." Joyce tilted the thick textbook up, displaying the cover.

The smile gracing her lips widened. She was practically beaming.

"I don't remember Psychology 101 making me this happy back in college," he said. "What's going on with you?"

His wife dug through her crammed purple backpack, unearthing a crumpled sheet of paper. She smoothed it out and handed it to him. He surveyed the page and broke into a bigger grin than the one on her face.

"I got an A on my chemistry exam," Joyce squealed. It earned her a smile from the librarian, to whom they were familiar with by now.

"Way to go," Kevin said. He was so proud of her. "I knew you could do it."

"Well, I wasn't so sure." She reached for his hand. "Thanks for all of your help."

He glanced at the graded exam and gently

squeezed her small hand. "You did it, sweetheart. The accomplishment is all yours."

"If you hadn't stepped in with tutors and a housekeeper twice a week, I'd probably still be flunking."

Kevin released her hand. Guilt still ate at him. "I should have been supportive from the start. How could you study in a war zone?"

He felt her fingertips on his forearm.

"I thought we agreed to put it behind us," she said.

"I know, but . . ."

"Behind us," she reiterated in the tone she'd used when the boys were young and behaved badly.

"Hear me out, sweetheart. There's something I need to make up to you."

"There's no need."

"Yes, there is." He reached into the inner pocket of his suit jacket and handed her an envelope. "I rescheduled our Hawaiian honeymoon to coincide with your Christmas break."

"Oh, Kevin," she shrieked. She threw her arms around his neck, and he pulled her close.

"You're so good to me," she whispered in his ear. Then she stiffened in his arms.

"What's wrong?" Releasing her from his embrace, he rubbed his thumb against her cheek.

"The boys. They'll expect to spend Christmas with us. It's one of the few times we're all together."

He took the envelope and pulled out their itinerary. "I don't want to miss being with them either," he said. "We don't leave until the day after Christmas. By then they're usually tired of hanging out with their boring, old parents and have run off with their friends."

"Sounds like you've thought of everything."

"All you have to do is pack a bikini." He winked. "Or not."

She laughed. The sound made his heart beat double time. Damn, it felt good to be back on track with his wife.

He smoothed one of her short curls behind her ear. "I want you to be happy. It's all I've ever wanted." Kevin looked down at his watch. "We'd better get cracking on that algebra. Your class is in a half hour."

"Actually, algebra is canceled for today. The professor is out with the flu."

"So you're free for the rest of the afternoon?" He raised a brow.

"Yes." She countered his raised brow with one of her own. "You?"

"I am now."

Fifteen hours of driving and Grant didn't feel at all fatigued. He was too excited. Besides, he'd already wasted so much time, he refused to squander a single moment on something as trivial as sleep.

A line his father used to say, when he was a kid and exhausted from studying, popped into his head. "You can rest when you're dead."

Spotting the road sign pointing in the direction

of Melody's hometown, he pressed his foot to the accelerator. In the past month, Grant had not only resigned from his job, he'd also sold his condo, put his things in storage and talked with Dirt.

But most of all, he thought about Melody.

Before she left he'd implored her to trust him, and when she couldn't, he'd stupidly let her walk out the door and out of his life. Grant sighed as the events of the last time he saw her replayed themselves in his head.

It had been a mistake to let her go. Now he hoped it wasn't too late to correct it.

He pulled his car into the lot in front of the town's ballpark. Dirt, his childhood hero-turned-friend and business partner, was standing in front of the minor league team's clubhouse waiting on him.

Grant uncurled his body from the car's cabin, exhaled and stretched his arms over his head. Dirt greeted him with an eager handshake and a slap on the back.

"How was your trip?" he asked.

"Good." Grant nodded, eager to get to the business at hand. "Is everybody in place?"

"Our lawyer reviewed the paperwork and the funds have been wired. All they need are our signatures and we own the Cosmos," Dirt said.

Grant looked up at his friend and grinned as the reality hit him. Now he truly understood what Melody meant about the yarn store being a dream come true.

No, he would never play in a major league game;

however, he would be a part of the game he loved. "Then let's go in and make it official, partner."

Later that afternoon, he pulled his bags from the trunk of his car and strode up the walkway toward the familiar house.

Ruth was looked up at him and went back to watering the flowers in her yard.

"So you decided to show your face after all." Ruth's tone was as dry as it had been when he'd called to reserve a room, but he had no idea why. They'd been on friendly terms by the end of his first visit, or at least, he'd thought so. She'd even given him a list of Melody's favorite desserts.

The scent of baking cinnamon wafted out the screen door, distracting him. It made his stomach growl and his mouth water simultaneously. He took a deep breath. Pure heaven.

"Is that cobbler I smell?"

"Apple pie," she corrected. "And it's not for you. It's for the church."

"Can you spare a slice for a weary traveler?"

"No."

Something was definitely wrong. "Do all of your paying customers get hostile hospitality, or just me?"

His host's eyes narrowed into slits. "I warned you not to hurt her," Ruth said. "The last thing Melody needed was some sweet talker with dollar signs in his eyes—"

"Whoa!" Grant dropped his bags and held up his hands in protest, stopping Ruth's rant midstream.

303

"What? You don't like somebody calling you on your smarmy ways?" The vein in her forehead pulsed angrily.

"You've got it all wrong."

"No, I was wrong when I thought for a moment you actually cared about my girl. How could you just dump her like that?"

"Melody left me."

Ruth's mouth fell open, forming a perfect o.

"Who said I dumped Melody?"

"I just assumed . . ."

"You're wrong."

Ruth's shocked expression gave way to one of skepticism. "Well, if she dumped you, what are you doing here?"

"I love her."

"I see," Ruth said. She put down her watering can and laid her small, wrinkled hand on his forearm. "Maybe there's an extra piece of pie after all. Take your bags on up to your room while I put on some fresh coffee."

Grant settled in quickly, driven by the aroma of homemade pie. He hurried into the kitchen. Ruth was pouring coffee to accompany the two generous hunks of pie already on the table.

Ruth didn't speak until he had swallowed the last bite of his second piece.

"So what are you going to do?" She eyed him over the rim of her coffee mug.

He debated having a third slice of pie, but decided to hold off. "I'll keep it to myself if you don't mind. I don't want it spread all over town just yet."

"Not to worry," Ruth said. "Edith is on a cruise with her sister, so the town grapevine's been on temporary hiatus."

She rose to clear the table, but Grant told her he'd take care of it. He put the plates in the dishwasher and refilled her coffee cup.

"So? What are you going to do?"

He smiled. "I'm going to prove to Melody Mason there's a man not interested in her for money."

Melody suppressed a muttered curse as the knitting needle slipped from her left hand. She'd been dropping things all morning—ever since Edith's daughter had mentioned seeing Grant at Ruth's house yesterday.

Picking up the needle with a huff, she turned the blanket she was knitting and started a new row of stitches. The shop was quiet, giving her a chance to knit. It was her special time, but the rumor that Grant was in town had ruined it.

An idiot could have figured out what he was doing back here, she fumed. It was obvious. His father had sent him back to give their job offer another shot.

"Well, he's just wasting his time," she muttered.

She dropped her needle again.

"Damn," she said aloud.

She bent over to pick it up off the floor, but another hand beat her to it. She recognized the hand and the sexy, dark chocolate forearm it was attached to. Her gaze followed the trail to his face.

Grant.

Melody hadn't heard him come in, and she couldn't suppress the joy filling her traitorous heart. Suppressed memories of the night they'd spent together rolled to the forefront of her mind. Her gaze caught his. For a moment it seemed he could read her thoughts, and he too, had been transported back in time.

Then she remembered what he was doing here. "Give it up, Grant," she said, snatching the knitting needle from him. "I'm not taking your job."

"Good, because I'm not offering you one."

"Then why are you here?" She didn't look up from the blanket and tried to focus on purling the next row of stitches.

She stiffened as he sat down next to her on the love seat.

"For you," he said softly.

A wave of sadness washed through her. "I thought we'd already been through this," she began.

"I'm not going to ask you or tell you to trust me," he said.

"Then why . . ."

Grant rested his forefinger against her lips, forestalling her question. "Listen to me, Melody. I was wrong to ask for your blind trust when I did nothing to warrant it," he said. "So I'm not here to tell you why you should trust me. I'm here to *show* you you can."

She grasped his wrist and gently moved his hand from her mouth. Willing the tears behind her eyes not to surface, she rearranged her knitting on her lap. "It won't work. In the back of my mind, I'll always wonder when you're going to start a campaign for me take a job with Price."

"I can't offer you a job. I don't work there anymore."

"What?" Melody asked incredulously. She dropped the needle again, and Grant retrieved it. "Did your father fire you?"

She knew Grant's father was serious about securing her services, but she didn't think he'd fire his own son.

"Actually, he promoted me, and then I quit," he said. "And came back here."

Melody shook her head. "You quit your job . . . for me?"

"Yes, partly for you, but most of all *because* of you."

He took her left hand in his. "In one short week, you not only captured my heart but freed me to follow it," he said. "Dirt and I bought the Cosmos. I'm here to stay."

It was all so much to take in, Melody didn't know what to say. Before she could, Grant pulled a gold bracelet from his pocket and wrapped it around her wrist.

"What's this?" she asked as he closed the clasp. She held her arm up and looked at the two tiny gold charms.

"One is a knitting basket and the other is a ball of yarn," he said. "You put me on the path to following my dream. I want you to look at this bracelet and know I believe in yours."

The tears Melody had held in check up until

now filled her eyes and rolled freely down her cheeks.

"Don't cry," he said, smoothing a tear away with his thumb. "I thought the bracelet would make you happy."

Melody sniffed. "I am happy."

"Then you don't mind having a new neighbor in town?"

She smiled through her tears. "Not at all."

He leaned in, touching his lips to hers in a kiss that touched the core of her very soul. When they parted, he looked deep into her eyes. "I love you, Melody."

Again, the words in her heart tumbled out on their own accord. "I love you too."

For a moment, he simply stared at her as if he couldn't get enough of looking at her. Melody felt herself blush under the heat of his scrutiny.

"Then I have another offer for you."

"Oh, no." Melody laughed. "I'm not working at the ballpark. What do you and Dirk want me to do? Take tickets? Mow the field?"

Grant chuckled. "I'm offering you a whirlwind courtship full of yoga classes, dinners out, holding hands and watching thunderstorms." Then his tone grew serious. "After which, I want you to be my wife."

He retrieved a black velvet box from his pants pocket and opened it. A brilliant golden stone surrounded by white diamonds blinked up at her.

Melody clutched at her chest with one hand while the other covered her open mouth. His words finally began to sink in and she threw her arms around his neck. "I love you," she whispered in his ear.

"Is that a yes?" he asked, the ring poised near her finger.

She smiled up at him as he slipped it on. "I couldn't possibly refuse."

JENNIE KLASSEL
IT HAPPENED IN SOUTH BEACH

If she's a beauteous, bodacious babe, gettin' down, gettin' it on, gettin' her man, she's definitely *not* good old Tilly Snapp. So what's the safe, sensible twenty-six-year-old Bostonian doing in Miami's ultra-hip, super-chic South Beach?

She's on the trail of the fabled Pillow Box of Win Win Poo—the most valuable collection of antique erotic "accessories" in the world. And she's after the fiend who murdered her eccentric Aunt Ginger. And while Tilly might not know the difference between a velvet tickle pickle and a kosher dill, with the assistance of the sexy yet unhelpful Special Agent Will Maitland, she's about to get a crash course in sex-ed.

Meet the new Tilly Snapp, Sex Detective.

South Beach ain't seen nothin' yet.

IF THE SHOE FITS

STEPHANIE ROWE

Run hard. Run fast. Just don't try to run in heels. Especially if your name is Paris Jackson and you're fashion-impaired. Designer labels and stilettos aren't exactly Paris's thing. Give her a pair of sneakers and she's a happy woman. That's why she's spending nights designing running shoes for her start-up company, and why she doesn't have time for an ex-husband on a therapy quest, a boyfriend who's changing all the rules, and a confusing attraction to the boss about to fire her from her day job.

And now people are telling her the way to succeed is through high-fashion shoes. Those will only trip Paris up. Won't they?

She's about to find out.

JENNIFER ASHLEY

CONFESSIONS *of a* LINGERIE ADDICT

The fixation began on New Year's Day: Silky, expensive slips from New York and Italy. Camisoles and thongs from Beverly Hills. Before, Brenda Scott would have blushed to be caught dead in them. Now, she's ditched the shy and mousy persona that got her dumped by her rich and perfect fiancé, and she is sexy. Underneath her sensible clothes, Brenda is the woman she wants to be.

After all, why can't she be wild and crazy? Nick, the sexy stranger she met on New Year's, already seems to think she is. Of course, he didn't know the old Brenda. How long before Nick strips it all away and finds the truth beneath? And would that be a bad thing?

NAOMI NEALE
CALENDAR GIRL

Name: Nan Cloutier

Address: Follow the gang graffiti until you reach the decrepit bakery. See the rooms above that even a squatter wouldn't claim? That's my little Manhattan paradise.

Education: (Totally useless) Liberal Arts degree from an Ivy League university.

Employment History: Cheer Facilitator for Seasonal Staffers Inc. Responsible for spreading merriment and not throttling fellow employees or shoppers, as appropriate.

Career Goal: Is there a career track that will maybe, just maybe, help me attract the attention of the department store heir of my dreams?

No way. That's a full-time job in itself!

- -